KEEPING THE SCORE

KELLY JAMIESON

Boldwood

First published in Great Britain in 2025 by Boldwood Books Ltd.

Cover Design by Head Design Ltd.

Cover Images: Shutterstock

A CIP catalogue record for this book is available from the British Library.

Paperback ISBN 978-1-83633-693-8

Large Print ISBN 978-1-83633-692-1

Hardback ISBN 978-1-83633-691-4

Ebook ISBN 978-1-83633-694-5

Kindle ISBN 978-1-83633-695-2

Audio CD ISBN 978-1-83633-686-0

MP3 CD ISBN 978-1-83633-687-7

Digital audio download ISBN 978-1-83633-689-1

This book is printed on certified sustainable paper. Boldwood Books is dedicated to putting sustainability at the heart of our business. For more information please visit https://www.boldwoodbooks.com/about-us/sustainability/

Boldwood Books Ltd, 23 Bowerdean Street, London, SW6 3TN

www.boldwoodbooks.com

To all the hockey players who believe that having a frozen rubber puck shot at you at 80 mph is the most fun thing you can do

1

FORD

"You're not done! More! More!"

Sweat stings my eyes and my muscles burn. I hop laterally onto my left leg, bending that knee, and touch my right knee to the mat. Then the opposite. One side, then the other.

"Explosive!" Victor yells. "*Explode* up from the mat!"

I push harder.

"Faster!"

"Mother*fucker*!" I'm dying.

"Two more!"

Hop-bend-explode. Hop-bend-explode.

"Last one!"

Oh, fuck, yeah. I finish, my legs trembling like cranberry sauce that just slid out of a can. I drop onto the floor, flat on my back, arms spread wide. "You're trying to kill me," I gasp.

Victor, the evil fucker, laughs. "And you're paying me to do it."

I huff out a laugh too, staring at the ceiling of the Long Island warehouse that holds Victor's training facility. He's not wrong. I'm paying him a lot.

"The faster you are, the more coordinated you are, the more conditioned you are, the more shutouts you get."

"I get lots of shutouts." I smirk.

"How many last season?"

"Six."

"What's the most an NHL goalie has ever gotten in a season?"

Fuck. He knows I know this. "George Hainsworth. Twenty-two."

"Uh huh." He crosses his arms and grins. "Something to work towards."

"That was in 1929!"

"Still. Lots of goalies have gotten more than six in a season."

"I can do more than six this season." I was proud of six shutouts last season. It was the most in the league, and I only played about half the games. Damn him.

"Cocky bastard."

I grin. "Just confident."

He nudges my leg with the toe of his running shoe. "Okay, we're done for today. Go eat some protein and hydrate."

I've been coming here five days a week for the last three months, pretty much the whole off season after our playoffs ended in May. Victor trains elite hockey players—I'm not the only one here, but I'm the only goalie. Victor has his own unique philosophy about training. He watched me play and analyzed my biomechanics and movement patterns, and designed a program specifically for me. We've been working on it all summer and now it's only a few weeks until training camp starts. I swear he's rewired my brain. In a good way.

I roll over and climb to my feet as a woman walks into the gym. She's pretty and blonde and carrying a baby on her hip. She waves at Xander, one of my training companions, just coming out of the locker room. He breaks into a big smile at the sight of his wife and baby.

"Hi, Sage." I've met Xander's wife a couple of times.

"Hi, Ford. Looks like you've been working hard."

"Oh, yeah." Sweat is dripping off me. I stop near her and look at the baby. "How's the little guy?" Shit, I can't remember his name.

"Good! He's getting so big! Want to hold him?"

"No." I take a quick step back. "That's okay. I'm, uh, all sweaty." I give the baby a fake smile. "Hey, kid. Do you like sharks?"

The baby gazes back at me with a tiny wrinkle between his eyes.

"Sharks?" Sage laughs. "What?"

I shrug. "I like sharks. They're fascinating. Did you know they can't swim backwards?" I ask the kid. "And they don't usually want to eat humans. They just want a taste to see if it's anything good."

The baby's bottom lip pushes out. Uh oh. That doesn't look good. Then his mouth opens and his eyes squint up. "Waaaaah!"

I blink at him. Wow. He can really yell loud.

"Oh, no. Leo, shhh." Sage bounces him and tries to comfort him. He continues to wail loud enough to pierce eardrums. "Shhh. It's okay. There are no sharks here." She casts me an unhappy look. "Let's go."

Xander frowns at me and follows his wife out of the building.

Yikes. The kid can't understand about sharks, can he? I was just jabbering.

Oh, well. I shake my head and head to the locker room to change and head home. Babies never like me. Kids do, sometimes, because I'm fun. But it doesn't matter. I don't want kids. Or a wife. I don't need anyone else in my life. My work is my life.

My condo is in Hoboken, a nice place in a trendy neighborhood. I park in the underground garage and ride the elevator to the seventh floor. There are only two units on each floor, which is a bonus. I walk into my place and hang my keys on the hook near the door where I always hang them, then head to the kitchen. I left my planner on the counter there and I sit on a stool and look it over. I still have to meditate and do my eye exercises. And eat dinner. This morning I did a load of laundry before I left, but I have to put it all away and I've scheduled cleaning the fridge for today. I decide what order I'll do things in and then get busy.

Dinner is leftover tahini-lemon chicken that I grilled yesterday, along with a salad. No cucumbers. Half an avocado. I guzzle down water while I prepare it.

I like meditating on the rooftop deck of the building when the weather cooperates. It's a nice late summer day so I go up there with my yoga mat, dressed in my white taekwondo Dobak —pants only. It's warm up here.

This is a nice spot with lots of shrubs and plants in natural wood planters. Peaceful. There's a gas barbecue and patio furniture, but I'm usually the only one up here. I roll out my mat onto the wooden deck and get myself comfortably seated.

First, I focus on my breath. Then I do a body scan. Yeah, I'm sore. But it feels good. It feels like I accomplished something. Like I'm getting stronger. Better. *Breathe.*

I think about my goals. To be the best goaltender. To be the number one goaltender for the New Jersey Storm. I've been part of a goaltending tandem for the last three seasons, but this year I want to be the number one goalie. Everyone knows I'm better than Pavel Bendik. I should be getting most of the starts. This past summer, I worked my perfectly shaped ass off to make myself even better.

Breathe.

How do I feel about my goals? Pressure? Excitement? Right now... I feel positive. Challenged. I can do it. I *will* do it.

After my meditation I do some eye-strengthening exercises that help me track the puck—looking side to side, up, down, diagonal, without moving my head.

"What on earth are you doing?"

Standing off to the side is Andi Marsh, my next-door neighbor, the woman who lives in the other condo on my floor. She's watching me with wide-eyed amusement, on the verge of outright laughter.

There was a time in my life when that would have stung me. Now I just go with it. If you're going to be weird, do it with confidence. "I didn't hear you come out here." I push up to stand.

"Clearly." Now she dissolves into giggles, almost doubling over. "That looked so weird!"

"I don't care." I smile back at her. "I'm strengthening my eye muscles."

"Oooookay."

She looks good. Better than she did a year ago after her dickwad of a husband cheated on her and left her. I run my gaze over her, taking in her messy dark blonde hair, brown eyes dancing with mirth behind big tortoiseshell glasses, and wide, inviting smile. She's wearing a loose white shirt and cut-off denim shorts. Yes, my eyes might linger on her long, smooth legs. "You must have had Lucky Charms for breakfast today."

She blinks. "What? Why?"

"Because you look magically delicious."

Her lips quirk but she rolls her eyes and shakes her head. "That is so bad."

I grin. "But true. So, what's up?"

"I need a favor."

I groan with exaggerated dismay. "Another one?"

I'm just razzing her. She doesn't ask me for many favors, and when she does I always agree. I've never been able to say no to her.

That makes it sound like she takes advantage of me, and she totally does not. I know it bugs her when she needs help with something. Sometimes I step in and offer to help before she asks because I know she'll break her brain trying to put IKEA furniture together before she'll admit she needs help. After her divorce, she bought a new bed and built it herself. The next morning, it collapsed with her on it.

I teased her about headboard-banging sex, but I knew she was alone. And I grabbed an Allen wrench and got to work so the slats were in right side up. While definitely not thinking about how I was making her bed safe for headboard-banging sex.

I'm a selfish asshole focused on one thing and one thing only —my career. Especially this year. But even a selfish asshole like me has some compassion. There's something about Andi that makes me want to keep an eye out for her. It was hard seeing how low she was after her marriage ended, when she's usually so cheerful and spirited. And she's a single woman used to having a man around. Is that sexist? Probably. I don't give a shit. I'll watch out for her since Trevor the Tool screwed her over.

I can't believe I was friends with that guy. Fuck him.

I *am* still friends with Andi, however. Yes, she's a woman. Yes, I'd fuck her on the nearest available surface if she gave even a hint she was interested. Which she has not. But I don't have time for romantic crap. Anything more than hookups leads to plans, obligations, and responsibilities I don't want.

"And this one's huge." She flashes an entreating smile.

"That's what *she* said," I smirk.

She cracks up laughing again. "Okay. I need a date for the awards dinner next week."

Right. She told me she's been nominated for some award by some business association.

"Are you finally asking me on a date?" I grin. "*You're* single now. *I'm* single. Coincidence? I think not."

I always make jokes like that. She knows I'm not serious. We're just friends.

"It's not a real date. I just don't want to go alone. Elodie was going to come with me." She names her friend. "But she just got word she has to go to Dallas next week on business."

"What about all those men you smash and dash?"

She frowns. "Ew."

"Hit and run? Screw and shoo?" I pause, thinking. "Ride and hide?"

"Jesus. You make it sound so sleazy."

"No judgment here, Marsh." I shake my head. "I don't blame you for getting back on that horse." No judgment because I'm the same. Hit it and quit it.

"Like you're any different." She lifts an eyebrow.

I shrug. "I don't deny it."

"So... can you come with me?"

Ugh. I'd do almost anything for her, but it's getting close to training camp and I'm really trying to stick to my plan. My schedule. "What day is the dinner?"

"Thursday. The season hasn't started," she adds cajolingly.

It hasn't, but my work has. "Thursday is the night I clean my floors."

She bites her lip in an adorable yet hot way. "I know." She gives me an apologetic smile and blinks her long eyelashes at me. Oh, hell. "Maybe you could do that a little earlier that day?"

"I don't know. I have training most of the day."

"Maybe you could do it Friday?"

I consider that. At length. The last thing I want to do is go to an awards dinner where I'll sit around eating rubber chicken with people I don't know. I also despise changing my schedule. "Maybe. What do I get in return?"

She taps a forefinger to the center of her chin and looks skyward. Cute. "Hmmm. How about my special beer meatballs?"

She made these for me once before and I loved them. The meatballs are cooked for hours in equal parts ketchup and beer. It sounds gross but it's really delicious. Apparently, her mom used to make them.

I sigh. "More food. When are you going to start trading sexual favors?"

Again, she laughs at my cheesy flirting.

"Fine," I say. "I'll do it."

Wait, did I just agree to it? The words somehow popped out of my mouth. Goddammit.

"Thank you!" She claps her hands together and her relief and glee make my heart trip. "I really appreciate it."

"You know I'm here for you."

"I know." She beams a smile.

"Do I need to wear a tux?"

"Do you even have a tux?"

"Of course I have a tux. Once a year I wear it for some charity event the team puts on."

"Oh. Okay, well, no, it's not that fancy. A suit is fine."

"Okay."

"Wait. Do you have a normal suit?"

I give her an offended look. "What does that mean? My suits aren't normal?"

"Please. You dress only slightly tamer than A$AP Rocky."

"That's an egregious exaggeration. I have never worn a kilt."

"True. Just please don't wear that red plaid suit."

"I love that suit."

"I know, and it would be great for a Christmas party, but this is an awards dinner."

"I dunno, Marsh. If you want me to do you a favor, I don't think you're in any position to criticize my wardrobe."

"You're right." She nods, abashed. "Wear whatever you want."

I can tell she doesn't mean that. "The leopard-print jacket is pretty sick. It looks great with black pants."

She nods, feigning enthusiasm.

I laugh. "Okay. What time should I pick you up?"

"We live next door to each other. I'll meet you at the elevator at five-thirty. I'll call an Uber."

"Okay. I'll be there."

"Thank you. Again. Are you done with your, uh, eye-strengthening exercises?"

"Yeah. But I'm going to practice some taekwondo patterns."

"Okay." She hesitates, her eyes dipping to my bare chest. "Okay. I'll leave you to it."

2

ANDI

In the divorce, I got the condo, the Le Creuset cookware, and Ford Archibald.

Yes, Ford is a person and can't really be considered part of our divorce settlement, but in my mind, he's mine. A friend. He was *our* friend, but now he's *my* friend. Unlike most of the other friends me and my ex-husband shared, who deserted me before the ink was dry on the final judgment of divorce.

Ford and I have known each other for a few years, since my ex-husband and I moved into this building and next door to Ford. Ford and Trevor are both pro athletes, Ford playing hockey, Trevor baseball. They connected over that, but because their seasons were so opposite, Ford was around more when Trevor was away on road trips. It was nice having someone close to help out when my bedroom doorknob broke or I needed help moving the stove so I could clean under it and Trev wasn't there.

Now Trev is gone for good, having dumped me for another woman.

I go into my condo and close the door behind me. I was tempted to stay up there and watch Ford do his martial arts exercises, or whatever they're called. I've watched him before—bare-foot and bare-chested, wearing loose white pants that sit low on his hips, bare back rippling with smooth skin over tight muscle as he moves. And the intense look of focus he gets on his face is mesmerizing. Not only is he ripped, but he's a very good-looking man, with vivid green eyes, carved cheekbones, and perfect dark beard stubble. He's lean and powerful, and his workouts are an erotic show of control and sensuality.

My mouth goes dry remembering.

I've seen him kick a leg up so high and straight I winced with a sympathetic pull in my inner thighs. Once, I held pads for him to practice his kicking and ended up with bruises up and down my arms. That man can kick *hard*.

Anyway. I got my nerve up and asked him to be my date at the dinner. And he said yes.

I already told him I've been nominated for Best Branded Series Campaign by the East Coast Digital Marketing Association. I'm super pumped about it. I really want that award. I really want to show my asshole ex-husband and his new girlfriend how good I am and what he's missing out on. I also want to show the digital marketing world that I'm succeeding at starting my own business. I don't want to be at the dinner alone.

I still haven't decided what to wear to the awards dinner. Elodie took me shopping the other day and I bought three new dresses. Three! Craziness. After my divorce, when she got tired of me shlepping around in joggers and old T-shirts, she gave me a makeover and I willingly participated since my self-esteem had taken a hit. I got new hair, new makeup, new clothes, and a new social life. As Ford alluded to earlier in his crude way.

It's fine. Trevor was my college boyfriend. We got married young. I never really had relationships with other men and now

I'm single, why not? I've been having fun learning how to flirt and hit on men. Men are fun.

Except Trevor. Bastard.

I open my closet and pull out one dress. This midnight-blue one-shouldered dress is sexy, but probably not right for a business function. Maybe I should just wear a suit. Nah. I don't want to be that business-like. I can look a *little* sexy.

This gray sheath is form-fitting and flattering. I really like it. It's a safe choice.

This red dress, though... wow. Do I have the nerve to pull it off? It's a lot more attention-grabbing than I'm used to wearing.

Trevor would be surprised.

But who cares about him? How about the guy I'll be with... would Ford like it?

Phhht. Why am I thinking that? I don't need to impress Ford. I should be worried about impressing my clients and colleagues and Haven fucking Gray. Or maybe I shouldn't be worried at all about how I look. I should be more concerned with the smarts and skills that got me this award nomination. I could go to the dinner in a burlap sack tied with a rope and a boatload of confidence.

But a little help from a nice dress never hurts.

3

FORD

How did I get myself into this again?

Oh, yeah. Andi.

Here I am in a suit and tie ready to go to an awards dinner where I will know nobody, except Andi of course, and listen to boring speeches. And I'm edgy about not getting my cleaning done. I keep thinking about it. It's important to get it done. Thinking about it makes my skin itch.

I take a deep breath. I know it's a cognitive distortion that not getting my laundry done is a catastrophe. I know how to challenge that thought. My therapist will be proud of me for questioning myself. *The world won't end if I don't wash my floors today. I'm holding myself to an unreasonable standard. I can do this. Especially for Andi.*

I'm even wearing one of my tamer suits tonight—navy blue, with brown brogues. I had to add some fun with my shirt—red and blue paisley—and solid red tie. I don't care what people think about how I dress, but even a selfish prick like me knows tonight is about Andi.

At least my hair looks good.

I grab my phone, wallet, and keys and head out.

And stop dead in my tracks upon seeing the woman standing at the elevator.

I guess I've never seen my neighbor like this before. After a rough few post-divorce months when every time I saw her she was wearing baggy sweats or pajamas, she's been looking better. She mostly works from home and dresses in casual clothes. She also volunteers at an animal shelter and wears jeans and T-shirts for that. She has a banging body, when it's not shrouded in sweats, and tonight... that body is unmistakable. She's not just a snack, she's a whole goddamn meal. And I am here for it.

I mean, as a friend.

The sleeveless red dress hugs her curves, and when she turns to face me, the front of the dress is wrapped across her, leaving an opening above the knees that reveals those absolutely stellar legs. Her pouty lips match the color of the dress—my favorite color. Her glasses are absent, showing off tawny brown eyes and long eyelashes. Her caramel-colored hair doesn't look much different —it's always in a loose wavy style that brushes her shoulders— but the whole package is giving Little Caesar's Pizza—hot and ready.

"Hi." She smiles and gives me an up and down look that I might think is checking me out except for when she says, "Thank God you're not wearing the plaid suit."

I heave a sigh. "You have no faith in me."

She grins. "Of course I do. I'm just kidding."

"Bust my balls, sure." I smooth a hand over a lapel. "I look great and you know it."

"I suppose."

"You also look decent," I say with a quick appraising look that isn't necessary because I already took in every detail of her appearance.

"Decent. Thanks for that effusive praise."

I grin and push the elevator button. "You'd look even better in my bed."

"Oh my God." She rolls her eyes and it's cute.

"How's my hair?" I tilt my head.

She studies it. "It looks fine."

"Fine." I shake my head. "It's *perfect* tonight." I may have a slight obsession with my hair.

The car arrives out front of our building just as we do, and I open the back door and help Andi in, getting a flash of leg as a reward.

It's about a twenty-five-minute drive to the hotel in Midtown Manhattan where the dinner's being held.

"There's something I have to tell you," she says on the way, as I try to ignore the scent of her perfume that fills the car—sweet, almost like caramel, with a light flowery note as well. Sexy.

"Okay. What is it?"

She presses her lips together briefly then says, "Trevor is going to be there tonight."

"Oh." I pause. "Why?"

"His new girlfriend is in the business."

"Right." I remember hearing this when they split up. Andi actually worked with the woman Trevor left her for. So fucking shitty.

She nibbles her bottom lip. "So I really appreciate you coming with me."

Yeah. Now I get why she didn't want to go alone. Seeing her ex and his new woman has to suck. "Free dinner and drinks is never bad."

"Er... I don't think the drinks are free. We're not rich professional athletes."

"Damn. Well, I hope you have your credit card."

She gives me a chiding look. "Yes, I do."

Like I'll let her buy me drinks.

I assume she makes good money. Condos in our building aren't cheap, she has a nice car, and works a lot. I sort of understand what she does but not really—some kind of online marketing work. She started her own business shortly after Trevor cheated on her, working out of her home mostly, and now she's nominated for an award so she must do well. She can probably afford to buy me a few drinks, but that's not happening.

Once we've been dropped off in front of the hotel, we take the elevator to the fifth floor where the dinner's being held in one of the ballrooms. The room is subtly lit by fancy chandeliers hanging above round tables topped with flower arrangements. Once inside, Andi stops and greets people with smiles. It seems like she knows everyone, getting congratulations on her nomination. She introduces me and I smile and shake hands with people I'll never see again. Some of them recognize my name and their eyes widen. One guy wants to have a whole conversation about the upcoming season for the New Jersey Storm, but I manage to disengage and follow Andi.

"We're at table twelve." Andi peers at a sign on one table. "Oh, right there."

"Who are we sitting with?"

She gives me the low down on the dinner companions she knows. "There's the bar." She points to the end of the room where people mill about an elegant glass and chrome bar with illuminated shelves of bottles behind it.

We both order glasses of red wine and I nudge her aside and tap my card to pay for them, ignoring her thwarted pout.

"Thank you," she says with a crooked smile. "But I owe you for this."

"Cheers." I touch my glass to hers and move away from the bar.

We pause at a small high-top table by a window. Andi keeps looking around the room, clearly uneasy. I want to make her feel better. "You're obviously going to win tonight. Do you have an acceptance speech prepared?"

She presses her lips together and meets my eyes. "No. I was afraid to jinx it by preparing."

"I didn't know you were superstitious."

"Not like you." She tilts her head. "I've never met anyone as superstitious as you."

"Thanks."

"That wasn't a compliment."

I laugh. "Oh. I thought it was."

"Superstitions are irrational."

"True."

"So you know that but you still act on them."

"Yes." I drink more wine. "They serve a purpose."

"Like what?"

"Why did you not prepare a speech?"

"Because..." The small furrow between her eyebrows deepens. "I said, I didn't want to jinx winning."

"But why? Did it make you feel better?"

She tilts her head. "Yeah, I guess."

"You're probably nervous about the award. It helped you deal with that. It gave you a sense of control."

She purses her pretty red lips. "Right."

"That's why superstitions are always about something we're insecure about, or afraid of. Something we don't have control over."

"Hmmm. Also true. I don't have control over the award."

"Exactly. There's a lot in life we don't have control over." Which pisses me off. But I'm working on it.

"Yeah. But I *want* to control it."

I smile. "Don't we all? I'd like to control every shot that comes at me so I can block it, but that's not how it works. And not having that control creates anxiety."

She looks at me searchingly as she lifts her wine glass to her lips, then says, "You get anxious about games?"

We've known each other for a while, but our friendship is pretty casual. We've never had a conversation like this.

"Sure. Nerves are normal. You have to learn how to use them to your advantage."

Nerves are normal. Anxiety is a normal reaction to stress. I learned that from the therapist my parents made me see years ago, when they got concerned about how stubborn and obsessed I was about having a routine. How I got so focused on hockey to the exclusion of everything else. I think they were worried about a neurodevelopmental disorder, and maybe I do have a disorder, but it was never bad enough that it was diagnosed as that. I did a bunch of cognitive behavioral therapy and talk therapy. I got medication for anxiety and learned why I needed so much routine and structure.

"Also," I add, "superstitions can enhance performance."

She bites her lip and her eyes dance. "Are you talking about athletic performance or sexual performance?"

Damn. I respond to her playful question with a smile. "I'm not superstitious about my sexual performance."

"Ohhhh. Okay. I get it. Confident in the sheets, anxious in the crease."

I burst out laughing. "Hey, that was good."

She grins. "Thanks."

"Although I am not anxious in the crease. I'm the Net Ninja."

She bites her lip on a smile. "Okay, then."

"But seriously, there is evidence that the psychological benefit of reducing anxiety can improve performance." I lift one shoulder. "Even little things like saying 'good luck' or 'break a leg'."

She nods, lips pouting thoughtfully. "Hmmm. Interesting."

"And then if it works, you don't want to tempt fate by not doing it anymore."

"So that's why you have so many. They work for you."

I nod. "Of course, my natural talent and hard work help, too."

"Of course." She tucks her tongue into her cheek. I seem to have distracted her from her nerves. "The lucky socks? Those work?"

"Well, even if they don't, they don't hurt anything. It's easier to wear the lucky socks than take a chance on things going horribly wrong."

"Sure. But could it get to a point where superstitions can become a fixation? Could it actually interfere in your life?"

Ugh. Nailed me on that one. I shift my gaze across the room. "Sure. It could happen."

"That would be terrible if you missed a game because you couldn't find your lucky socks." She says it with amusement, but it's not really funny.

"Terrible," I agree uncomfortably. "So you don't have any superstitions?"

"Well... I do always make sure my bra and panties match."

Oh, Jesus. My tongue sticks to the roof of my mouth.

She immediately regrets saying that, I can tell. Her eyes dart around. "Uh..."

"What color are they tonight?" I ask, trying for smooth operator, and not a drooling dork.

"Never mind!"

"Hi, Andi!" A woman approaches us with a bright smile.

I immediately sense Andi tensing up. But she smiles too and turns to greet the woman. Her smile freezes, though, when she takes in the woman's pregnant belly.

Oh, no. Is this Trevor's new girlfriend?

"Look at you!" the woman says to Andi. "You look so nice when you make an effort!"

My face stiffens. I set my hand on Andi's mid-back and gently rub.

"Thank you!" Andi says, as if that were a real compliment. "Haven, this is Ford Archibald. Ford, this is Haven Gray. We used to work together at Design Edge."

Haven turns her attention to me, eyes widening. "Ford Archibald? You play for the Storm!"

"I do." I smile and shake her hand. "Nice to meet you."

"Oh, wow, this is amazing! Andi!" She slides Andi an arch look. "I heard you have a hockey player neighbor."

Yep. This has to be the girlfriend. So where's Trevor?

Oh, there he is, walking toward us across the room, carrying two glasses. He's first looking at Andi in her sexy red dress, his eyes wide with appreciation, then he sees me and breaks into a smile.

"Hey, Ford," he says. "I didn't know you'd be here." His forehead creases and he looks at Andi. "Hi, Andi."

"Hi." She's doing a really good job of hiding her discomfort. "Ford was nice enough to accompany me tonight."

"Huh." Trevor divides a still-puzzled look between us. Then his gaze lingers on Andi. "You look really good."

"Thanks." This smile is stilted.

Haven blinks and also looks at Andi. "Congratulations on your nomination. I was so surprised when I saw your name."

My jaw tightens. I'm ready to deck this lady. (I would never hit a lady, just so you know.)

"Thank you," Andi says. "And congrats to you as well!"

Wait. They're both nominated. For the same award? I try to keep a poker face. Why didn't Andi tell me that?

Haven gives a light laugh. "Thanks. We're really pumped about it."

A few more people join us and soon there's a small group around us chatting. They're all talking business so I don't have much to say, but that's okay. I'm not one to fade into the background but I can handle it for a little while. I keep an eye on Andi and Trevor to make sure she's okay. Her smile is bright and brittle and I can tell she's putting on an act.

That conversation we had earlier went deeper than I expected. I was trying to ease her nerves but she's easy to talk to. I've never hidden my weirdness from her, since we're just friends, and I like it that she seems to like me even though she knows how weird I am.

4

ANDI

As a server places a plate in front of Ford, he reaches into an inside pocket of his suit jacket and pulls out a small package. I watch as he unwraps a set of eating utensils—knife, fork, spoon—and sets them on his plate.

I blink but say nothing, picking up my own fork to dig into my salad. I'm just happy he's here. My insides are writhing with jealousy and nerves.

She's pregnant.

It's bad enough that I have to face my ex with his new girl-friend, and that she's nominated for the same award I am, but she's *pregnant*? Sweet baby Jesus and his tiny toes.

Trevor never wanted kids. Neither did I. He was focused on his baseball career, and I was focused on my job. Focused on supporting us while he followed his dream. But this... kind of hurts.

I feel like I'm eating and talking and smiling in a fog. I can't stop thinking about Haven's cute pregnant belly. How they're going to be a family. How I'm alone.

And she was a bitch to me!

I have to win this award. I will probably die if I don't.

Okay, that's a bit hyperbolic. Or maybe not.

"What's wrong?" Ford asks in a low voice near my ear.

"What? Nothing. Why?"

"You made a noise. Like a growl."

I press my lips together. Oops. "I'm fine."

"I wanted to smack her, too."

I jerk my head around. His eyes are warm with compassion.

"Is Haven nominated for the same award as you?"

"Yes."

"Sucks for her."

I can't stop the smile tugging at my lips. "I appreciate the support."

"Did you know she's pregnant?" he asks in a low voice.

I shake my head, looking at my plate, my throat full of sand. "No."

He curses under his breath. "I'm sorry."

I blink rapidly and smile. "It's okay. It's not like I wanted kids. I thought Trevor didn't either, but... well."

After our salad, we're served a New York strip steak with peppercorn cream sauce and then a chocolate brownie with fresh fruit. It's all delicious, but the knots in my stomach are growing tighter as we get closer to the awards part of the evening.

My self-esteem has taken a beating the last few years, with my husband dumping me for another woman, a woman I considered a work friend, then leaving my secure, high-paying job to start my own business. To basically start over. And she's pregnant.

I really want to win tonight. I need to win at *something*.

Which means I'm going to be crushed when it doesn't happen.

I wind my fingers together in my lap and look down at them.

Ford bumps my shoulder with his. "Are you going to eat your dessert?"

I glance at him. "Yes. No. You can have it."

He takes my plate and finishes off the brownie while I fret over watching Haven win the award, imagining Trevor's enjoyment and her gloating.

So what if she does? It doesn't really matter. I'll be fine.

I keep telling myself that.

By the time speeches and awards start, I've accepted that Haven is going to win and that's okay because I'm my own boss now, I have a great new life as a single woman, and I'm here with a hot professional athlete. There's always something positive!

So when my name is called I blink in confusion. Did I hear that right? I turn to Ford, who's smiling broadly.

I'm afraid to stand up in case I've made a terrible mistake and I'll humiliate myself.

Ford takes my hand and pulls me to standing. "Congratulations," he says in my ear. "Get up there."

Still blinking, mouth open, I make my way through the tables to the dais, trying not to stumble. The presenter, a man I vaguely know through networking functions, smiles and nods at me. I guess it's for real? I'm not up here stealing Haven's award?

Still forcing a smile, I try to get my shit together as I speak into the microphone. "Oh, wow. This is really unexpected. Holy shit." That gets me a big laugh, and heat floods up into my face. Dammit, I have no idea what to say! I break out in a sweat as I search for words. "I'm so grateful for this because it comes from my peers," I stammer out. "I know all of the nominees personally and they are all incredible at what they do." I'm calming down a little and I smile and make eye contact with a few people. "So it really means a lot to me, and I want to thank all the other nominees for the work you do to inspire and motivate, and thank you especially to Haven for all that you taught me in our years working together." Yeah. I can be the bigger person.

I straighten my shoulders and thank other people—my former bosses, mentors, and friends who've supported me. "And despite economic concerns, there are so many reasons to be optimistic that business will improve."

I return to the table holding my small crystal trophy, determined not to look at Haven. And Trevor. Now the adrenaline is flowing and I practically float through the room, beaming and accepting congratulations from the others at our table. The room is a blur around me. Ford stands as I arrive beside him and I exuberantly throw my arms around him. His hands close on my hips, sending a dart of heat to my belly, which I ignore.

"I just fucked that up," I say.

He chuckles. "You did great, Marsh. Congratulations again." And he slides his arms around me, pulls me against him, and gives me a gentle squeeze that makes my skin tingle everywhere.

It's a normal physical reaction. He has an amazing body, exuding heat and energy and masculinity, and he smells incredible. And I'm high enough from my win that I just go with it.

I'm about to take my seat when Haven appears.

"Andi," she says tightly.

My first reaction is to smile, assuming she's here to congratulate me.

"I can't believe you won," she says.

I blink, sensing Ford's body tense next to me.

"But you only won because you stole Mirabella Cosmetics from me," she snaps, leaning in. "That was dirty. You don't deserve that award."

I actually gasp out loud. "What?"

Ford slowly stands, scowling at Haven, waves of fury emanating from him. "Excuse me?"

She glances at him and actually takes a step back seeing the look on his face from his six-foot-four height. But she doesn't back down. "You heard me. She's a fake. She cheats. She went behind my back and stole a client away from me."

"I did not!" Outrage heats my veins and I stand too, facing her. "That is a lie. You take that back."

"I will not." Her eyes narrow. "Losing that client cost me at Design Edge. And it was because of you. That was your plan all along."

"You're..." I stop and slide my gaze around, taking in the people around us watching. I lower my voice. "This is not the place for this discussion."

It's not a discussion, though. She's lost her mind.

"Walk away," Ford says softly, staring her down. He slides an arm around my waist in a protective gesture, pulling me to his side and slightly behind him as if Haven's going to punch me or something. "Andi did not do that. Just leave."

Haven's face floods with color and she glares at him, then at me. And she moves toward me. Instinctively, I take a step toward her too.

"Oh, hell, no." Ford pushes me behind him, putting himself between me and Haven. "Don't even think of touching her," he growls.

His protective presence obviously deters her. Others at our table have stood, sensing an impending bitch battle, or something. Much as I'd like to, I can't fight with a pregnant woman.

Haven presses her lips together, her face in rigid lines, then pivots on a heel and marches away.

Suddenly I'm trembling, leaning against Ford's back. "Oh, dear God."

He turns and steadies me with those big hands. "Are you okay?"

I swallow. "I think so."

"What is her problem?" he rumbles. "Jesus."

"She's... I think she's jealous."

"Yeah, I'd say so." He rubs my back in gentle circles that both comfort me and send sparks down my spine. "What the fuck?"

"Thank you." I draw back from him, gathering my composure. I glance around. "Thanks for standing up for me."

"Of course. She's a loon."

"That was not cool," the woman next to me says. "Wow."

"Unprofessional," her partner says, frowning.

"I think... I'd like to leave now." I gaze up at Ford.

"Yeah. Let's get out of here."

I grab my little purse and my trophy, holding myself together long enough to say good night to the others sitting with us, then Ford leads us out of the room, down to the ground floor, and out into the city night. The sun has set and the lights of Manhattan glitter and sparkle around us.

I pause. I don't know which direction to go.

"Should we get an Uber?" Ford asks.

"I need a drink. Let's walk." I stalk along the sidewalk toward West 46th.

Ford falls into step with me. "You okay in those heels?"

"My feet are killing me," I admit. "But I'll make it."

There are lots of restaurants on this street just up ahead. We pause at one of the first we come to, an Italian place with a tiny patio in front. Miraculously, there's an empty table and we are quickly seated there.

I pick up a cocktail menu and study it.

"Are you warm enough?" Ford asks.

I realize I shivered in the evening breeze. "I'm fine."

He shakes his head and takes off his suit jacket, moving around to drape it over my shoulders. His warmth and scent—

like warm leather and spice—envelop me and for a moment I feel a wee bit dizzy. I resist the urge to drop my chin and press my nose into the lapel to breathe in more. "Thank you."

He sits back in his chair and loosens his tie, all smooth and sophisticated in his expensive clothes, a contrast to the sweaty, half-naked guy doing martial arts, or the athlete on the ice, or even the automaton he appears to be at home, all regimented and organized.

A waiter appears and I order a dirty martini. Ford gets a beer.

"So," he says. "Did you steal her client?"

"No!"

His lips twitch and I see he's teasing.

"I didn't steal them," I say more calmly. "They were a client I worked with at Design Edge. We had a good working relationship. When I left Design Edge, they had a couple of months left on their contract, and they decided not to sign with them again and came to me. But I had no idea they were going to do that."

He nods.

"Some of the people at Design Edge were upset about it," I continue. "Especially Haven, who took over their account when I left. The thing is, Haven's good at what she does. Mirabella just preferred working with me. But she doesn't need to be jealous of me."

"You're too nice to her."

"Probably," I say with a glum smile. "Thanks again for defending me."

"She was way out of line. For a minute I thought I was going to have to break up a cat fight."

I snort-laugh. "You almost were."

"The only reason I stopped you is because she's pregnant and you were gonna take her down." Amusement shades his voice.

"I thought hockey players like fights."

He grins. "I'm a goalie."

"So goalies never fight?"

"Uh... rarely."

Intrigued, I lean forward. "Have you? Gotten in a fight?"

"Maybe a few times."

My mouth drops open and a little laugh escapes me. "Seriously?"

He gives me a look with a crooked smile. "I have a bit of a temper."

I tilt my head. "I've never seen that."

"Mostly when I see something unfair." He pauses. "That sparks my temper. Like whatshername blaming you for losing a client."

Tonight was the most emotional I've ever seen him. No, wait —he had seethed a bit when he found out Trev had left me for another woman. So there *are* things that rile him up... "So you fight in hockey when something's not fair?"

He rubs his chin. "I guess? One time this player for the Bears —Jake Colman—kept skating through my crease, kept bumping me. He was pissing me off and I told him if he touched me again he would, er, eat my hockey stick."

A laugh bursts from my lips. "And he did?"

"Yeah. So he had it coming. I warned him."

"Did you get a penalty?"

"Oh, hell, yeah."

"Was that the only fight?"

"No."

Our drinks arrive and I pick up my martini to take a swallow. It heats my mouth and warms me all the way down my esophagus. When the server has gone, I say, "Okay, tell me."

He shakes his head, a smile playing on his lips. "There were actually a few times when I was a kid. But the other time as a pro,

I wasn't the only one who got in the fight. One of the other team's guys crosschecked Shawzy, right in front of my net, dropped him to the ice. I was pissed and I came out of the net and jumped the guy. A few other guys got involved and then the tender from the other team came down the ice and he and I got into it."

I cover my face with my hands, wanting to laugh, even though I don't approve of physical violence. Getting riled like I did earlier is out of character for me. "That's crazy."

"Yeah, it kind of was. Anyway. You didn't need to get into a donnybrook with a colleague at a fancy awards dinner. That's a little different than mixing it up on the ice."

"True." I take another sip of my drink. "I'm calming down. Thanks for distracting me."

"Good. Sorry that happened. Don't let it ruin your night. You should be proud."

I give a firm nod. "I am." But... I wrinkle my nose. "I thought winning the award would make everything okay. But I'm still divorced. Haven and Trevor are still together. And she's pregnant."

Ford purses his lips as he lifts his glass. After he swallows, he says, "I thought you were over him."

My eyebrows tug together. "I... am. I guess."

"You guess? Do you still want to get back together with him?"

His question takes me aback. There have definitely been times I've imagined Trevor coming back to me, apologetic and begging for forgiveness, admitting he made a terrible mistake. It's a fantasy to imagine the man who broke your heart is also broken-hearted and repentant, hurting as much as he hurt you.

But if that happened, how would I react? Would I really forgive him? Would I really take him back after what he did?

"I... I don't know. I mean, he's with someone else. And they're having a baby. So no."

"What if he wasn't with someone else?"

I meet Ford's eyes, but it's uncomfortable because he's looking at me so steadily and intently, and I look away. "I don't know. It was more than just him falling for another woman."

"What was it?"

"It was... the fact that I'd supported him all those years. We got married when we were young. I put myself through college and supported us so he could play ball. So he could pursue his dream. I..." I stop, my throat closing up. "I wanted to be a veterinarian. But that takes years of school. So I did a business degree instead. Trevor always told me that I'd get my turn to follow my dreams once he'd made it. But then..." I clear my throat. "Just when that happened, when he finally made it to the big league, and I was starting to apply to vet schools, he... lost interest in me."

It fucking hurts to admit that. Even though it's been almost two years since it happened, I still sometimes question why I wasn't good enough for him. Why wasn't I enough?

And yeah, my friends have tried to shut that down and reassure me that I *am* enough, that he just wasn't the right man, and I mostly believe that, but there are times when I'm feeling low and those doubts creep back in.

I watch Ford's face change, going from relaxed to stony with narrowed eyes, then neutral. "He's an idiot."

I smile. "Thanks. You're good for my ego." He's been so kind and compassionate tonight. I'm not sure why I'm a little surprised; maybe it's because I've mostly seen his cocky, dirty, flirty side.

His shoulder lifts in a barely-there shrug.

I drain my martini glass, feeling a welcome buzz. The waiter instantly appears. "Another one?"

"Sure." I look at Ford, but he lifts his half-full glass and shakes his head. "Anyway." I look down at the table. "It's over between us. He's moved on."

"And you seem to have moved on, with all those guys you date."

I make a face. "Yeah. That's the only kind of relationship I want. Not serious. Just fun."

I'll always love Trevor, in some ways. I'll always love the Trevor he was when things were good—when we were young and in love and had so much fun together. But that Trevor is gone. I'll never have a relationship like that again. And that's okay. Obviously my judgment about men is flawed. Professional athletes clearly are only concerned with themselves—with their careers and getting ahead.

And as supportive as Ford is, I know he's exactly the same.

And that's why we're just friends.

5

FORD

Thank God the season is starting soon. Summer makes me crazy —all that free time. I like structure, so I make sure my off season is busy with taekwondo, yoga, and of course hockey workouts with Victor.

My teammates are back in town—those who left for the summer—and it's great to see them and hang out again. I stayed here in Hoboken instead of going home to Erie because I wanted to work with Victor.

Today I'm at the grand opening of a new facility for the organization Keeping Kids Safe. Our newly anointed team captain Benny is being introduced up on the dais. I'm glad he's our new captain. He's a quiet guy who doesn't say much (although he can chirp with the best of them on the ice) but he's a good leader. Along with the progress the team made last season, I like our chances this year of not only making the playoffs but making a deep run for the cup.

Which is why I was so determined to improve my game over the summer.

We all clap and hoot exuberantly for our new captain as we watch him walk up to the mic.

"Thank you, Sue," Benny says. "I'm thrilled to be a part of this group and to give back to the community. I'm proud to use my voice and platform to give kids who need it a voice. Hockey is a team sport and we all know how important it is to stand together, and kids who've experienced abuse also need a team around them."

Yeah, it's a team sport. But as the goaltender, I feel a unique pressure to be the best. There's nobody else on the ice I can blame when a puck gets by me and into the net.

After the short ceremony, Benny's girlfriend, Mabel, turns to us and beams. "He did great."

This is Benny's first time in public as captain. He's kind of shy and public speaking isn't his favorite thing, but yeah—he did great. And seeing his new girlfriend all proud and admiring of him gives me a pinching feeling in my chest. I'm happy for them.

"Of course he did," my teammate and Mabel's brother, Smitty, says.

Benny makes his way over to us. "Thanks for coming, guys." He looks around. "Where's Alfie?"

Carson Alford, AKA Alfie, had been here earlier, but he disappeared part way through the ceremony. Last year, he and his wife were in a terrible car crash and their baby died. Alfie was injured and even though he's recovered now physically, he's still not doing great mentally.

"He had to go," Mabel says. "I think this was hard for him."

"I'm sure anything to do with kids is hard for him," I say quietly.

"Yeah." Dilly, another teammate, nods with a sad smile. "I'm glad he came, though. Hopefully we'll see more of him."

"We have to make sure we invite him," Benny says. "Even if we're just hanging out."

"I'm afraid I'm going to say something stupid around him." I rub my jaw. It's one thing to deal with a guy with a broken arm. But when it's a guy with a broken brain, it feels awkward.

"I think we all are," Benny says. "But if we say something stupid, we apologize. It's better than not saying anything or ignoring him."

"Yeah, for sure." Nash nods.

"I'll tell you this," I say. "I am *never* having kids. After hearing about abused kids this morning, and Alfie losing his son, it's never happening." Not to mention scaring them into tears by talking about sharks.

"Oh." Mabel purses her lips. "You shouldn't let that stop you."

"Well, that's only part of it. Can you imagine me as a dad? Ha! A kid would drive me nuts. And I'm probably not the best role model."

"Probably true," Dilly agrees too easily. But I don't react. "You and your routines. I don't think strict routines and kids go together very well."

"Exactly. I'm too selfish," I say. "And weird."

"Who knows what the future holds?" Mabel says. "Maybe someday you'll meet a woman and fall in love with her and want a family with her."

I snort. "Not gonna happen."

I've always been different. I embrace my weirdness now, but I know from experience as a kid how much it hurts to feel excluded. Belonging and fitting in are important when you're a kid. In hockey, I found people with a common interest, somewhere I can feel secure and fit in even though I'm kind of offbeat. Hey, goalies are supposed to be different. Everyone knows that.

Outside of hockey, I don't think anyone will ever see past my peculiarities to see the real me. I mean, my peculiarities *are* the real me; they need to accept that. So relationships aren't for me. And that's fine. Like my neighbor, Andi, casual hookups or a few dates are fine for me.

I had fun with Andi the other night. Even though I didn't want to go. I'm glad I was there for her when that crazy bitch accused her of stealing a client. She was so pumped about winning that award and then that happened.

Then I remember her saying she wants her ex to know what he lost. Like she still cares what he thinks. For some reason, that annoys me.

I shake my head. "Okay. Where are we going for lunch?"

We end up at Waylon's, a barbecue place on Newark Avenue. Since the weather is still nice, we sit out on the sidewalk patio beneath a red awning. I order burnt ends and coleslaw. "What kind of beer would go best with that?" I ask the server.

"Oh! We have a new one. A meat beer."

"Oh my fuck," Smitty mutters.

I like trying new beers. Intrigued, I ask, "What is it?"

"Pork Porter," she says. "It has a smoked pork flavor."

"Perfect. I'll try that."

Dilly makes a retching noise. I ignore him.

"That sounds disgusting," Smitty says.

I ignore him, too.

"How'd your training go this summer?" Dilly asks me. "How's that new trainer?"

"He's great." I nod enthusiastically. "He has a whole different philosophy and I really like it."

"What is it?" Smitty asks.

"He's basically rewired my brain."

Dilly laughs. "Finally someone has."

I grin. "Seriously." I tell them more about Victor and the exercises he has me doing. "We worked on them over and over until my brain just does them now. He doesn't just look at just the athletic side of things but the artistic side."

They all look at me like I just said I want to jump off the Statue of Liberty.

"I'm not just a machine," I tell them.

Benny scratches the back of his head. "Are you sure?"

"I get it," Mabel says. "Hockey's not just physical. It's mental. It's not just analytical and scientific; there's an artistry to it."

"Hockey is not an art," Smitty says to his sister.

"I'll argue with you about that," she says.

Mabel's got her quirks, too. I like her. We've kind of gotten to be friends since she moved here.

"What's the definition of art?" she asks her brother.

"I don't know. Art. Creation."

"Hang on." She grabs her phone. "Okay, here it is. It's the expression of human creative skill and imagination to produce a work that is appreciated primarily for its beauty or emotional power." She looks up from the phone. "See? Hockey is beautiful to watch. Also you guys make people feel a lot of emotion. Think of the fans!"

Smitty snorts. "I think they're talking about painting, or sculpture."

"Sure, that too," she says calmly. "I stand by my argument."

"She's right," I say.

Mabel reaches across the table for a fist bump.

"Anyway, the point is that I'm not just a machine. I'm an athlete, but I have a craft. So do all of us." I lift my chin.

"I'm not convinced," Dilly says. "But okay."

"It's really changed my game," I add.

I see the skeptical looks on their faces, but I don't care. I'll show them once training camp starts. I can't wait.

"Are you still doing martial arts?" Mabel asks.

"Yeah. I went to the dojo twice a week over the summer."

Another thing they think is weird. Again, I don't care. It works for me.

After lunch, Mabel has to go back to work but the rest of us stay for another beer. We talk about training camp, workouts, and get in an argument about whether Dilly is a "himbo."

"I don't even know what that means," he complains after telling us a woman called him that.

"I'm not sure either," Smitty admits.

"It's a guy who's big and buff but nothing going on in his head," Benny says.

"Fuck. Thanks a lot." Dilly scowls.

"I'm not saying that's you," Benny adds hastily. "But I think that's what it means."

"I think it just means a guy who's nice. Not necessarily stupid," I put in.

"Like a golden retriever," Smitty adds.

"Shit, we need Mabel," Benny says. "She'd know this stuff."

"Ask her about it," Dilly says. "For a friend. Like, for real. Don't tell her it's me."

"How's she going to weigh in on whether you're a himbo if she doesn't know it's you?" Benny asks.

Dilly throws his hands in the air. "I don't know!"

"Ask her if she thinks any of us are himbos," Smitty says.

Benny gnaws on his bottom lip. "I don't know. I guess I could ask her."

"Do women like himbos?" I ask, a little confused about this conversation. "Or no? Was she trying to insult you?"

Dilly scrunches his face up. "It didn't sound like she was trying to insult me."

"Why would it be a good thing if it means a guy's stupid?" Smitty says.

"Maybe some women like stupid men. Maybe it's easier for them."

"That's bullshit. I don't think that's what it means. I think it's a nice guy."

"But women don't like 'nice guys'," Dilly says with a touch of bitterness. "Don't they all want a bad boy alpha male?"

"We need Mabel again." Benny rubs his forehead. "I don't think that's always true."

I grin. "You're going to be having a fun conversation with her tonight. Be sure to report back."

"Speaking of himbos..." Dilly gives me a serious look. "Did you ever try that Minoxidil like we suggested?"

I narrow my eyes at Dilly. "No. I don't need Minoxidil."

They love to drag me about my hair. I have great hair. I just like to make sure it looks its best.

My phone rings. Thankful for the interruption, I glance at it to see it's my mom. "Ah. Better get this." I stand. "Who's buying?"

"You are," Dilly says.

"Nope. I think it's your turn. Thanks, man." I hit the button to take the call. "Hi, Mom. Hang on." I move the phone away from my face. "See you later. I have to get going." It's my day to clean the big bathroom. "Hey, Mom, how are you?"

"Hiiiii, honey! I'm sooo good!"

I swallow a sigh. She's baked. Again.

6

FORD

When I was eight, I accidentally got stoned on a pot cookie.

My parents loved me and brought me up with an emphasis on peace, love, and nature. I was encouraged to follow my own path. My path turned out to be hockey, which wasn't what my parents had in mind. Hockey is not exactly a peaceful and loving sport.

Don't get me wrong; I love my parents and I appreciate everything they've done for me. Raising a hockey player kid who gets to the NHL is never easy, but for my parents it was miserable. Practices, games, tournaments—so much scheduling! For people who live their lives moment to moment, without rules and limits, it was excruciating trying to keep track of everything. Also, as people who practice peace and love, they hated the brutishness of the game and especially the fights. Somehow, they did it, though, and I'm grateful.

Now that I'm an adult and on my own, I can keep my life balanced and structured. Which is how I like it. And they're free to live their life the way they like it, too—footloose and freewheeling, protesting weapons of mass destruction and gun violence, and traveling. I paid off their mortgage so they could retire and do the things they want to. When I was a kid, there was never money left for travel, after paying hockey registration fees and all my equipment and travel to tournaments (which wasn't the kind of travel they had in mind; hanging out in cheap hotels with a bunch of hockey parents was painful for them). Also, there was never time. Even in summers they paid for me to go to elite hockey camps. They never got to backpack across Europe like they wanted to as young adults, but now they are. But I'm not letting them backpack and stay in hostels. I'm paying for hotels and air fares and car rentals so they can experience it in comfort. They're not twenty anymore, although they sometimes act like it. They leave on their trip in a couple of weeks.

"How's it going?" I ask my mom.

"Great! We've been planning our trip. We've been looking at places to stay in Vienna."

"Oh, good." I hope she's not too high. Lord knows what she's booking. Probably Australia instead of Austria. Or Paris, Texas instead of Paris, France.

"I had the craziest dream last night," she says, totally off topic.

"Yeah?" She really does have crazy dreams, and she remembers them all.

"We were in Malaysia. Penang. It was kind of scary. There were ghosts."

I look up at the sky.

"What if our dreams are just glimpses into parallel universes?" she asks. "Those ghosts could be real beings."

"Mom."

"Sorry. Anyway, we wanted to check with you about hotels. Some of them are expensive."

"That's okay. Stay somewhere nice."

I talk to her more while I drive. When I get near the building

I say, "Gotta go, Mom. I'm about to park and the cell service isn't good down there."

"Okay! It was good to talk to you. I love you! Your dad does, too."

"Love you, too."

I stop in the lobby to get my mail and notice a woman sitting there on one of the black chairs. There's a baby carrier on the coffee table in front of her.

What's with the babies, lately?

I look down at the envelope in my hand, then jerk my head up again. That woman... she's looking at me now, and jumps to her feet. I know her.

"Willa?"

"Hi!" She buzzes across the lobby toward me, hands clasped in front of her. "Ford. I was waiting for you."

Willa and I went out about a year ago. I remember it was last summer. We met at a bar one night, went out the next evening, had a night of smash and dash at my place, and never saw each other again. My usual.

Why is she here? And after all this time?

I'm staring at her speechlessly, trying to gather my wits. "Waiting for me?" I repeat. "Uh, why?"

"I need to talk to you. It's important."

I rub one eyebrow, confused. "Um. Okay. You want to come up?"

"Please." She hurries back to the seating area, picks up the baby carrier and joins me at the elevators. "This is Matilda."

I peer into the carrier. Another baby. She's asleep so at least I won't make her cry.

We ride up in silence and she follows me into my place.

"Would you like something to drink?" I offer. "Coke, water, Gatorade?"

She shakes her head. "I'm good, thanks. Is it okay if we sit?"

"Sure."

She sets the baby on the floor near the couch and sits so she can watch her. I sit across from her. I'm feeling kind of warm. Like my skin is too tight. I'm not sure what's going on here.

"You're probably surprised to see me," she says with a strained smile.

"Yep." That sounded rude. I don't want to be rude. I'm just baffled about why she's here.

Or... I look at the baby again. I narrow my eyes. Is she going to tell me I'm the father? One night! We used protection. I always use protection. And that was over a year ago!

That can't be it.

But... I swallow.

"This isn't easy so I'm just going to come right out with it. Matilda is your daughter."

I throw up my hands. "No way. Come on."

She wrings her hands. "It's true, Ford. I'm sorry."

I move my head side to side, staring at her. "No."

She holds my gaze steadily and fuck me, I think she believes it. "How can that be? How old is she?"

"She's three months old. Almost four months."

"Oh. But... but... how did it happen?" I swipe at beads of sweat that are popping out on my forehead.

She scrunches up her face. She's pretty enough, with pale blonde hair and blue eyes. I don't remember her being this thin, but truthfully, I don't recall much about our brief time together. "It happened." She shrugs. "Sometimes condoms fail."

I let that sink in. "Shit."

"I know."

"Are you sure it's me? I mean..."

"Yeah, I'm pretty sure."

"But not 100 percent?"

She bites her lip. "Ninety-nine? We can get testing done. I knew you'd want that, and that's fine. I actually brought a home test."

"Whoa." I blink. "Are you... looking for child support?" I'm not being critical; that would be reasonable. In fact, that would probably be the only reason someone would show up a year later with a baby.

Her eyebrows slope down and she closes her eyes briefly. "No," she says quietly. "Not exactly. I have a bit of an emergency situation and I need your help."

"Is she okay?" I glance at the baby, suddenly alarmed.

"Yes, yes. It's not her. It's my... parents."

* * *

A couple of hours later, my place is packed with all kinds of baby equipment. There are baby bottles and formula spread out on the counter in my kitchen. A huge bag of diapers sits in the hall.

I'm alone. With a baby. My daughter. This is fucking bonkers. I feel like I'm living in an alternate reality.

But the screams coming from that tiny human are definitely real. She's awake, her mom's gone, and she is not happy.

7

ANDI

"Your Ideal Customer Profile, or ICP, is the pool of accounts within your total market," I say to my computer monitor. The faces of my clients in our virtual meeting look back at me. "But it's a huge population, so we want to narrow things down."

I pause at the noise I'm hearing from the condo next door. It sounds like a baby crying.

Can't be.

"First we look at foundational segments," I continue. "Like good, better, and best fit customers. Then we can go even further to next-level segments."

"Is that... a baby crying?" Maria asks.

Oh my God. Can they hear it, too? I glance at the wall between my place and Ford's. My office is right next to his living room. I've never heard noises from there before, but apparently the walls are paper thin.

"I didn't know you have a baby," James says.

"I don't," I quickly say. "I'm not sure what that noise is. It seems to be coming from next door. I'm so sorry."

"It's fine," Maria says, but she's frowning and her tone indicates it's not really fine.

"Let's move on," I say, hoping that if I keep talking they won't hear the other noise. "So, all these segments help us better understand your audience, so we can confidently target and personalize their content."

Another wail sounds from the other side of the wall. Dear lord, it does sound like a baby, and it sounds like the baby is in pain. It's very hard to ignore that. What is going on?

We finish up our meeting with a plan in place for categorizing my client's customers and they seem on board with it. A soon as I've ended the meeting, I push my chair back from the desk, stand, and hike out of my apartment and down the hall to rap on Ford's door.

I hear the baby crying.

The door is yanked open and Ford stands in front of me, an infant on his shoulder. His hair, usually artfully tousled, stands up in all directions, his clothes are rumpled, and he seems to be sweating profusely. His presentation is extremely disturbing, given that he's always so meticulous about his appearance.

"What is going on in here?" I demand. "I was trying to have an online meeting and my clients heard the baby crying!" I stare at the child. "Whose baby is that? And why do you have it?"

Ford closes his eyes briefly. "She's my baby."

My eyes pop open wide. I stare at him. My brain scrambles, trying to make sense of this. Is he adopting a baby? Why would he do that? Did he really say that? I must have misunderstood. Meanwhile, the baby is screaming her little head off.

I shake my head. "I'm sorry, what?"

"She's my baby," he repeats, louder, over the howling.

I blink and take in the stress etched on his face, the tightness of his jaw, the lines at the corners of his eyes. "I don't understand."

"Honestly, I'm not sure I do either." He growls out a sigh, patting the child awkwardly on the back. "Come in."

I eye the baby as if she might attack me. "That's okay. I just need you to keep her quiet."

"I'm trying! Jesus! You think I *like* listening to this sound?"

I suck my bottom lip between my teeth. Oh, yeah. He's stressed.

I know nothing about babies. To be honest, I'm a little afraid of them. Tiny humans whose existence depends on you. Who cry for hours for no reason. Or maybe there is a reason—it's because they're dying, and you don't know what to do about it. Terrifying!

"Come on, Matilda, stop crying, *please*."

Matilda. I swallow. "I have no advice to offer, but I have another meeting in half an hour and I need for my clients to *not* hear screaming. They'll think someone is torturing her."

I turn and march back to my apartment.

In my office, I sink into the chair in front of the computer.

Why do I feel guilty? That's not my baby. But... poor Ford. He looked stressed. And I just left him there.

How can it be his baby?

Okay, yes, I know how babies are made. Ford has never had a serious girlfriend, but he's been with a lot of women. Yikes.

Did he know about the baby? I guess it's possible and he never mentioned it to me? No, it's not possible. I would have seen the baby. Heard the baby before now. Why did the baby just show up? This is so bizarre.

I can't stop thinking about it and I'm still distracted when it's time for my next meeting. I don't hear the baby anymore, which is a good thing, so I manage to compartmentalize and focus on business.

Until we're wrapping up and the wailing starts up again.

I see the startled looks on the faces of my clients.

"Sorry," I say with a tight smile. "That's my neighbor."

"Wow, that's loud," Oliver says. "Everything okay?"

"Oh, yes!" I nod reassuringly, although I'm not at all certain. "Fine, fine! So we'll meet again next week, same time... does that work for everyone?"

We all confirm and after I end the meeting I enter it into my calendar, trying to tune out the baby cries. It's not so easy, though. Anxiety tightens my shoulders and my stomach. Is the baby okay? I mean, Matilda. Is *Ford* okay? He did not look okay.

I have no more meetings, but still a ton of work to do. In my determination to succeed, I may have taken on more clients than I can handle by myself, but I don't mind working long hours. I love my work. Right now, though, I abandon my work and stride to Ford's place. When I knock, he answers quickly, still holding the baby but on the other shoulder.

"I'm sorry!" he bursts out. "I'm trying my best! I took her into my bedroom so you couldn't hear her, but I had to come out here to get a diaper."

"That's probably what she needs." I step into his condo. "A clean diaper."

"I don't think that's it," he mutters, turning to walk into his living room. "I tried that a while ago and it didn't seem to help."

I follow him. There's a stain on his shoulder and all down the back of his shirt. I think it's baby vomit. "Oh. Is she hungry?" That's the extent of my baby knowledge. Feed them or change their diaper.

"No." He forks his fingers into his thick hair. "I fed her."

I eye Matilda, her cries amplifying the fear inside me. "How did this happen?"

Ford lifts an eyebrow.

"I know, I know." I wave a hand and perch on the edge of a chair. "But who is the mother? And how did you just end up with this tiny human now? Were you keeping her secret?"

"Long story." He paces, shifting the baby to cradle her in his arms and bounce her a little. "I'm still in shock."

"No doubt."

"Willa and I had a one-night stand. About a year ago."

I'm doing math in my head. "Matilda is about three months old?"

"You got it. Well, actually almost four months. But the math is mathing."

"Ohhhh, boy." I pause. "Are you sure you're the father?"

"Yeah. We're getting testing done, but when you see her eyes you'll know."

I purse my lips and nod slowly. "And where is... Willa now?"

"She had to go home to Fargo to take care of her parents. They were in a bad car accident and they're both hurt."

"And she couldn't take the baby with her?"

Ford makes a face. "She says she needs time to focus on her parents. They're both in the hospital."

Do I buy that? I don't know. "So she dumps the kid on you."

He winces. "Basically, yeah."

"Wow." I pull in a breath and exhale slowly. Then I cover my ears with my hands. "That noise is making me crazy."

"You and me both."

I pull my phone out of my bra. "Hold on." I google *how to stop a crying baby* and study the results. "How about a warm bath?"

"I'd love one."

I give him a slanted, chiding look. "For the baby, Ford."

"Yeah, I guess I could try that." He looks as fearful as I feel.

I read some of the other suggestions. He's already walking

her, patting her back, and making soothing noises. "Oh! Does she have a pacifier?"

"Yeah, but Willa said she doesn't like it."

"Did you try?"

"No."

"Where is it?" I stand.

He points to a bunch of baby paraphernalia on the floor in the corner.

"Whoa. That's a lot of stuff." I approach it cautiously.

"I know. This place is a disaster. Jesus." He hates clutter and mess. "The pacifier's in the diaper bag."

I open the pink bag and dig around in it. I produce a clear plastic case with two pacifiers in it. I pick out one and go over to Ford. Matilda's little face is red and scrunched up. Not a good look. I hesitantly poke the pacifier at her but she doesn't see it. So I touch it to her lips.

She turns her head away.

Ford takes it from me and continues to try to get it into her mouth but when he does she spits it out. Over and over.

"See?" he says, sounding defeated.

"Damn."

"Watch your language."

I burst out laughing. Then I meet his eyes and see he's serious. "She's three months old," I remind him gently.

"Right, right."

"Okay, back to the bath. Does she have a little tub or something?"

"No, she has a bath seat that you put in the big tub." He walks over to the pile of stuff in the corner that could rival the inventory of Babies"R"Us and nudges it with his toe. "There's a bag of bath stuff here."

I locate the bag and carry it and the seat to Ford's bathroom.

I've been to Ford's condo lots of times, but now I realize this bathroom doesn't have a tub.

"My room," he says. "I have a tub in the en suite bathroom."

"Okay."

We walk through Ford's bedroom, which I have never seen. It's gorgeous—a massive king-size bed with a gray upholstered headboard fills the center of the room, with modern marble cubes as nightstands. Big glass globes provide light, and dark floor-to-ceiling curtains are open to let in late-afternoon sunlight. His bed looks luxurious. Comfortable. For some reason, though, looking at his bed disturbs me. I look away.

In the bathroom, he rocks Matilda while I run warm water and rummage around for a small cloth, some baby wash and shampoo—the girl's got a head of thick, dark hair—as well as lotion and a cute hooded towel.

By the time everything's arranged and there's enough water in the tub, Matilda's cries have eased off somewhat. Her eyes are puffy and drooping closed. "I think she tired herself out," I say quietly. "Should we still do this?"

"I have no fucking clue."

"Language." I catch his eye and reluctant amusement tugs his lips. "I guess we need to get her clothes off her." She's wearing a little cotton dress in a pink and green floral pattern with a matching pair of... shorts?... under it.

"Right. I'll take her to the bed." He carries her back into the room and carefully lays Matilda down on the puffy duvet. He pulls the dress up to her chin and she starts fussing again.

Gingerly, he tries to ease her arms out of the sleeves. "I'm afraid I'll break her," he mumbles.

"Don't break her." I watch anxiously. "Babies are fragile."

"I know." Eventually he has her out of the dress. Her chubby arms and legs are constantly kicking and waving. I almost laugh.

"Did you put this on her?" I ask him.

"No. This is how Willa brought her."

"Hmmm. Do you think she's crying because she misses her mom?"

He looks up at me, open-mouthed. "Jesus. Of course! Why didn't I think of that?"

"Well, there's not much we can do about that."

"You could hold her. Maybe she needs a woman."

"No, no." I shake my head violently, backing away with my hands raised. "I can't hold a baby. I don't know how."

He gives me a look as if I just deserted him in the high Arctic and peels the shorts down her legs. Now the little girl is just in her diaper.

"I'm afraid to take this off," he says. "She might pee or poop."

"I think we have to risk it."

He takes off the diaper and picks her up with awkward care. I have to say, the sight of his big man hands holding a tiny naked baby gives me a twinge in my previously unnoticed ovaries.

He carries her back to the bathroom and stands and looks down at the water.

"Well, put her in the tub."

"She could drown in there."

I nod seriously. "Valid concern. How do people do this?"

"Christ. Willa went over a bunch of stuff with me." He scrubs a hand over his face. "But when it comes to actually doing it, I'm lost."

"I'm afraid I'm not much help. I know nothing about babies." I give him a glum smile. "Trevor and I both agreed we didn't want kids." Which makes the fact that his new girlfriend is pregnant that much more depressing.

"I don't want kids either," Ford mutters, looking down at Matilda's face. "But I apparently have no choice in this matter."

I feel for him. I really do. This is a life-changing surprise.

"Okay. I'll just get in with her." He lays her on the bathmat and pulls his T-shirt over his head.

Gulp. "Whoa. What are you doing?"

"Getting in the tub." He undoes his belt and zipper and shoves his jeans down. He steps out of them, leaving him in a snug pair of black boxer briefs. He hooks his thumbs into the waist band.

"Jesus!" I wave my hands. "Stop!"

He shrugs, as if being naked in front of me is no big deal. "Fine." And he picks up the baby and steps into the tub, still wearing his underwear.

Sweet Jesus. I've seen his bare chest before but this... this is magnificent. His body is hard and fit, with perfectly proportioned shoulders and hips. My eyes linger on the grooves of his abs then lower to his powerful legs. I swallow. "Is it warm enough?"

"I think so." He sits in the shallow water and places Matilda in the baby seat facing him.

"We should have scrubbed the tub first," I add fretfully. "There could be germs in there."

"Not in my house," Ford retorts.

"Right." He has a meticulous cleaning routine. I tease him sometimes about how he could afford to hire a cleaning lady, but he's tried that and apparently they can't meet his standards.

Matilda is snuffling and hiccupping but not screaming. She puts one fist in her mouth and looks up at me.

Oh, yeah. Those are Ford's eyes.

It kind of knocks me sideways, seeing that miniature replica of him, with the pale green irises ringed in darker green, thick eyelashes, and mop of dark hair.

I hand Ford the little cloth and bottle of baby soap.

Chomping on her fist, she does seem distracted as he gently

moves the soapy cloth over her skin. Ford squeezes the cloth over her hair and I give him the shampoo bottle to lather up her locks. His massaging fingers calm Matilda even more, and we exchange hopeful glances.

While he's doing that, I dig out a little comb for her hair, some lotion, and a clean onesie. I also find a pink sack sort of thing that I think she might sleep in.

While I wait for him to finish, I look around his bathroom. It's lovely, too, sleek and clean with a huge glassed-in shower, gray and white tile, and a square modern vanity. My gaze lingers on the shower and the bottles lined up on a shelf inside. That's an extraordinary amount of hair-care products.

Ford stands, water running down all his sleek muscles, the wet cotton of his underwear plastered to a fat bulge at his groin. I blink rapidly and vacate the bathroom so he can dry himself off. He emerges with a big towel around his waist and Matilda in his arms, now swaddled in the hooded towel.

"She's not screaming," I whisper.

"I know." Once again he lays her on the bed and carefully dries her off everywhere. She's still kicking and flailing, but her eyes are bright and open, watching his every move. It takes a while, but eventually she's dressed again with only a few squawks as Ford maneuvers her little limbs into the clothing. He straps the pink sack around her with Velcro and her eyes are drooping.

"I think she's going to sleep," he murmurs.

"Yeah. Where does she sleep?"

He points to the apparatus beside the bed and carries her over to it to gently lay her down.

I'm holding my breath as he straightens, waiting for screams, but other than a couple of huffs and grunts, Matilda stays silent.

I tiptoe out of the room. Ford follows moments later, now wearing a pair of gray sweatpants and a T-shirt. Who knew he even owned a pair of gray sweatpants? I have to admit to a weakness for such attire; Trevor may have betrayed me, but he was also a pro athlete with a great body, and when he wore gray sweatpants I was a total floozy for him. I'm sure this reaction to Ford in the same clothing is just Pavlovian.

I take my time looking away as he fiddles with a device on the coffee table, then collapses onto the couch. "Holy shit."

I sit, too. "Yeah. Holy shit."

He rolls his head on the back of the couch and looks at me with anguish filling his green eyes. "Andi. What the hell am I going to do?"

8

FORD

I still can't believe this is happening.

Since the moment Willa appeared at my door, my life has devolved into out-of-control chaos. My living room is stuffed with baby things, my kitchen is full of bottles and nipples and formula, and I can still feel Matilda's cries scraping against every nerve ending in my body. The helpless frustration at not being able to soothe her has me exhausted.

"This is really... wild," Andi says. "Did you know you have a child?"

"No! Jesus." I close my eyes. "I had no idea."

"Why didn't she tell you?"

"She said she wasn't sure I was the father. She'd been with a couple of other guys around the same time. She decided to have the baby on her own, but around Matilda's three-month birthday her eyes started changing color and Willa realized I had to be the father. And then... her parents got in that accident and she... well, she said she needed me."

"That's not fair to you," Andi says quietly. "To dump all that on you out of the blue."

"I agree. On the other hand, I don't want to be that guy. Who doesn't take responsibility for his own child. I just... I just don't know how I'm going to handle this." I turn to look at Andi again. "Training camps starts in a few days. I can't exactly bring her along."

"Well, no. You need a babysitter. Or a nanny."

"How the hell do I find one of those?"

"I don't know! I'm just trying to help. Come on, you're a smart guy. You have to have some problem-solving skills."

"I do not," I say tiredly. "I think every brain cell in my head was destroyed by all that crying."

"I do understand that," she replies, slumping into the couch. "It's a terrible, horrible sound."

"Right?"

"Again, you're smart enough to figure things out. I found out about the bath on Google. We'll look up some other strategies for calming her down. We'll look for a nanny."

"I'm not going to find anyone before Thursday."

She grimaces. "Probably true. But you never know."

"I can't do it right now. I'm exhausted."

"Maybe you need a nap."

"I never nap when it's not a game day." I close my eyes.

I roll my eyes. "I think you can deviate from your usual routine, since your routine didn't include a baby."

"True." I lift my head which feels as heavy as planet Earth. "Okay." I grab a cushion, shove it behind my head, and stretch out on the couch.

Andi stands, giving me room, but then walks toward the door.

"Where are you going?" I ask sharply.

"Home." She blinks at me.

"Don't go."

She gives me big brown eyes from behind her tortoiseshell-framed glasses. "What? Why?"

I don't even know why I said that. Except this feels easier with someone else. "What if she wakes up and I don't hear her?"

She rolls her eyes. "Oh, you'll hear her."

"I might not."

"I have work to do." She blows out a breath. "But fine. Go ahead, have your nap." She waves her hands at me. "But just know, I'm not much help when it comes to babies. I know nothing."

"That's about the same as me, eight hours ago. And the knowledge I've acquired since then is minimal." I close my eyes, trying to relax my tight muscles.

This is so fucked up.

* * *

I do wake up when Matilda cries. The sound comes through the baby monitor. I blink my eyes and try to pull myself out of the depths of sleep.

"Ford."

"What?"

"She's awake."

"I know. I hear her." I push myself up to sitting and rub my face. "What time is it? How long did we sleep?"

"Nearly two hours."

"Oh, man. I needed that." I head into the bedroom to pick up the crying baby, then take her over to the bed. I have a pad that I lay her on to change the diaper. She stops crying, thank fuck, as I fumble around and change her, waving her little arms and watching me with eyes that are weirdly discerning. I feel judged.

And found lacking. "Okay, princess, are you hungry?" I lift her up again and take her to the kitchen.

"Can I help?" Andi asks. "Although I don't know how to make a bottle."

"Do you want to hold her?"

"No! Just tell me what to do."

"Willa wrote down the instructions for making a bottle." I reach for them. "She brought this machine."

"Fancy," Andi says. "It's like a Keurig for baby bottles."

I snort-laugh.

Moments later, Andi hands me the bottle. "Here you go."

I pop the nipple into Matilda's mouth and she immediately starts sucking. "You were starving, weren't you?" I say to her. "Attagirl." I carry her back to the living room so I can sit.

"You've got this," Andi says.

"I feel like an idiot." I'm holding the baby and the bottle awkwardly. Matilda gazes up at me. "She knows I don't have a clue what I'm doing."

Andi laughs. "Now that she's not crying, she does seem very... wise."

"Right? Like, if she could talk she'd be bossing me around."

"Just wait."

I look up and catch her smile.

Jesus. One day Matilda will be talking. And walking. And then she'll be graduating from high school. My mind boggles. I seriously can't deal with this.

I have a daughter.

"I missed my meditation session this afternoon," I complain.

"I'm sorry. I know you like to stick to your routine."

"Yeah." It makes me twitchy to have everything in disarray. My chest feels vaguely tight and my stomach is percolating.

Matilda finishes the bottle. I set it on the coffee table. "Willa said I have to burp the baby after she eats." She showed me a couple of different ways, so I lift Matilda to my shoulder and pat her back. "Come on, little girl, give me a big belch."

Andi chokes on a laugh.

I'm rewarded with a good burp.

"What do you do with her while she's awake?" Andi asks. "Or does she go back to sleep now?"

"Willa said she'll be awake for maybe a couple of hours at a time."

"Yikes."

"I know. Be glad she's not crying." I look around. "We'll do tummy time. I'm supposed to do that."

"Tummy time?" Andi rises and follows me over to the baby equipment.

"Yeah. It strengthens her neck or something. Can you spread out that blanket?"

Andi lays out the brightly colored quilt and I crouch down to place Matilda there on her belly. She immediately fusses. Crap. "Hey, you have to stay here for a while." I rub her back. "It'll be fun."

"It doesn't look fun," Andi says. "I think you need to move her arms up."

I frown but carefully adjust Matilda's little arms to support her better. She still doesn't seem happy.

"Maybe she needs a toy?"

"Yeah. I think Willa said something about that." I dig around and find a thing that folds into a triangle. One side is a mirror. I prop it in front of Matilda.

Immediately, she's intrigued, lifting her head and pushing higher onto her forearms to peer at her own reflection. I look at Andi and we both grin.

"Who's that pretty baby?" I ask Matilda.

Matilda makes a noise.

"That's right! It's you."

When she tires of that, I find a red ball with holes in it and roll it in front of her. She watches it, then reaches for it, but it's too far for her. So I move it closer and she curls her little fingers into it.

"Attagirl."

"I can tell she's so smart," Andi says.

I grin again. "Yeah? With all your baby experience?"

She laughs. "You just know these things."

"Well, I agree. Obviously she's smart."

Between the two of us, we keep Matilda happy on her tummy for about half an hour. That's a half hour of blessed no crying. Matilda does make noise, though, with lots of screeches and high-pitched squeals. "Aaaye ah!" she says. "Aaaaaaah!"

"Listen to that," I say to Andi. "She's trying to talk already."

"It sounds like it!"

After a while, I pick her up and walk her around the condo, showing her everything and explaining things. "That's the award I got in college." I point to the trophy on a shelf. "And that picture is the American Olympic hockey team celebrating in Lake Placid when they beat the Soviet Union."

Andi watches with amusement. Matilda seems to be taking it all in. Then it's bedtime. Thank Christ. I'm exhausted.

When Matilda's asleep, Andi and I fall onto the couch again. I let out a long exhale. "This is a lot of work."

"It really is." She bites her lip. "No wonder new moms are exhausted."

"What am I gonna do?" I ask again. "I don't have time for this! My schedule is all messed up. I should be at the gym, training with Victor. I didn't meditate. And it's bathroom cleaning day."

She presses her lips together, nodding slowly, giving me a long look. She opens her mouth, then closes it.

"What?"

She speaks hesitantly. "I think you might have to let go of your schedule while you have the baby."

Panic seizes me. My nostrils flare and my blood runs cold. "No. I can't do that."

"You have to find a nanny," she reiterates. "But until you do... you're on your own."

Fuck. I really am. My hockey teammates and buddies aren't going to be any help with a baby. My parents are leaving for Europe soon. An overwhelming sense of helplessness fills me, my breathing quickening. "I don't know how to be a dad."

"Look," Andi says quietly. "I'll do what I can to help. But I'm in the middle of a big new contract and I just signed deals with two more clients. And I already said, I know nothing about babies. But I can try to help out until you find a nanny."

Relief slides through me. I'm not entirely comforted, because I know Andi's busy. Her business is important to her. And she's kind of terrified of Matilda. But at least she's another adult. Although I know I can't ask her to look after Matilda for hours while I go to the gym.

This is really going to fuck up my plans for this year. I've made so much improvement to my game. I'm eager for training camp to start so I can show off my gains. But now... that's all trashed.

My teeth grind together and my muscles tense.

"What's wrong?" Andi asks warily.

I close my eyes briefly on the rush of heat through my body. "I'm pissed."

"Um... why?"

"Why do you think?" I snap. I open my eyes and see her expression. "Sorry. Sorry. I'm..."

"Pissed," she replies helpfully.

"Yeah." I suck in air. "I've worked so hard all summer. I've grown my game so much. And now... I have a baby left on my doorstep—"

She snorts softly.

"Well, almost. I have all this responsibility dumped on me out of the blue and it's fucking my whole life up. Training camp starts Thursday and I need to be in top shape to perform!"

"I get it." She pauses. "Do you have any family who could come help?"

I shake my head. "My parents are leaving for Europe soon for a few months."

"Whoa. Okay."

"I can't ask them to give that up. They've wanted to do this forever. And they gave up so much for me, my whole life." I can only imagine their reaction to me knocking up someone in a one-night stand and ending up a father. Jesus.

"And you're an only child."

"Yeah."

She regards me with a look on her face that makes me want to squirm. "So who are you mad at? Them? Me?"

"No! Not you." I shake my head. "I'm not mad at anyone. I'm not mad at Matilda. It's not her fault, for Chrissake. Maybe I'm a little mad at Willa. I'm just mad at..." I gesture widely. "All of it."

And I don't say it out loud, but I'm mostly mad at myself, because I know I'm acting like a selfish asshole. Because I *am* a selfish asshole. And I *hate* needing help. When I was a kid, I vowed I would never need anyone else. I would only rely on myself. Asking for help makes me feel weak. I hate feeling like that.

I've been focused on my career and I'm too selfish to look after someone else. And right now, I'm pissed that someone *is* depending on me. And apparently I *do* need someone.

"You can do this," Andi says calmly. "I'll help. You'll find a great nanny. It'll be hard, but you got this."

Her calm optimism and faith in me takes my anxiety down a notch. She's always positive. Even after being betrayed and dumped by her ex, she got through the heartbreak and pain and regained her ability to always see something good.

I can try that, too.

9

ANDI

Luckily, Ford finds a nanny quickly. I guess when you're desperate you can make things happen. Also, he has money, which probably helps. So I only have to help out with Matilda for a few days.

I admit that I'm nervous around her. I don't know what her sounds mean. I don't know what the crying means. I don't know what to do with her.

She is kind of cute, though. Those intelligent eyes just like Ford's watch my every move. When she tries to talk, her little mouth forms into the cutest shapes and it's adorable. And when she smiles... oh dear God, that melts my insides into slush. Her smiles are getting more frequent, especially with Ford, but also with me. When I hand her a toy and her eyes light up and she beams a smile and reaches for it with both hands, I get weird sensations in my chest.

But there are times I'm frustrated and her cuteness doesn't help. The day training camp starts, I obviously have to look after her. Ford can't miss that. He's skipped taekwondo classes, workouts, meditations, and has started carrying Matilda around in a baby sling on his chest so he can get his cleaning done. But I have a virtual meeting today so this could be tricky.

I bring her to my apartment so I can hold my meeting. She's really good and happy as I play with her, although I'm anxiously checking the clock, watching the time pass. I have to get her to sleep before my meeting starts. So even though she's still bright-eyed and energetic, I try rocking her to sleep then laying her in her bed. Her eyes close and she's quiet. Yay!

Just in time for my meeting.

But as I present to my clients, she starts wailing. I have the baby monitor on, so the sound is *loud*. Crap.

I see the startled looks on my clients' faces. I don't know what to do. I can't mute myself because I'm the one presenting. I reach over and turn off the baby monitor. I can still hear Matilda in the other room, but I'm not sure if others can. I continue talking, but fuck! I can't concentrate with the baby crying like that. Maybe she's dying!

"I'm so sorry," I say with as much apology in my tone as I can muster. "Can we break for just a moment? I have something I need to attend to."

They agree and I mute and jump up to run to the living room where Matilda's in her little bed. She lifts her arms to me pleadingly, her face contorted. What can I do but pick her up?

"What do you need, sweetheart?" I gather her into my arms, only slightly more comfortable holding her than I was a few days ago. "Are you hungry? Wet?" I feel her little padded butt. The diaper seems dry. I'll try a bottle, but dammit, I need to get back to my meeting. Maybe I can feed her with my camera off?

That's really going to impress a client.

Shit. I thought I could handle this today.

I make a bottle of formula as quickly as I can then carry Matilda back to the office. She grabs the bottle with both hands and eagerly chows down. As I approach my computer, I realize I left my camera on... and I'm not wearing pants. I was running out of time before the meeting, so I just grabbed a suit jacket and threw it on over my T-shirt.

They must have had quite the view when I ran out of my office.

Fire climbs from my chest up into my face as I quickly take my seat, turn off the camera and turn on the mic. "I'm so sorry. I'm helping out a friend today and this little one isn't cooperating." I laugh lightly. "I'll just keep my camera off while we talk for now. So back to where we were." *Where were we?* I fumble with one hand for my notes. Okay. "Pay-per-click advertising lets us reach audiences on news and other websites and digital platforms through paid ads. We can set up PPC campaigns on Google, Bing, LinkedIn, X, Pinterest, and Facebook. These campaigns segment users based on their demographics or their particular interests or location, which is hugely powerful."

"Which platforms would you recommend for us?" Joe Edison asks.

"Definitely Google and Facebook," I reply, and launch into more details about click-through rates, conversion rates, and social media traffic. Meanwhile, Matilda is happily sucking down her formula and I'm relaxing a little. When she finishes, I manage to sit her up on my lap and pat her back as I talk. I'm pretty proud of myself... until she lets out the biggest belch I've ever heard from her. Right in the middle of a pause in my presentation.

Luckily they can't see my face, but I can see theirs. Joe looks startled, and Hugo bursts out laughing.

I guess laughter is good?

"I am so sorry," I say again. I can't help thinking how proud of her Ford would be. He's unreasonably obsessed with her bodily noises. I almost want to laugh, but I rein it in. "Let's move on!"

Somehow, we get through the rest of the meeting and as I end it, I can only hope that the unprofessional interruptions don't lose me this client. I blow out a breath and look at Matilda, who is holding a toy to her mouth and sucking on both it and her fingers. She gazes back at me placidly. "You better not have cost me that job." But I say it in a gentle tone so she knows I don't mean it. I mean, she probably doesn't understand, but I don't want her to think I'm really angry at her.

I may be a little frustrated.

I stand. "I hope your dad is killing it at training camp." I carry her to the living room. "Today is medicals. I remember spring training for Trevor. You don't know him. He's my ex. He's a…" I pause, mindful of language. "He's a jerk." I remember how important training camp is. It's when players compete for places on the roster. I remember all the time Trevor spent working out —weightlifting, agility drills, core strengthening, not to mention the on-field training—and I remember all the disappointing years he was assigned to extended spring training because he wasn't ready for a full season in the majors or the minors. I don't think the NHL is like that and I don't think Ford is at risk of not making the team, but I know he wants to do well. "Hopefully your dad…" I pause.

Ford *is* her dad. We may have been doubtful, but he already got the results from the DNA test he did. The results were 99.999 percent certain that he's Matilda's father.

"Hopefully your dad is passing with flying colors. When are you going to sleep? I have work to do, Tilly." I've started shortening her name. Ford doesn't like it. I think it's cute.

The new nanny starts Monday, so after tomorrow I'm in the clear. I just have to make it through one more day, entertaining a baby with toys and goofy games and changing diapers. I can handle this.

* * *

"I fired her."

I gape at Ford. "What?"

It's a week later. I just got back from volunteering at Bright Side Animal Shelter. I had to miss a couple of days I was supposed to go in because of looking after Tilly, and I was happy to be there today with the animals. I love animals, especially dogs. There's a new guy, a lab mix named Draco, who I took for a walk today. He's so sweet.

I've been blessedly baby free as the nanny cared for Matilda while Ford was at training camp, even in the evenings when he had exhibition games. Hanna's been very flexible and accommodating, thank goodness. I met her briefly one day and she seemed nice and has a lot of experience with babies, although she is very young. I got a little uneasy at the way she looked at Ford, but I shook that off. Ford and I are just friends, so I don't know why I felt weirded out.

Now he's fired her.

"Why?" I demand.

"She wasn't working out. She wasn't adhering to the schedule I came up with for Matilda."

Yes, it wasn't long before Ford had a strict schedule for the baby. And I know babies do need routine and stability, but he got so upset when she wouldn't go to sleep at the time he thought she should, or wasn't hungry when he wanted to feed her. I don't know how realistic his schedule was or how he came up with it.

"Oh. But is that really that important?"

"Of course it is! Also... she..." He stops.

"What?"

He looks away and rubs the back of neck, his face etched with discomfort. "I caught her snooping in my bedroom."

"What!" My mouth drops open.

"Yeah." His sigh could knock over a Zamboni. "She's a big hockey fan. Like, a crazy fan."

"No!"

"Yeah. I was worried that she wasn't really looking out for Matilda. She was just trying to steal my underwear."

"Jesus!" I know I'm swearing in front of the baby, but I can't help it. "That's insane!"

"I know. Fuck."

Our eyes meet. We both make a "yikes" face and shrug.

"This kid's gonna have a mouth like a sailor," Ford says.

I wave my hands. "You have time to get used to it and adjust your habits before she starts talking." When *do* babies start talking, anyway? I need to do some research.

Or not. She's not my baby.

"What are you going to do?" I ask.

"I've talked to a few others from the agency." He shakes his head. "None of them sound any better."

"You've got to be kidding me. Nobody?"

He shrugs.

"Nobody is good enough to look after your baby girl."

He shrugs again.

To be honest... that's kind of hot.

No. I mean, I like it. He didn't want this. But... it seems like he does care about his baby.

"Does that include me?" Oh, shit. Why did I ask that? I'm not going to help. I *can't*.

He blinks at me, lips parting. "No. Of course not."

Well. I'm glad he trusts me. Although I'm probably the *least* qualified person. I open my mouth, then snap it shut.

We stare at each other, the air thickening around us.

"Help me, Andi," he eventually says, his voice low and rough.

Shit. I know how hard it is for him to ask for help. Not that he often needs it. But... he's always been there to help me.

I turn and walk away from him in his condo, over to the window overlooking the street. I can't do this. I just can't. This business is everything to me. After losing my husband, my work friend, and my job... this is all I have left. I *have* to be a success at this. How can I do that and look after a baby? We've already had one Zoom fail. I can't keep doing that.

Thoughts roll through my head. I hate seeing Ford so dejected. He cares about that baby and obviously wants her to be safe and looked after. But he's also dedicated to his career. I get that, too. This season is important to him in breaking out as the team's number one goalie. He's clearly conflicted about those two competing interests.

He's always been there for me—after my marriage ended, he made sure I was eating and not drowning my sorrows in boxed wine and popcorn, making sure I got dressed some days by taking me out for lunch, and making me laugh with proposals like *Let's play carpenter. First we'll get hammered, then I'll nail you.* He helped me with so many things—repairs around the condo, killing spiders, watching movies with me when I didn't want to be alone. I feel an unreasonable obligation to him. Maybe it's not unreasonable. We're friends. That's what friends do, right? Help each other. Support each other. Make each other laugh.

Maybe I'm not being a good enough friend to him. It's about give and take, right? Yes, I'm busy. Yes, my new business is important to me. And yes, it's important to me to succeed. But Ford's important, too. And okay... so is Matilda, the little scamp.

Think positive. That's always my motto. Like my mom always says, nobody ever damaged their eyesight by looking at the bright side.

I can look after a baby. It's natural! How hard can it be?

I turn to face Ford. "I'll help. We'll get through this together. But we need some rules."

He smiles. "I like rules."

10

FORD

Andi and I sat down with my hockey schedule and her schedule and mapped out exactly when she'd need to look after Matilda. I shared the schedule I created for Matilda, although Andi seemed unsure of it. I let her look at my planner so she knows what days I schedule various things like cleaning and laundry and other appointments. She agreed to go for CPR training, but also made me agree that I have to respect her business time and also, I made her promise she would not post any pictures of Matilda on social media.

I haven't said a word to any of the guys about Matilda. Which means I've been acting weird, but that's the usual for me so they haven't even wondered what's going on.

I don't know why I haven't told them. Maybe because it's so huge. And weird. Like, who really gets a baby dropped on their doorstep?

Me. That's who.

I guess I'm a little afraid of how they're going to react. They know I'm not good father material. They'll probably call child protection services. I don't know.

On the other hand, announcing I have a baby is the kind of bizarreness they expect from me.

I at least need to let Coach know that I'm dealing with some stuff in my personal life. I've tried not to let it impact my play, but I know it has. I worked so fucking hard all summer and I don't feel I've really shown everyone what I can do. I'm the Net Ninja. My self-discipline and focus is legendary. And here I am all rattled by a twelve-pound girl.

So I'm meeting with Coach in his office. Training camp is done and our last practice before the regular season just ended. He's going to freak out.

"So, I, uh, have some news to share with you," I begin. "A few weeks ago, I became a father."

He blinks at me, his expression wooden. "A father."

"Yeah."

"You had a baby?"

"Well, not me. But yeah."

"I didn't know you even had a girlfriend."

"I don't." I swallow. "It was a one-night stand about a year ago."

He looks at me. The silence expands. "But you said... a few weeks ago."

"Right, right. She's four months old now. But I just found out about her." I pull air into my lungs. "Her mother had to go to look after her parents after a bad car accident and needed to leave the baby with me. So right now, I have full custody. And I'm not sure how long that's going to be for. Willa said it could be a couple of months."

He leans back in his chair. "Okay. Wow. That was a total surprise to you?"

"Yeah." I tell him a few more details about it, about my failed nanny hire, and that a friend is helping me look after Matilda.

"I've really been trying not to let it interfere with my game, but I thought you should know. Being a single dad might, uh, impact my schedule."

"Jesus." He rubs his mouth. "Yeah." He looks across the room, then back at me. Then he asks the same question Andi did. "Are you sure you're the father?"

"Yeah. She has my eyes."

Coach continues to regard me enigmatically.

Did that sound hopelessly gullible? Probably. "We also did a DNA test," I add.

"Family's important," he finally says. "We're here for you. Let us know what we can do to support you."

He's not freaking out.

"I just want you to know that I've worked really hard to prepare for this season." I lean forward. "I won't let this interfere with that. I want to start as many games as I possibly can. I want to win them all."

"Yeah, it shows," he replies. "How hard you've worked. But Ford... family is a priority."

"Sure, sure." I nod vigorously. "But I'm totally committed to being the number one goalie."

He nods. "Good. Like I said, let us know what we can do to help."

He's not freaking out. He's supporting me.

"Do your teammates know? I assume they do."

"No. I haven't told anyone yet. I've been trying to adjust to things. I don't know." I press my hand to my forehead. "Maybe I thought this was all going to go away before the regular season starts."

His eyebrows elevate. "Babies don't just... go away."

Shit. "That sounded bad, didn't it? I know that. I just meant... fuck, I don't know what I meant. This has really rattled me."

He nods. "Understandable."

We end the meeting. That didn't go as badly as I feared. Maybe the guys won't wild out when they hear.

I head to the players' lounge where everyone is eating post-practice lunch. They're lounging around at tables and on leather couches, drinking energy drinks, eating healthy lean proteins and veggies. I stand looking around at everyone for a moment until guys start taking note of me and giving me weird looks.

"S'up, Archie?" our new captain, Benny, calls to me. "Did you miss the chicken shawarma? It was really good."

I make a face. Damn. I like chicken shawarma.

"No, there's some left," Dilly calls. "Here, I'll make you a bowl."

"No cucumbers!" I call back. "I hate cucumbers."

He shrugs and starts spooning food into a big bowl.

"I have an announcement to make."

All heads turn toward me. Silence descends.

"What is it?" Benny asks, shifting on the couch to fully face me, concern etched on his forehead.

After last season's tragic car accident involving Alfie and his wife and child, they're probably all afraid I'm going to say something terrible. I swallow and lift my hands. "It's okay. It's just some, uh, unexpected news." I pause, then square my shoulders. "A few weeks ago I had a visit from a woman, I, uh, hooked up with last year."

Some eyes widen. Some brows furrow. The silence deepens.

"Yeah. She had a baby with her. A little girl. Who is mine." I pause for a deep breath, then lower my ass to the arm of one couch.

"Holy shit," Benny says, and other guys mumble similar curses.

"Right? Well." I explain the rest of the story to them, trying to gloss over how much this has completely derailed my life. I don't need everyone feeling sorry for me. I'm doing enough of that myself. "My friend next door has agreed to help but I still have to keep looking for a full-time nanny. Except I'm not really sure how long Willa's going to be gone."

"Oh, man." Turks bounds up. "We'll all help! You're not in this alone."

Everyone mutters agreement.

"Absolutely," Benny says, nodding. "What can we do?"

"Holly and I can help," Turks says, naming his wife. They have two young kids. "Holly can babysit if you need."

"Maybe you should check with her before offering her services."

He freezes. "Riiiiight. But I know she'll be willing, she loves kids."

"Us, too," Shawzy speaks up. "We have our hands full with three, but we can help. Do you need diaper lessons? I have lots of sleep tips."

"I need all the tips I can get." I rub my forehead, my heart turning the consistency of pablum in my chest at all their support. "Thank you."

"When can we meet her?" Shawzy asks. "What's her name?"

"Her name is Matilda. Matilda Grace. She's four months old." Some weird emotion presses behind my sternum. "And I guess you can meet her whenever you want. Tomorrow?" We have a day off before our first regular season game on Monday night.

"Okay, great."

Not everyone can come, and notably Alfie is quiet. I totally understand. It would be so fucking hard to see Matilda when he just lost his little guy so tragically. But the rest of the guys all make arrangements to come over Sunday afternoon.

I pull my utensils out of my pocket and eat my shawarma

chicken bowl, without cucumbers. It's delicious. The chef here spoils us with all the meals and snacks they provide. Then I take off to relieve Andi. It's Saturday so she doesn't have meetings, but she still has work to do and also, she might like a little time to herself.

I really am grateful for her help.

I let myself into my condo and find the two girls on the living room floor. Andi's leaning against the couch, legs bent, Matilda on her thighs facing her. "What does a cow say?" Andi asks. "Mooooooooo." And Matilda giggles with that infectious, enchanting baby laugh. My feet halt for a split second as I watch Andi laugh, too, and God... she's beautiful. Her smile for Matilda is tender and affectionate and real.

She looks up at me and her smile broadens. "Hey! Daddy's home!"

Daddy. Jesus. Something winds tight around my chest and windpipe. I feel like I can't breathe. I force myself to walk toward them and crouch down. I smile back at Andi. "Hi."

"Hi."

Then I look at Matilda. She holds her arms out to me and kicks her legs, making little grunting noises. I laugh and pick her up, my fingers brushing Andi's thighs as I do so. I ignore that. "Hey, pretty girl. What are you doing?"

She's wearing an outfit I haven't seen before, little cable-knit pants and a matching sweater in a cream color. "What are you wearing? You look cozy."

"We went for a walk." Andi slides away from the couch then stretches out flat on the floor on her back. "So we got out the woolly clothes." She turns her head and peers up at me. "She might need a few more things for winter. All her clothes are pretty summery."

I guess that makes sense. "We can do that. It's important to be well dressed, right, Tilly?"

I realize I've said the nickname without even thinking.

"Ha!" Andi lifts her head, grinning. "You called her Tilly!"

"Fine, fine. It's easier than Matilda all the time."

"I like it. Okay." She rolls over again and stands, stretching. "I'm outta here. Got stuff to do."

"Don't you want to come shopping?"

She tilts her head, looking conflicted. "Nah. That's okay. You have some daddy time with her."

My public outings with Tilly have been minimal. Once to a doctor's appointment we set up to make sure she's on track with all her immunizations and growth, and once to the bodega down the street when I needed milk and Andi wasn't here. But I guess I can handle it.

"Also, I have a date tonight. I need to get ready."

My head snaps around. "What?"

She nods. "Yeah! It's been a while. It's Saturday, though, and I knew you'd be home so I get to go out and drink adult beverages —woohoo!" She pumps a fist in the air as she walks toward us. She bends down to kiss Tilly's cheek. "Bye, honey bunny. Be good for Daddy."

The scent of Andi's hair drifts to my nose as she leans in, that sweet-like-sugar-and-flowers scent. Sexy.

No. I just mean it's different than baby lotion. Which is the only female scent I've smelled recently.

"I should go shower so I don't smell like poopy diapers." She shakes her head. "What has my life become? Okay, bye!"

I watch her walk out, her tight ass perfectly outlined in a pair of black yoga pants.

"What about tomorrow?" I call to her.

She stops at the door and frowns at me over her shoulder. "You have a day off, right?"

"Yeah." But... but what? "The guys are coming over to meet Tilly."

Her frown morphs into a huge smile. "You told them!"

"Yeah. And Coach. It went better than expected."

"Oh, good! I'm glad they're coming over. But... you don't need me for that."

"No, no. Just letting you know."

"Great! See you Monday, then. I have your morning skate on my schedule, and the game that night. Call me if you need me when you try to nap." She holds up her hands, palms out, in a reassuring gesture. "All good."

"Okay. Yeah. See you Monday."

The door closes behind her and I look down at Tilly, also watching Andi leave, her bottom lip pushing out. "Oh, man. You want her to stay, too?" I move with Tilly on my hip, distracting her. "But we don't need her! We can have fun together, right, baby girl?" I pick up a soft toy and shake it for her. It works. She forgets Andi.

But I don't. She's going on a fucking date?

11

ANDI

On my way out for the evening, I stop at Ford's door and knock.

He opens the door and rakes his gaze from my face to my toes and back up. "Oh, hi," he says smiling. "I was just having dirty thoughts about you."

I snort. "You're a father now. You need to behave." I hold out the little stuffed bear. "This was at my place. Tilly really likes it so I thought I'd drop it off on my way out."

"Oh." He takes it. "Okay. Thanks."

He continues to look me over.

Maybe it's my top? The snug, black asymmetrical shirt leaves one shoulder bare. My jeans are long and loose and my pointy-toed flats peep out from beneath the hem.

"Okay!" For some reason all my breath has evacuated my lungs. "Bye!" I head to the elevator.

Did he like how I'm dressed? I know he was joking about having dirty thoughts about me, but the way he looked at me... eh. Probably not. But it's fun to wear sexy, grown-up clothes for a change.

In the lobby I book an Uber and wait for it to arrive to take me to the rooftop bar in Manhattan where I'm meeting Elodie.

I didn't exactly lie to Ford. I am going on a date. But it's a date with my best friend. I don't know why I didn't mention that. I just got this weird vibe from him. Like he didn't want me to go on a date.

Does he expect me to spend every minute of my life helping him with Tilly?

I reflect on this in the back seat of the car as we travel into Manhattan. I don't think he does expect that. He's been very reasonable about how much he's asking of me. I can tell he hates it that he needs help. But everyone needs help, sometimes.

We sat down with his schedule and my schedule for the next month. His is a lot more involved. I just have a few meetings scheduled. We figured out when Tilly needs care based on his practices, workouts, and games. There will be travel; they open the season with two games at home, but next weekend they travel to Washington. That's not overnight, though, just a late night. But the week after that they'll be gone for three days.

I'm not nervous about looking after Tilly by myself for three days.

I'm terrified.

Deep breath. I can do it.

I wanted to do this for Ford, to pay him back for being there for me. But I have to admit that Tilly is cute and I kind of like seeing her. And seeing a new side of Ford.

The car stops on West 26th Street in front of an elegant hotel. I text Elodie and she replies that she's in the lobby so I hurry in. I see my friend near the elevators, with her chin-length blond bob and bright red lips. "Hi!"

"I haven't seen you for so long!"

"You've been busy traveling."

"I know, and you've been busy, too."

"Wait till you hear."

She gives me a wide-eyed look. "Let's get a drink."

We ride up to Nakuru, the rooftop bar on the fiftieth floor. It's chilly for sitting outside so the glass doors are closed, but we score a table for two right in front of windows with a view of the Empire State Building.

"Wow." I gaze out. "This city never fails to amaze me."

"Gorgeous, isn't it?"

We order frosés—vodka and rosé wine, frozen to a delicious and potent slush.

"Okay, tell me everything."

I blow out a breath. "Okay."

She listens as I talk, mouth falling open, leaning closer, making noises of astonishment. "Holy shit," she says as I finish.

"I know, right?" I sip my drink.

"You don't even like babies."

"I know." I wince. "Although Tilly's pretty cute."

"I can't believe that mother just abandoned her child."

"I know! I feel very judgmental about it. But I'm trying to be fair; things must be pretty bad for her to do that."

"I guess so." Elodie drains her drink.

Mine is still full since I've been talking so much, but we order two more anyway.

"If you need help, I can come over," Elodie says. "At least I have two nieces."

"I might take you up on that. The week after next, Ford will be away for three days."

"Uhhh... I'm in Seattle that week."

"Well, shit." I fake cry. "I don't know how I'm going to do that."

"Maybe he'll find another nanny by then."

"Maybe." I'm doubtful. He's pretty picky.

Three guys walk into the bar and are seated at the table next to us. I give them a quick glance as they're all tall and wearing nice suits.

Elodie and I catch up on other things—how her job is going, how my business is going, how I'm feeling about Haven being pregnant.

"I was shook," I admit to her. "When I saw her. It really bothered me." I shrug. "I guess I've accepted it."

"You've accepted that you and Trevor aren't getting back together?"

I think about that. Ford asked me about that, too. "I guess I have. Too much has happened now to go back."

"He betrayed you."

"Yes. He did."

The guys at the next table are eyeing us. When I catch the eye of one, he smiles.

He's pretty good-looking—dark blond hair, tawny scruff, and a great smile—but young. Younger than my thirty years, anyway. But I smile back at him.

He lifts his glass in a toast.

"Who are you smiling at?" Elodie starts to turn.

"Don't look! Those guys over there. One of them just smiled at me."

"Ahhhhh. Excellent."

I roll my eyes. "I'm not here on a man-hunt. I'm here to have drinks with you."

"We can do both."

I do like the excitement of flirting with a man. The anticipation of what could happen. Maybe sex—honest, physical pleasure. It's been a while and I miss that. So I catch the man's eye again. And sure enough, a moment later he rises and strolls over to our table.

"Hi, ladies."

I look up—way up. "Hi."

"My friends and I are wondering if you'd like to join us. We have a bottle of Casamigos Blanco and we really don't want to drink it all ourselves."

"Oooh, tequila," Elodie says. "I love tequila."

"Perfect. Let's get your chairs moved over to our table."

They're ordering bottle service and all three are dressed in nice suits. This seems promising.

We make introductions. The guy who came over is Ryker, and his friends are Tyler and Kevin. They pour us shots of the sipping tequila, smooth with hints of vanilla and oak.

"So what do you guys do for a living?" I ask. "You're still in suits, so I'm guessing..." I put a finger to my chin. "You had late business meetings."

They all laugh. "Nope," Tyler says.

"You don't know who we are?" Ryker asks.

"Uh..." Elodie and I exchange glances. "Should we?"

Are they famous? Actors?

"We play hockey," Tyler says. "For the Bears."

My eyes pop open as round as hockey pucks. "No!"

They all smirk, thinking they've impressed me.

"My, uh, friend plays hockey, too!" I say. "For the Storm."

"Uh oh."

I grin. "Yeah. We're drinking with the enemy."

"Who's your friend?" Ryker asks.

"Ford Archibald."

Now they seem surprised. Did they think I was making that up?

"Hey," Tyler says. "I'm a goalie, too."

"Really?" I tilt my head. "Are you as, um, eccentric as other goalies?"

"Nah."

"Yeah, you are," Ryker says to him. "You told us once that being a professional hockey goalie was punishment for something you did in a past life."

I roll my lips in on a laugh.

"Well, yeah." Tyler nods. "Having frozen pucks coming at you a hundred miles an hour is like being stoned in today's day and age." His forehead creases. "I just don't know exactly what I did to deserve being stoned."

Okay, this guy is making Ford's idiosyncrasies seem mild.

"Archie's a good goalie," Tyler says. "Really good."

Warmth spreads in my chest, as if I'm somehow responsible for Ford being a good goaltender.

"He stopped me once on a breakaway and I still don't know he did it," Ryker says, shaking his head.

"That's why they call him the Net Ninja," Kevin says with a laugh.

I grin. I've heard that nickname. It's hilarious.

Well, so much for getting with one of these guys tonight. There's no way I can sleep with a hockey player from a rival team.

And honestly? I don't really want to. I keep thinking about Ford. I don't think he'd be mad if I did that, but... I don't know. The idea has lost its appeal.

* * *

Sunday afternoon, the thin wall between my place and Ford's becomes apparent again. This time it's not Tilly crying, thankfully. It's a lot of deep voices and booming laughter. What the hell? Is he having a party over there?

Oh, right. He said some of his friends were coming over to meet the baby. I hope they're having fun. I'm trying to work on a new ad campaign for one of my clients. The noise is distracting.

There's no way I'm going over there to complain, though.

12

FORD

I can't believe they did this.

My teammates started showing up at one o'clock with food and gifts.

"We're throwing you a baby shower," Benny explained with a grin as he carried in a charcuterie platter.

I don't like spontaneous surprises. I like things planned and organized. Preferably by me. So this stresses me out. I'm trying to resist the urge to kick everyone out, worried about how this will affect Tilly, and pissed about all the junk food.

This is a bad attitude. I *know* that. I just have a hard time dealing with all these feelings, and on top of everything else, I'm pissed at myself for being pissed. My muscles are all tense and my heart is thudding as I carry Tilly and watch others arrive with chips and dip, chicken wings, sliders, and a big tray of brownies.

I know how to deal with anxiety. Slow breathing. The 3-3-3 rule—looking around and identifying three objects, three sounds, then three body parts. But I don't have patience for that right now. Tilly seems to sense my tension and fusses in my arms.

I don't know what to do, but I'm afraid I'm going to blow up and say something I'll regret.

Andi.

Before I've analyzed why I think of her, I'm out the door of my condo and down the hall to hers. I don't think the guys even notice me leaving, they're so busy arranging food and gifts. I rap on her door.

She opens it and gives me a blank look, taking in Tilly and my probably pissed expression. "What's wrong?"

"Can I come in?"

"Uh... sure." She steps aside and I stomp into her living room. She follows.

"The guys are throwing us a baby shower – gifts, buffet, the lot."

She grins. "No!"

"Yes."

"That's amazing!"

"I didn't know about it. I'm..."

"Freaking out."

"Yeah." I rub my forehead. Tilly squirms. "They didn't tell me! They didn't even ask me, they just did it."

Andi walks up and takes Tilly from me.

She's come a long way since that first day when she wouldn't hold her.

"Hi, sweet girl," she says with a kiss to Tilly's head. She looks back at me. "It's okay, Ford."

"I know. I know." I start pacing. "I'm just not good with unexpected events. I'm so mad."

Her lips curve. "I see that. But are you really mad?"

My forehead tightens. "Yeah."

"Usually anger starts with something else." She looks back at

Tilly. "Why are you wearing pajamas to a baby shower, young lady? You need to dress up!"

I screw up my face at that. "Shit."

"It's fine. I'm kidding. Sort of."

Tilly is staring at Andi, somewhat calmer. I shove a hand into my hair and cross the living room again.

"So what else is it?" she asks.

I huff. "I don't know."

"Yeah, you do. Think about it."

"I feel pressured."

She nods. "Are you afraid?"

I narrow my eyes. "Afraid of what?"

She looks at me steadily. "Not being in control?"

I gaze back at her. "Shit."

"That's what it really is, isn't it? You want to be in control. And they took that away from you."

I roll my eyes as I pace the room.

"They're just trying to help," she says. "They care about you. I think that's so nice of them to do that."

"Yeah. It is."

"They're good friends."

"They should know I don't like surprises."

"They probably didn't think about that. After all, it's a nice surprise. Not a bad surprise."

"Like having a baby show up at your door."

"Yes, like that. But even that's not all bad. Look at this sweetheart."

I exhale sharply. "Yeah." Some of the tension in my shoulders eases as I regard Tilly.

"Don't let your need for control and perfection cause you to miss out on things. Happy things like a baby shower. Those things are important."

I go mannequin-still and stare at the wall. Jesus. She's right. I know that. I just didn't... get it.

"Where does this need for control come from?" she asks quietly, neutrally.

I almost spill my guts. But I don't need to tell her about my whole weird childhood. "I just like order. Stability."

"Right." She purses her lips, then says, "Breathe. You've got this."

I try to moderate my breathing. Yeah. I can do this.

"Be grateful to your friends. Show them you appreciate all the effort that went into this."

"I do appreciate it."

"I know you do. And it's all for this little girl. Right, Tilly? They brought you presents! Aren't you excited about that?" She takes Tilly's little arm and waves it. Tilly smiles and makes a noise of agreement. Andi grins. "She can't wait to see the gifts."

It's for Tilly. This is all for Tilly. That calms me down more.

I sit on Andi's couch, elbows on my knees, and take a few deep breaths. I look over at her. She's always so... positive. Calm. My breathing eases a bit. "I'm okay."

"Good. How about I go back with you? I'll get her into a pretty dress and you can take control of the party."

I look up at her and catch the twinkle in her eyes. I smile. "I'm an asshole."

"Did you yell at them to get out?"

"No." I pause. "I wanted to."

"But you didn't. So you're not an asshole. Right now, anyway."

I snort, her disclaimer amusing me. "Okay." I pull air into my lungs and let it out slowly. "Let's go back before they think I've abandoned them."

Andi carries Tilly, following me down the hall. "I heard the noise from your place. Sounds like they're having fun."

"*They're* having a great time," I say dryly.

We walk in and a couple of guys look up and see Andi.

"Hey, everyone, this is Andi. My neighbor. Andi, this is... everyone." I wave a hand.

She smiles. "Hi, guys. I'm just going to borrow this princess for a few minutes. She wasn't expecting a party." She disappears into the spare room where I've got all Tilly's things arranged now.

I take in the chaos of food spread out on the kitchen island, drinks on the counter, and a pile of gifts on the coffee table. *It's fine.* "How'd you guys do this in such a short time?"

"We have ways." Benny grins. "We may have had a little help from the WAGs."

"They gave us some party games to play," Shawzy adds.

"Jesus." I shake my head. "Like what?"

"Baby bottle bowling," Shawzy replies. "Also baby shower charades, where we act out things like painting our nails or folding laundry." He pauses. "They're meant for chicks, obviously."

"Well, if we get bored, we can do that," I say, meaning, *Hell no, we're not doing that.*

"You need a drink, bro." Crusher hands me a beer. "Here you go."

I do need this. I lift it to my lips and take a big swallow. "Thanks." I check out the food offerings and pick up a cracker from the charcuterie board. "Who made this?"

"I bought it," Benny confesses.

"Looks great."

"Let's open the presents," Smitty says. "You're supposed to sit in a decorated chair to do that, so we brought this..." He holds up a big pink bow then sticks it onto the top of one of my leather chairs.

I bite back a smile. "You guys are whacked."

"Yep. Have a seat." Smitty gestures at the chair.

Andi emerges from the bedroom with Tilly, now wearing a pink ruffled dress and a pink headband with a ridiculously huge bow on it. I stare at her. I didn't even know she had those things.

She starts to hand Tilly to me, but Smitty says, "He's gonna be opening gifts. I'll take the baby."

I blink at him. Andi hands Tilly over to him and she regards him with a tiny crease between her eyebrows and a pouty bottom lip. He grins at her. "Hey, Matilda. I'm Uncle Marek."

Damn. I clear my throat.

"Here." Dilly hands Andi a beer. "Have a drink."

"Oh." She takes it hesitantly, glancing at me. "This seems like a guys' party."

"It's a shower," Dilly says. "You can stay."

She looks back at me and I dip my chin in agreement.

Smitty hands me the first gift and the next hour is spent unwrapping all kinds of things—clothes, toys, little rattles that go on her wrists and feet, and another tummy time mirror toy. While I'm opening gifts, Dilly is writing things down.

"I see you already have one of those," Crankster says. That's the nickname we gave Noah Lawson, a rookie who never smiles. "I can return it."

"That's okay," Andi puts in. "We can take one to my place. She spends lots of time there."

The guys all exchange looks. What? I told them about my neighbor helping me.

"Alfie sent this." Benny hands me one more gift. "But he couldn't make it today."

I take the gift, nodding somberly. His baby was about the same age as Tilly when the car accident happened. I don't blame him for not being here.

"Thanks, guys," I say, looking around the room. "This is really unexpected and awesome. You didn't have to do this. But it means a lot."

Andi beams at me and I smile back at her.

Later, in an aside, Smitty asks, "What's with you and your neighbor?"

"What? Nothing." I look over at Andi, standing near Benny who's holding Tilly, and laughing.

"Uh huh." He nods knowingly. "You went to get her. Why'd you do that?"

"I..." Fuck. "I have no idea."

He hoists his eyebrows. "She's hot."

I can't argue with that; Andi is objectively hot. "We're just friends. Look, don't get any weird ideas. I told you guys about her."

"You told us your neighbor was helping. We all pictured a little gray-haired old lady. Someone grandmotherly."

I choke on a laugh. "Oh. Well, that was wrong."

"No shit."

We go join Andi and Benny.

Andi says, "Hey, I met some of your competitors last night."

I frown. "Who?"

"Three players from the New York Bears."

Everyone in the room bellows with disapproval.

"Who?" I demand. "Where?"

"I was at Nakuru. It's not far from their arena. They'd just finished a game. Now what were their names? Oh, one of them is a goalie! Tyler Something."

"Tyler Kadner," I growl. "Jesus."

"He said you're a good goalie." Andi meets my eyes, and I see the amusement at my reaction.

I grunt.

"The others were Kevin and Ryker."

"Kevin Beaven and Ryker Murphy," Smitty says. "Were they trying to pick you up? You shouldn't date a Bear."

"That's not what most women say," Andi says.

Everyone cracks up laughing, even me.

"I don't get it," Crusher says.

"Oh, come on," Smitty says. "Haven't you heard about that big debate on social media? They asked women if they'd rather be trapped alone in the woods with a man or a bear. And women all said the bear."

"And a bunch of men got mad about it," Andi adds.

Crusher's brow wrinkles. "Huh. That's kind of depressing. I'm not mad, though. I get it."

"Anyway, I think Tyler was flirting with me a little," Andi says. "But he's kind of young for me."

Heat simmers in my belly. "I thought you were on a date. He was flirting with you in front of your date?"

"I was on a date with Elodie," she replies gently.

"Oh." That's good. But also, fuck Tyler Kadner.

"Okay, listen up, everyone." Dilly waves a piece of paper. "I wrote down all the things Archie said when he opened the gifts." He pauses, holding the paper in front of him. "This is what was said the night Matilda was conceived. Number one: it's so small."

Everyone roars with laughter.

"Number two: where does this go? Number three: this is really cute. Number four... isn't that a choking hazard?"

As everyone guffaws, Dilly finishes reading the things I did, in fact, say, although not the night of Matilda's conception. Even I laugh.

Andi takes Tilly and lays her on a blanket on the floor, fastens the little rattles to her wrists, then puts the rattle socks on. Tilly's intrigued, waving her arms and kicking her legs, and looking at the noises. Andi takes her little feet and lifts them up so Tilly can see them. She stares intently.

Jesus Christ, she's cute.

"She's been almost finding her feet," Andi says. "These are great."

My attention moves to Andi, sitting cross-legged on the floor, dressed in ripped jeans and a striped blue sweater. Her shiny gold hair falls over her face as she plays with Tilly's feet, the curve of her lips warm and affectionate.

Jesus Christ, she's gorgeous.

Something seizes in my chest. I can't be thinking things like that.

Last night when she stopped by on her way out, I was jarred, seeing her in sexy clothes, no glasses, and shiny lipstick. She looked extremely fuckable. I beat myself up for the rest of the night for thinking that. Then I dreamed about undressing her. Fuck.

Andi's my neighbor, my friend. Trevor's ex. Also, the only person I trust to help with Tilly. I cannot mess that up.

Also, Andi's never given any hint whatsoever that she's attracted to me. Why would she be? I'm an oddball. I've never hidden that from her. On top of that, now I have a baby. And I'm certainly not looking for a relationship. I don't need anyone. I mean, I do have a healthy sex drive, to put it mildly, and it's been a while. No wonder I'm getting horny thoughts about Andi.

But those have to stop. Right now.

13

ANDI

"Ford Archibald makes it look so easy—he just goes down on his knees and swallows it up."

Wait, what? My attention was distracted from the TV by Tilly, but I look back. What the hell are they talking about?

Oh. Ford just made a nice save.

Do these hockey announcers know how dirty they sound? Does Ford know what they say about him? Knowing him and his dirty mind, he'd love it.

It's the first game of the regular season. Ford's in net, and the Storm are leading one-nothing early in the first period.

I don't know much about hockey, but I'm watching anyway. And I'm making Tilly watch because she should see her dad play hockey.

Just kidding. She's too busy sucking on her toes.

She's lying on the floor and I'm sitting cross-legged in front of her with a view of the TV. I give her a tickle and am rewarded with a baby giggle. That has to be the best sound in the world. It makes me smile.

I watched Ford at the start of the game go through his routine

—part of it is looking rapidly side to side only moving his eyeballs. It's like the eye exercises he does and definitely looks odd.

It's weird to think all those players were just here in Ford's condo yesterday. They seem like good guys. They threw a shower for Ford! That made my heart go all squishy. They were all so easy with each other, like a family, but with some good-natured ragging... also like a family.

The crowd on TV starts roaring and I look up again. My eyes fly open wide. Ford is out of his net, *way* out of his net, as a player on the other team comes in on him with the puck. *What is he doing?* It happens fast, but Ford goes down, the other player trips over him and falls. I gasp, my hands going to my mouth.

He's okay. He gets up. But another player from the Caribou hits him and he goes down again, his mask flying off.

"Oh my God!"

The whistle blows sharply and the play halts. I can hear the ref yelling, "Are you okay?" at Ford. I watch with my heart in my throat as he gets up, retrieves his mask, and then, in his trademark move, shakes his hair back. I hear the panties of women all over North America dropping.

He seems to be okay. He goes to the net to squirt water on top of his head, fastens his mask back in place, skates around a bit, then positions himself in the goal to prepare for the faceoff.

Holy shit. Why did he do that?

"Your dad is crazy," I tell Tilly. "But you'll find that out when you get bigger."

Well, I guess he may have saved a goal with that daredevil move. As I watch, he makes save after save. The TV announcers are beside themselves with wonderment. I don't know enough to be impressed, but after a while even I can tell he's on fire tonight.

I'm so happy for him! It's a great start to the season.

While he's protecting the Storm's net, his teammates are scoring goals at the other end. By the middle of the third period, it's four-nothing for the Storm.

"He could get a shutout!" I tell Tilly. I need to get her to bed, but I'm having a hard time moving away from the TV. She's cradled in my arms, a little drowsy from the bottle she just sucked back. I turn down the volume of the TV and stand to walk around with her, still watching intently.

As the Caribou pelt the Storm net with pucks, the announcers say, "And Archibald's down on his knees again! He likes to go down."

Jesus. This is giving me extremely inappropriate thoughts about Ford.

And then it happens. The puck gets past Ford and into the net.

Damn!

Ford shakes his head and skates back and forth in front of the net.

So much for the shutout. Oh well. They're still going to win. Probably.

I get Tilly into her bed, turn on the monitor, and hustle back to the TV to catch the end of the game. It ends up five-one for the Storm, so yay! Great start to the season. And Ford only let in one goal!

He said he'd be home as quickly as he could after the game, but the media wants to interview him about the forty-four saves he made, and also that wild play out of his net. I watch him as he talks, sweaty but confident, his smile cocky when he talks about his taking down the Caribou player. "People probably think I'm crazy for doing that. I prefer the term 'mentally spicy'."

The reporters all laugh.

I smile reluctantly. He's spicy, all right.

After his interview, I change the channel, then turn the TV off and pick up my phone to scroll on social media. The next thing I hear is, "Hey. Andi. Wake up," with a gentle touch to my shoulder.

I blink Ford's face into focus. His hand is still on my shoulder, his eyes on mine, his face close enough to see the ring of darker green around his irises.

"I fell asleep," I mumble. His hand is warm and strong on me.

"I see that." The corners of his mouth lift. "Tilly's asleep, too."

"Yeah." For a moment, I just look at him, all irresistible pheromones and athletic beauty. Images of him coming down next to me on the couch, moving over me, letting me feel his heat and energy on my entire body, flash through my head.

I push to sit up and he steps back.

I shove my hair back and blink a few times. "Okay! Congratulations on the win! You played amazing."

"Thanks. I did." He smirks.

I have to smile. "Tilly was impressed. I made her watch."

He chuckles. "Somehow, I don't believe that."

"Well, I tried." I shrug. "She's a little young. But you have to start them young, right?"

"Uh. Yeah."

"I better get home."

"Oh. Okay." He sounds disappointed.

I pause. "What?"

He shrugs. "I need to wind down."

I shift on the couch. "You want to talk?"

"Yeah." He takes off his suit jacket and drapes it over a chair, then unbuttons his cuffs. I watch him roll up one sleeve, then the other, exposing his strong forearms dusted with dark hair, the veins on the backs of his big hands prominent. "I'm really wound up."

Oh, God. Me too. I swallow and try to collect myself as he sits on the couch, trying not to stare at his forearms. "You should be exhausted," I choke out, sweat breaking out on the back of my neck.

"Well, I am that, too." A small smile touches his lips. "But the adrenaline is still pumping."

Oh, yeah. Something is pumping.

I pick up a cushion, turn sideways to face him, and sit cross-legged. "It must have felt good to play so well your first game."

"Yeah. It did." He nods with satisfaction. "It's what I worked for all summer."

"Yeah. It was interesting seeing all your little habits. The TV announcers said you talk to the goalposts."

"Damn right I do. When I hear that clank of the puck hitting the post, I'm like, fuck yeah, buddy! And I give them some high five love taps with my paddle. The crossbar, too," he adds.

I grin. "But when it hits the goalpost, don't you feel like it got past you?"

"Sometimes. But mostly, I feel good because I'm on my angles and they couldn't get a better shot."

"Or they just missed."

"Hey. Don't take away my cope."

A laugh pops out of me. "Sorry. You're right, you tell yourself what you need to."

"I also tap the posts at the beginning of every period. I have a whole routine I do."

I stare at him open-mouthed. "Okay. I didn't notice that."

"That's okay."

That makes me laugh again. I lean forward. "So how does taekwondo fit into all this?"

"Believe it or not, there are a lot of similarities between martial arts and goaltending. Physical and mental. One of the tenets of taekwondo is self-control, and that was something I really wanted to work on. Discipline. It was important to me to show up consistently and to train hard. I wanted to control my behavior and my emotions."

"We all have weaknesses."

"Speak for yourself."

I laugh again. "Okay."

"No, I'm kidding. You're right, we all have weaknesses, and you need to know what they are to be able to work on them. Taekwondo helped with that. Discipline is the bridge between goals and success."

"That's really... admirable."

The corners of his mouth quirk. "Thanks. I feel like it was selfish, in a way. I had a goal and I was going to achieve it."

"And you did."

"To be honest, I'm still working on it. There's always something to learn."

"And physically? How does taekwondo help that?"

"So, physically the goalie and the martial artist both start in a static stance. Both are done in a confined space. In taekwondo, it's the mat. Then you read and react to what's in front of you, and for both, you have to be fast and flexible and agile. Hockey is fast and you have to react fast, and, like sparring with an opponent, you never know what's going to happen."

"I don't know how you react so fast and stop that puck."

"Well, the secret is, I actually don't."

"What?"

"Nobody's reflexes are fast enough to stop a puck at the speed players shoot it. I stop the puck because I've been watching the play, and I've anticipated what's going to happen and where it's going to come from."

"Ohhhh."

"Although I do have amazing reflexes," he adds modestly.

"I'm sure you do." I bite my lip on a smile.

"Mentally, the pressure is similar too. It's you against your opponent."

"But you have a team playing with you in hockey."

"Yeah, but being in goal, you're pretty much on your own. Any mistake you make is obvious. And these days, teams expect perfection."

"You *are* a perfectionist."

"Yeah. But really? There's no such thing as perfection."

"That's true." I regard him, transfixed.

"In taekwondo you learn patterns, and you practice the moves over and over until you don't have to think about them. That helps with goaltending, too. That kind of training helps you react fast without having to think. It helps you keep your composure."

"So that's how you stay calm in net?"

"More or less. I also think a lot about sharks."

I choke on a laugh. "Sharks?"

"Yeah. Sharks are fascinating." He flashes a grin. "Thinking about them keeps me from getting too in my head, otherwise I overthink moves, get hesitant, and start to panic."

"Panic." I snort a laugh. "I thought for sure you were going to get a shutout tonight."

He rolls his eyes.

"I even told Tilly you were going to," I add. "We were excited."

"Wait, what? You told Tilly I was going to get a shutout?"

"Yeah..."

"You said it? *Out loud*?"

"Yeah..." My smile droops.

"Shit!" He stares at me. "You can't do that!"

I blink at him and push my glasses up on my nose. "Can't do what?"

"You can't say it out loud! The word shutout!"

"Oh, no. Is that another superstition?"

He takes a breath, his strong chest rising. "Yes. But everyone knows that. If you say it, you jinx it."

I narrow my eyes at him. "So you're saying it's my fault you didn't get the shutout?"

He stares at me.

Holy shit! I think he really does believe that!

"Sorry I missed the baby shower."

I look up to see Alfie standing in front of me in the locker room. We just finished practicing. Everyone else has headed out but I stayed on the ice for a while with Pete, our goalie coach.

"I get it, man." I incline my head. "You doing okay?"

He sits on the bench and huffs out a sigh. "Not really."

"Fuck. I'm sorry. What can I do?"

He looks at me. "Nothing." Then he drops his gaze to the floor again. "Ayla's having a hard time dealing with things."

"That's understandable."

"Yeah. I know. But..." He forks his fingers through his hair. "At some point you have to get on with your life."

"I guess it can take a while. And it's probably different for different people."

He moves his head up and down without looking up. "I'm worried about her."

Shit. I have no experience with this to draw on. When my grandparents passed away a few years ago, it was sad, but not unexpected. When your child dies... Jesus. I can't even imagine, especially now that I have Tilly. "Is she getting help?" I ask carefully.

"Yeah. We're both going for therapy. Together and alone. And she's been seeing her doctor. But she hasn't gone back to work. She doesn't seem to have interest in anything." He pauses. "Including me."

Oh, Jesus. I stare at my buddy, a knot forming in my gut. "I'm sorry," I manage to say. "I don't know what else to say."

He looks up with a crooked smile. "Yeah, I know. Don't worry. I'm just venting."

"It's good to talk things out. I know it's not always easy, though. And I can always listen, even if I can't do much else to help. Hey. Let's go get a beer."

"I should probably get home to Ayla. But..." He sighs. "Okay. Sure."

I send Andi a quick text to let her know I'll be home a bit late, and Alfie and I decide on a place to meet up. I don't suggest Uncle Ernie's, where we often hang out. Uncle Ernie's Café and Pizza is near where a bunch of us live, the food and drinks are great, and Ernie's a great guy and huge hockey fan, but... Ernie is also Ayla's grandfather. And Ayla used to work there.

So we meet at the Swan Dive on Palisade Avenue, a cozy little pub with lots of types of beer and decent food. The lunch crowd has mostly cleared out so we find a table in the back corner. I order a Raging Bitch IPA and Alfie gets a Three Sheets ale.

"So." Elbows on the table, Alfie turns his beer glass.

"Yeah. Life sucks sometimes."

"How are *you* doing?" he asks. "With the baby."

"Well. We've managed not to drop her on her head."

"We?"

"My neighbor. And friend. I tried to hire a nanny and it didn't work out." I make a face and tell him about Andi and how we've been coordinating schedules.

"Lucky you have her," he remarks. "You figured out diaper changes and all that?"

"More or less. I did put an outfit on her upside down one day. Andi thought that was hilarious. I wondered why it didn't seem to fit right."

"Haha. Yeah, there's a lot to learn. When Kane was a newborn, every time he made a noise I ran over to pick him up. Didn't realize he was just making noise in his sleep. He made a *lot* of noise in his sleep."

Alfie keeps talking about Kane and I just smile and listen. This is probably good for him. I bet nobody wants to bring up his baby, but clearly he wants to talk. I may not have any advice for how to deal with grief, but I can do this.

An hour later, Alfie seems happier and more relaxed. "Thanks for listening, man."

"Hey, no problem. Any time. We can do this again."

"Maybe some time I could meet Matilda."

I feel a bite in my chest. "Yeah. For sure. Whenever you're ready."

I head home, eager to see my little princess. How things have changed. I've gone from being terrified and dreading being alone with her to missing her. Wow.

I go to Andi's place because she took Tilly there this morning so she could work while Tilly sleeps. I find Andi flustered and pissed off.

"What's wrong?" I take Tilly from her. "Hi, sweetie."

"You're late!"

"I texted you."

"I know, but you didn't ask me, you just told me you were

going to be late! And I had a meeting scheduled and we had another Zoom adventure. Oh my God."

Oh, boy. "What happened?" I remember that other time Tilly caused problems in a meeting.

"She was crying because she had a poopy diaper. So I put myself on mute and yelled at her to wait just a few minutes, pleeeeease. But I wasn't on mute." She rubs her temples. "And then I did it again when I went to get her and it turned out she had a huge blow out and there was poop everywhere, and everyone heard me going, 'Oh no, Tilly, you have shat everywhere, what have you done?' and I think I probably lost that client."

I roll my lips in because I want to laugh. But I don't think Andi sees this as funny. Yet. She will. "I'm sorry. I wasn't thinking. I was talking to Alfie and he seemed like he needed to talk so I suggested we go get a beer."

"A beer. I lost a client so you could have a beer."

My amusement disappears. "It wasn't just getting a beer. He's going through hell. He and his wife are having problems because his wife can't get past what happened. Their baby died."

I've told her about that. She knows it was a tragic accident.

She takes a deep breath.

"He talked about his son," I continue, a little annoyed. "I think it was good for him."

She closes her eyes briefly. "I don't think it's fair to me that you did that without checking with me first."

Now I drag a big breath into my lungs and let it out. "You're right. I'm sorry. I should have asked. I'm just so used to being on my own."

She nods. "I get that."

"I could have met up with Alfie later. Maybe."

Her stiff posture deflates. "Okay. Thanks. I get that it was important to you to talk to him."

"It was. I just didn't think."

"Please don't take me for granted."

Shit. I jerk my chin down. "You're right. Absolutely. I do appreciate what you're doing for us, and I hope you didn't lose a client. I'm sorry."

"I was also worried because you don't do stuff like that on the spur of the moment. You always stick to your routine."

"True." I scrunch up my face and think about that. "I just... did what I thought I needed to do. He seemed really down."

She tilts her head. "I get it. I'm glad you were there for him."

"Okay."

We look at each other for a heavy moment. Then I say, "Did we just have a fight like a married couple?"

A slow smile tugs at her mouth. "I think we did."

"Yikes."

"Does that mean we get to have makeup sex now?" I give her a hopeful look.

Our eyes meet.

Uh... whoa. I've always made jokes like that around Andi. This time it doesn't land like it usually does. Because I'm actually thinking about sex with her. And usually she responds with a smart-ass comment and an eye roll. But now... the look in her eyes, her gaze locked on my face, then lowering to my mouth... I know what that means. My body responds.

What if we did it? What if we had sex?

No. That can't happen. Apart from the baby in my arms, Andi is off limits, obviously. As a friend. A neighbor. And now someone helping me with my daughter.

"Kidding!" I say lightly. "Wow, is it hot in here?" I wipe my brow. "Or is that just you?"

She laughs, but it sounds a little strangled. The air is still crackling around us.

"Alfie says he wants to meet Tilly."

Andi clears her throat. "That's great."

"Yeah. I think it's progress. Well. I'll take this little girl off your hands so you can get work done. Go suck up to that client."

"Good idea." She gives me a wry smile. "I cleaned her up and gave her bath so she's all good now." She looks at Tilly. "Matilda Grace, you rascal."

She says it so affectionately my heart expands hard against my sternum.

"Bye, baby," she adds. "See you tomorrow."

Tomorrow. I have nothing else going on today. "Hey. Let me make you dinner to apologize for being late."

"Oh. You don't have to do that."

"I know, but I want to. Come over around six?"

She tilts her head, purses her lips, and I see wheels turning in her head. Then she says, "Okay. Thanks."

This makes me happy as I leave her place and go home. I need to buy something to make for dinner, though, so first I make a shopping list and then Tilly and I head out again. I put her in her stroller and walk to Trader Joe's. I don't mind cooking but all I usually eat is what's planned by Victor—lots of protein and veggies. I can make something really good for Andi.

I pick up some of the sweetcorn, burrata, and basil ravioli. I'll serve them with a brown butter and garlic sauce. And a salad. I peruse various options and decide on a Caesar salad. I toss a chunk of fresh parmesan and a loaf of focaccia bread into the basket. Tilly sleeps through my shopping expedition, so I take my time collecting all the other things on my list.

Tilly's waking up on the way home, so we stop in the park. I stroll along the path and sit on a bench to take Tilly out of the stroller. A couple of young mothers sit across from me with their babies and strollers.

"Hi," one of them says to me with a smile. "How old is your baby?"

"She's four months."

"Aw. What a little sweetie."

"How about yours?" I ask, making conversation.

"Broderick is six months," she replies.

The other woman says, "This is Rebecca and she's just two months old. I also have a two-year-old. We were just talking about baby-led weaning."

Ha. I know what that is. When Turks and Holly came over to give me baby advice, they told me about that. "I've thought about introducing her to some solid foods," I say. "I think she's still a bit young."

"Yeah." Mom Number One nods. "But you could give her a slice of avocado or a cooked carrot just to give her the taste."

I chat with the moms for a few minutes. "Does your little guy sleep through the night?" I ask Mom Number One.

"Yeah, he does. He has been since he was about three months old."

"Wow. That's great." I rub my forehead. "I'd give just about anything for a full night of sleep."

"It's all about the routine," she says.

My ears perk up. "Routine?"

"Uh huh. You need an eat, wake, sleep cycle."

"Tell me more."

* * *

Tilly's a little fussy when we get home so I do the usual stuff to try to calm her. It seems she just wants to be held, so I tuck her into the baby sling so I can get things done. I try to get her to go to sleep, but she's not having it.

She kicks her legs and gums her ball toy.

"Hey, Tilly girl. Do you want to change, too? Let's get you into something nicer for dinner."

I look through the new things I bought her and pull out a little pair of knit pants and matching sweater in a greenish-blue color. There are matching socks too.

When she's dressed, I admire her. "That color really brings out your eyes."

She coos in agreement.

"Okay. Andi should be here soon. Let's go."

15

ANDI

I spend about fifteen minutes debating with myself whether to bring a bottle of wine to Ford's place. It's just dinner. We don't need wine. But wine is nice and it's always good to bring something when you're a guest. But I'm not really a "guest" since I almost feel like I live at his place these days. In the end, I grab a bottle of merlot and carry it with me down the hall.

All because of that moment earlier where he joked about having makeup sex. And because I actually have been thinking about sex with Ford, I didn't take it as a joke like I usually do. And he knew that. And it got really hot in my condo.

I spent even longer debating what to wear, and much of the debate was similar. It doesn't matter what I look like for Ford; he's seen me at my worst now. It's not like this is a date. But my need to look my best wins out, although I'm wearing jeans and a fitted black turtleneck sweater, nothing fancy. My hair is done in loose waves, and I did put on makeup—eyeshadow and mascara, and a shiny pale pink lip gloss.

I pause outside his door. *Be cool, be cool.*

I knock and walk in, as I've been doing lately. "Hi!"

Oops. He's asleep on the couch. I cover my mouth.

Tilly is with him, on her back on his chest, tucked into his arm. She's asleep, too. Both of their faces are so beautiful, relaxed in sleep, Tilly's little mouth soft, her cheeks round, Ford's carved and darkened with stubble.

Sweet Jesus. He's wearing gray sweatpants and a snug white T-shirt that hugs his biceps and chest. The shirt has risen up to reveal a strip of bare skin. This is both the sexiest and most endearing thing I've ever seen.

I stand and look at them for probably too long, until Tilly moves, lifting her little arms above her head in a stretch, scrunching up her face. When she lets out a squawk, Ford's eyes open. Blinking, he focuses on me. "Oh. Hey. What time is it?"

Pretending I just arrived, I saunter closer. "Just after six."

"Oh, man. Sorry. We fell asleep."

"I see that."

Tilly's squirming and he sits up and holds her. "See, was that so bad?" He looks back at me. "She didn't want to sleep. I should change her diaper. And change my clothes."

Tilly looks at me, kicks her legs and holds out her arms to me.

My heart. "Hello, baby girl." I reach out and take her from Ford, and give her a kiss on her cheek. "Did you miss me? It's been hours!"

"Sooo long," Ford says with gentle sarcasm as he stands.

"You go change. I'll change little miss's diaper."

"Thanks."

We meet up back in the kitchen. Ford has changed into a pair of dark jeans and a navy, orange, and sky-blue polo-style shirt. Despite the unusual shirt, I feel that punch of attraction that keeps happening.

I set the bottle of wine I brought on his kitchen island. "I brought this. But we don't have to drink it. Or we can. Or you can keep it for some other time." *Babble away, Andi. So not cool.*

"I have some, too, but we can open this." He checks out the bottle. "Oh hey, don't even need a corkscrew." While he opens the wine and pours two glasses, he says, "Dinner's mostly ready. I just have to cook the pasta and put it all together."

"Were you helping your dad make dinner?" I ask Tilly. "No? You wouldn't go to sleep? How can that be? Let's go have a chat." I take her and my wine over to the living room and set her in her bouncy thing, then sit in front of her. "You changed your clothes. Look at this pretty sweater. Tell me what you did this afternoon."

Ford joins us, sitting on the couch. "We went shopping at Trader Joe's. Then we stopped at the park and she went on the swings."

I blink wide eyes. "Oh, wow. Just like a big girl!"

"She liked it."

"Did you like it? Yeah?"

She smiles back at me. "Ammagaddagoo."

"Oh, that does sound fun," I reply. "Tell me more."

Ford laughs when she jabbers more baby sounds. He gives her a bottle and we play with her for a while with some of her toys. Then she starts to rub her eyes and lose interest in the toys. "I think she's ready for another nap," I say.

"Amazing. Maybe we can eat dinner in peace."

After we get her into her little cot in Ford's bedroom, I help Ford in the kitchen. He heats up the sauce he made for the pasta while I grate parmesan cheese for the salad. Then we sit down at his dining table to eat.

"I like your place," I tell him, looking around. "It's a little different than mine."

His décor is light-colored and airy, similar to mine, although his furniture is sleek leather and smooth wood, where I have a comfy sectional with a lot of cushions that you sink into and antique oak pieces I picked up at flea markets over the years when Trevor and I didn't have much money.

"Yeah. Yours is nice too. I wish I had a balcony like you."

"It's small, though. And there's the rooftop terrace. You use that a lot."

"I think I'm the only one who does."

I pick up another piece of ravioli with my fork. "This is so good. Is there corn in here?"

"Yeah. I got it at Trader Joe's. Don't think I made it."

"Well, you made the sauce. And it's delicious, too." I pop the pasta into my mouth and enjoy it. "So, do you have a mantra when you meditate?"

"Yep."

"What is it?"

"Be the shark."

I blink, then chuckle. "Okay."

"It was something I read once. You can be the shark and rule the ocean, or you can be a goldfish and wait for fish food in the aquarium. I don't like waiting. Especially for food," he jokes.

"Food is definitely important. How did you get so interested in sharks?"

"I don't know. They're just interesting. Big, dangerous fish. At the top of the food chain."

"Hmmm."

"There are lessons we can learn from them." He sets down his fork and picks up a piece of focaccia. "Keep swimming. Keep moving forward. Sharks can't swim backwards," he explains.

"Right. That's a good rule. Keep moving forward."

"Also, don't fear hold you back. Some sharks are afraid of dolphins."

"Oh, I love dolphins! Who could be afraid of them?"

"Right? Great white sharks are supposedly man eaters, but they don't really like the taste of humans."

"Good to know," I reply dryly.

He grins. "What about you? Do you have a mantra?"

"I don't meditate."

"You should."

I tip my head to one side. "Why?"

"It's good for you."

"So is fiber."

He barks out a laugh. "True. Meditation helps deal with stress and anxiety."

"Ohhh, like the stress of being in the net with players shooting pucks at you."

"Exactly." He gives me a look. "Don't tell me you don't have stress in your job."

"Oh yeah, I do." I pucker my lips up briefly. "Dealing with people is always stressful. Right now I have one client who is so indecisive I almost lost my mind the other day."

"There you go. Meditation would help that."

"Hmm. Maybe some time I'll try it. I do try to stay positive, though. I think about the tattoo on my back."

He blinks. "You have a tattoo on your back?"

"Yeah." Without thinking, I stand up, turn around, and pull up my sweater. The words *Rise above the storm and you will find the sunshine* are inked in script up my spine.

"Very nice," he says in a choked voice. "I like it."

I pull my sweater down. I probably shouldn't have done that, but I kind of like that I flustered him. I take my seat.

"How about yoga?" he asks. "Have you done yoga?"

"No."

He heaves an exaggerated sigh. "Andi, Andi."

"You're a hockey player. You don't do yoga."

"Sure, I have. It's great for flexibility. I'm *very* flexible." He wiggles his eyebrows suggestively.

I grin and shake my head.

"It's also great for staying calm and balanced. Sometime, I'll take you to a yoga class."

Sure he will. "Okay."

16

FORD

I started the season with a bang in that first game. I was proud of myself for that. I've been working my whole life to be the best goalie I can be. My play that night earned me the start in the next game. That game didn't go so well. We lost, four-three. I let in four fucking goals. And the game after that, I let in four again. Except that game we won, at least. But these numbers are not making my stats look good. Goals against average, save percentage—not looking stellar right now. I'm right in the middle of the pack, and that is not where I want to be. Goodbye, Jennings Trophy.

The season has just started.

And I'm so fucking tired.

I'm on my way to the arena for tonight's game, taking the route I always do. I'm starting tonight and much as I want to play every game I can, I have a lump of dread in my gut. I have to do better.

I take responsibility for my failures. I don't want to blame anyone else for my shitty play. But if I could just get a good night's sleep, I'd be performing a lot better.

I don't want to blame Tilly. But that little scamp is not sleeping through the night. After talking to those moms at the park, I've been doing research. I downloaded an app they told me about and I've been tracking everything Tilly does—sleeping, pooping, eating. I've read about eat, wake, sleep cycles and I'm drawing up a plan. I love planning, so this is perfect. It makes me feel like I have a little control. My last plan didn't go so well, but I had no idea what I was doing.

My mood is not helped by the fact that I am painfully horny. Since that moment when I made one of my off-color flirty jokes with Andi and she looked at me like she wanted to ride me like a bike, I haven't been able to stop thinking about that. Riding her. Railing her. Doing dirty things to her.

I think about that tattoo up the smooth curve of her back.

I've been lone-rangering every chance I get. It's a wonder I don't have a repetitive strain injury to my wrist. But it's not enough, dammit.

Think about sharks...

Or hockey.

Bender, our other goalie, started the two games after that and picked up wins. The team is really building off the progress we made last year. They've changed up our power play, and it's working a lot better. Luckily we haven't had any injuries. (Knock on wood. Please. Right now. I mean it.) And I'm pissed that I'm not rising to the same level.

But I'm so tired.

I park in the underground lot and head into the arena. As I walk in, the team's social media guy takes a photo of me. He gets pics of all the guys in our game day fits.

It's been almost two months since Willa left Tilly with me. She thought she might be gone a couple of months. I could try to find another nanny, but is it worth it if Willa will be back soon? I need to know.

And then what happens? I just give Tilly back to her?

It almost seems laughable that when she arrived, that's exactly what I thought would happen. But now? No way in hell am I giving her back to Willa. We're going to share custody of her.

I sent Willa a text message earlier, but I haven't heard back from her.

I change out of my suit and tie into shorts, a hoodie, and a ball cap, and walk out to the ice. It's quiet out here now, the stands empty. I sit on the bench and close my eyes to do my visualization. I do this every game. I visualize the saves I'm going to make and the plays I'm going to help. I imagine a breakaway happening in front of me. With closed eyes, I watch the play develop, position myself in the crease with the perfect angle and depth, and then I make the save.

Christ, I could fall asleep right here.

I rub my eyes.

Goalies usually have intense pre-game routines and I'm no different. I think it's because of the pressure; having a routine helps ease some of the stress of being between the pipes. But you can get carried away with having too strict of a routine.

I go to the gym and do a series of stretches. I feel tight in my hamstrings today, so I spend a few extra minutes doing high kicks and using a foam roller. Then I grab my ball and go out to the hall to bounce it off the concrete brick wall. I focus on driving it to the floor and wall with one hand, catching it when it bounces back with the other. Over and over. Faster and faster. I catch every single throw.

On the way back to the dressing room I stop in the players'

lounge to grab my usual pre-game snack: a cinnamon raisin bagel and a banana.

"Hey, Archie," Benny says to me as I walk in. Like me, he's wearing shorts and running shoes, taping a stick.

I'm usually one of the first to arrive, and Benny comes pretty early, too.

"Hey. How's it going?"

"Good. I keep meaning to ask you—Mabel wants to meet your daughter. Think we could set something up?"

"Oh. Sure. We can do that."

I get dressed following my strict routine. First my leggings and compression shirt. Then my cup, pants, and socks. I have to put on my right sock before I can even touch my left sock. One time my left sock was on top of the right and I asked Eddy to move it for me. This was before he knew about my superstitions and he was annoyed, so he chucked it at me. I screamed and ducked before it hit me to keep from touching it. Everybody else thought it was hilarious, but I was pissed.

With my chest protector and goalie pads on, I grab my gloves and again go out into the hall and do more stretching, then a series of fast hand, upper body, and head moves, imagining pucks coming at me. I have this all planned—it's almost like a taekwondo pattern. Trainers and equipment guys are walking past me, in and out of the dressing room, getting ready for the game, and they just ignore me. Everyone's used to this.

I go back in to tape my stick. This is another meditation time for me, where I listen to music with my earbuds, relax, and focus. Everyone knows not to interrupt me.

Time for warm-up on the ice. I finish dressing. First the right skate, then the left. Goalie skates have flatter blades that help when pushing around in the crease, and they have better protection. I get my helmet on (with sharks in a stormy ocean custom painted on it), grab my stick, and lead the way out. There are fans in the arena already, lots of kids lined up along the glass at our end with signs. Music blasts through the speakers. I skate straight to the net, shooting a couple of pucks out of my way. The first thing I do is grab the water bottle and squirt some onto the blade of my stick. Another superstition.

I do a sprint around our end of the ice with the guys to warm up, do more stretches, then get into net and face the shots from my teammates. The other guys all seem pretty fired up tonight, flying around the ice, shooting the pucks hard at the net. All their energy just makes me feel wearier. I challenge myself by doing some jumps on the ice, as high as I can, and more hand-eye movements.

As I leave the ice, I flip a puck over the glass for a kid with a sign that says "MY FIRST STORM GAME". He's ecstatic and jumps to catch it, but a man behind him grabs it in the air. I hope that's the kid's dad. I watch to see if he hands the puck to the kid... but he doesn't.

"Hey!" I glare at the guy. "That puck was for him!" I point at the kid who's now almost in tears. "Give him the puck!"

"I caught it," the guy says.

"I'll come up there and get it," I shout at him, starting toward the door.

He recoils and leans over to give the kid the puck.

"Good man." I knock the glass and give the boy a chin lift and a smile. He's happy again. "What an asshole," I mutter as I skate off.

"Who's an asshole?" Smitty asks.

We tromp down the tunnel. I tell him what just happened.

"Jesus. People suck."

Now I'm irritated. Not a good way to start the game. I throw myself down in front of my cubby and scowl at the team logo on the carpet. Apparently, my glare is enough to keep everyone away.

I let my eyes go unfocused and pay attention to my breathing. In. Out. In. Out. I acknowledge the things that pass through my head—that guy was an asshole; I'm so damn tired; what am I going to do about Tilly; and why do I keep thinking about Andi? —trying not to get involved with the thoughts. Trying to let them go. Let my mind be free. Eventually I let myself be aware of the hard bench I'm sitting on, my skate blades on the floor, the chatter of guys around me.

I need my sports drink. I'm into blueberry pomegranate right now.

"You okay?" Crusher asks me.

I start. "Me? Yeah. Why?"

"You're usually more animated before a game. You seem distracted."

I shrug.

"He is distracted," Smitty says with a smirk. "You met his neighbor, didn't you?"

I level an icy glare on Smitty. "This isn't about her." *Not totally*.

"Sure," he says.

"Oh yeah," Crusher says. "The neighbor is smokin' hot."

Yeah. She is. And I'm fucking desperate for sex. But I only want it with her. Jesus.

"Is Tilly okay?" Benny asks.

"She's fine." I guzzle my drink. "Growing."

"Good. Any word from her mom?"

"No. Last I heard, her parents aren't doing well."

"You got this, man."

"Hell yeah, I do." I give him an incredulous look, like, *is there any doubt?*

I've got this.

Back out on the ice, I do the routine I do before every period —a figure eight in the crease, then a turn into a crouch, a few fast side-to-side moves, then I drop into a squat and jump straight up to standing. I tap my pads, right, then left, then tap each goalpost, right then left. I turn and bump my forehead against the crossbar.

I've got this.

Forty minutes later, I'm forced to admit I don't got this.

Jesus Christ on a bicycle. I let in two soft goals in fifteen seconds, both of them on breakaways. The players both pushed the puck in front of them, I poked at it, missed, and they scored.

And then at the end of the period, Cassidy from the Condors pissed me off by digging for the rebound when I had the fucking puck. And I lost my shit.

"What was that about?" Coach shouts in the dressing room.

"I made the save," I shout back. "He wanted the rebound, but I had the puck, so he hit me. It's my fucking crease, right? I told him to get the fuck out of there. If there's a rebound, play the puck, otherwise don't fucking touch me."

"Jesus Christ." Coach shakes his head.

Tension crackles in the room.

"And how they hell did they get two breakaways?" Coach demands. "Hart was just out of the box, you gotta watch that, you gotta be on him. And the other one—Aaron and Noah, were you both fucking asleep on the blue line?"

Their faces tighten.

"Apparently," I mutter. I was pissed off about that, too. Two breakaways in a minute!

"Hey." Benny gives me a look.

Yeah, yeah. He's trying to keep things positive. But this was not a positive period.

17

ANDI

This is a last resort.

We're in Ford's SUV driving around Hoboken in the dark. I don't know what was going on with Tilly, but she would not go to sleep. I was trying to get her to sleep when Ford got home and he had no luck either, so we've strapped her into her car seat and hope the motion and noise of the car will put her to sleep.

So far, she's quiet.

I lean my head back in the passenger seat and let out a long exhale. "Wow."

"Maybe she's teething."

"I think it's too early for that." But I actually have no idea. I pull out my phone and open my friend Google. "Six months, usually." I really need to do more research. Maybe there are things we should be doing for Tilly that we're not. I've been winging it with help from YouTube and Google when I have a question, but I should know more about babies.

"I downloaded this app," Ford says. "I was talking to some moms at the park."

"Oh yeah?"

"I'm going to try to get Tilly onto a better schedule. I can't handle much more of this lack of sleep."

"That sounds like a good idea."

We drive in silence for a while.

"*I* might fall asleep," I say, as city lights slide past in ebbs and flows.

"Go ahead. I got this."

But I can't shut my mind off, despite my fatigue. "What are you most afraid of?"

"Right now?"

"No." I smile. "In general."

He slants me a look and moves his hands on the steering wheel. "That's a pretty deep question."

"Yeah. Tell me."

He's silent for a bit, then says, "Needles."

"Needles? Like medical needles?"

"Yeah. I've always hated getting needles. Getting blood drawn."

I smile slowly. "What happens?"

"I pass out."

"Shut up."

His lips quirk but he stares straight out the windshield. "No lie."

"I hate to tell you this, but Tilly is due for her four-month vaccinations."

"Oh, I can handle it when it's someone else."

"Okay, good." I study his shadowy profile. His nose is perfect, amazing for a hockey player and even more amazing for a goalie. But he does wear a big mask on the ice. I didn't mean that kind of fear when I asked.

"Actually," he says quietly, "my biggest fear is that I can't be a good father."

Oh. I roll my lips in. I think he's doing great at this parenting so far. "I'm sure every father is afraid of that."

"Yeah, probably. How about you? What's your biggest fear?"

This I already know. "I guess it's that I'm afraid there's something wrong with me, and that's what led to my divorce."

His head whips around, then jerks back to watch the road. "That's bullshit."

I shrug. "You can say that, but you don't know that. I blame Trevor for cheating on me, absolutely, but was there something wrong with me that led to him doing that?"

"There's never an excuse for cheating."

My mouth softens. "Really? You believe that?"

"Yeah."

"You've never cheated on a woman?"

"I haven't exactly had a lot of relationships. So no. But I wouldn't. If I was that unhappy in a relationship, I'd tell her."

"Sometimes those things are hard to talk about."

"True." He considers that. "But you have to."

I like hearing that from him.

"Anyway, the divorce wasn't your fault," he says.

"Maybe... I worked too much." I say it slowly, because I've never actually said this fear out loud. Not even to Elodie. "I worked a lot."

"Why?"

"What do you mean? Why did I work a lot?"

"Yeah."

That makes me think. "Well. I loved my job. I wanted to do well at it."

"Uh huh. Why?"

"Because..." I have to ponder that, too. Why was it so important to me? Why was winning that award so important? Because I'd taken some hits to the self-esteem, and I wanted to feel good about myself. But when Trevor and I were married... "Well, partly because I had to. I was supporting Trevor and me. He started to make a little money playing ball, but it took a long time for him to break into the big leagues and make real money."

Ford nods.

"And I guess it was an esteem issue," I add quietly. "It always seemed like his career was the priority. He was a good athlete, and talented. Maybe not the best ball player in the world, but he worked his butt off, too, and... athletes get a lot of attention, and..." I trail off. "I wanted to be good and talented at something, too."

I've never really articulated that. I did go for some therapy after the divorce, but I think it was almost too soon. I was still too angry and resentful to be able to look deep inside myself.

"But it worked out okay, because I have a great career," I add.

His lips twitch. "You always see the bright side."

I lift one shoulder. "I try." I pause. "Sometimes too much, maybe."

"What does that mean?"

"Well..." I look down at my hands. "Sometimes I think being too optimistic and too loyal kept me from seeing who Trevor really was."

"Ah." His jaw sets as he looks ahead out the windshield. "Anything else you're afraid of?"

I roll my bottom lip between my teeth. Having talked about my fear that I caused Trevor to lose interest in me makes it less scary. Now... what I'm most afraid of is falling in love again. And losing it. Again. Being rejected... again. Trusting the wrong person. Again.

But I can't say those things. Those are too scary. And so, like Ford, I make light of it. "Peeping Toms."

He chokes. "What?"

"Peeping Toms. I always have to have the blinds or curtains shut at night because I'm afraid there's someone out there watching me."

"Has that happened?" His voice sharpens.

"No." I shake my head. "I think it came from a movie I watched as a kid."

"Huh."

"So since you've never had a real relationship, I guess you don't believe in soulmates."

"Where are these questions coming from?"

"I'm just making conversation! We're sitting in this car driving around, we might as well have a conversation. Do you believe in soulmates?"

Again, he takes his time answering. "I believe in them for other people."

I tilt my head. "But not for yourself?"

"Well, I haven't experienced it yet. But I've seen buddies fall in love and absolutely lose their minds over a woman. Like Benny and Mabel. They're so different, and yet they found something together that goes deeper than just being introverted or extroverted. I guess that's a soulmate?" He shakes his head. "But my soul is freaky."

I laugh. "Oh my God."

He lifts one shoulder, flicks the turn signal and brakes to slow down.

"You're not a freak," I say. "Maybe a little eccentric."

"When I was a kid, people thought I was a freak."

Oh no. My heart bumps. I hesitate, then ask gently, "Why?"

"My parents were... different. They believed in following your own path. They were very loving, but also very hands off. As long as I wasn't hurting anyone, I could do whatever I wanted. But when you're a kid and you don't have any boundaries in your life, it can be... scary."

I nod somberly. "Yeah. I can see that."

"So I was different from the other kids. My parents didn't come to parent-teacher conferences or make sure I did my homework. I begged them for rules, like what time I had to go to bed."

I stifle the noise of distress that rises in my throat.

"But they just embrace spontaneity and following your id."

"That's not very... adult," I venture.

"Yeah. Exactly. They were like children."

"It's great to be free," I say. "But also scary."

"Yeah. Like, they were fine with it when I didn't want to go to school. And there were *lots* of days I didn't want to go to school."

"Why?" The word is almost a whisper.

"Like I said, other kids thought I was a freak. They made fun of me. Bullied me."

"Oh no. Because of your parents?"

"Yeah. And partly because of how I looked."

My eyebrows shoot up.

"I was tall and skinny and I wore glasses," he says with a shrug. "My clothes weren't always the latest styles. Mom liked to shop in thrift stores, even though we could afford new things. She has a unique style."

Hmm. He must get that from her. I exhale a long breath, working to keep my voice even. "I'm so sorry."

"Hockey saved me," he says. "When I discovered I loved hockey it gave me something to pursue. My own path to follow. It gave me a purpose. And there were lots of rules and boundaries. And I loved it."

"That's so great."

"It caused some conflict," he continues, merging into traffic on another street. "My parents didn't believe in rules and schedules. So when I had to be at a practice or a game, they waved it off. I got so..." He pauses. "Anxious, I guess. I was worried that I was like my parents. I saw their loosey-goosey way of life and it bugged me."

"Oh." I tilt my head, my chest aching.

"And I didn't want to be like that," he continues. "I was afraid I'd get kicked out of hockey. I didn't want to be some loser who didn't show up for games or didn't work hard and let the team down. As I got older, there were consequences for that. It's a team sport, and you just don't do that to your teammates. Mom and Dad didn't get that. So I was always nagging and arguing with them so I could get to the arena."

"Ohhhh." Okay. I'm seeing what's going on here.

"That's why I took up taekwondo. Self-discipline isn't something you're born with; you have to learn it. And like any other skill, if you want to master it you have to practice it."

He's kind of... amazing.

"Kids should be allowed to follow their own path," I say. "But I think parents need to lay the foundation for that. They should have been there for you to make sure you got what you needed to succeed in hockey." Oops. Maybe that sounded critical of his parents. "Obviously, they did. I'm sure they love you."

"They do," he says. "And yeah, over the years they started trying harder. They saw how important it was to me. And how well I was doing. But it made them miserable. They absolutely hated the weekend tournaments out of town. They had nothing in common with the other parents. They wanted to be sitting at home smoking weed or doing shrooms."

"Oh." I blink. "So I guess they couldn't exactly get mad at you when you did that."

"I have never smoked the devil's lettuce."

I burst out laughing. "Riiiiight."

He grins briefly. "Okay, I have. I still enjoy the odd edible. But you're right. That would have been hypocritical of them. So instead of giving me hell, they just didn't say anything."

"Ah. That lack of boundaries, again."

"Like I said, hockey saved me. Although, for a while my parents were worried about how obsessed with it I was. They thought maybe I had OCD or a developmental disorder." He pauses and shoots me a sideways glance as if he's afraid of how I'll react to that.

"What did they do about that?"

"They got me seen by a child psychologist. He didn't think I had a disorder, but when I talked about my anxiety, he helped me figure out that my need for routine and structure probably related to the lack of rules and boundaries growing up."

"That makes sense. Kids need limits."

"Yeah. And I never thought I would be a parent myself. But here we are. I'm gonna need to learn how to set limits for Tilly without being a total dictator."

"Hmmmm." Obviously, he's learned from his experience. And yet, there are things it seems he hasn't learned. "I'm sorry you were bullied."

"It's okay. I survived. I learned from it. You were talking about how you wonder if you're defective... well, I knew I was."

"That's not true."

"Sure, it is. That's why I've never had a relationship. But it's okay. As I kid, I learned that I don't need anyone else. Other than my teammates."

I'm silent. I hate that. I hate that for him so much. I hate that he believes that. And I hate that he's afraid he can't be a good dad.

"This has been quite the discussion," he says lightly. "Think we can go home now?"

I look back at the mirror that shows Tilly's sleeping face in the back seat. "We can try. Fingers crossed we can get her up and into bed without waking her up."

It feels like we're both parents, working together, like partners. We argued like a married couple. Then he made me dinner like we're a couple. But I'm not Tilly's parent. And Ford for sure is not my husband.

But is he still just a friend? I'm getting to know him so much better, and those idiosyncrasies that were amusing and baffling are making more sense. They're also kind of... endearing. I like this guy.

He parks in the underground parking and carefully carries Tilly into the elevator and up to our floor. We tiptoe into his condo and he gingerly lifts her out of the car seat and lowers her into her little cot. I'm right there beside him to help with the buckle and straps and slipping her knit hat off her head.

In the dark, we stand next to each other and wait in suspense to see if she wakes up. Her eyes stay closed, her tiny mouth a perfect little rosebud. She really is a pretty baby.

Close enough to feel his body warmth and breathe in his warm, spicy scent, I turn to look at Ford and he turns too. Our eyes meet. The quiet shadows close around us, heat building.

His gaze drops to my mouth. My lips part. Excitement twists in my belly. God, I want to taste him. To feel his mouth, the rasp of his beard stubble, the hardness of his body. His eyes go heavy-lidded and I'm drifting closer to him, lips parted, a heavy ache pulsing low inside me.

Then he glances down at the sleeping baby and steps back. He holds a finger to his mouth in a "shhh" motion then shoos me out of the bedroom.

Right. Right. There's a sleeping baby. Ford's baby. Sweet salty Jesus. What was I doing? I've lost my goddamned mind.

18

ANDI

Ford's on a road trip for three days. I did this once before and survived, but this time Elodie comes over to help. She came over this afternoon to babysit while I went out to a client meeting that had to be done at their office. And she stayed for the evening so I could catch up on work. I love her.

Ford really has to do something to find a nanny. Willa told him she needs at least another month, but she's not sure. It's been over two months and we're both exhausted. I may have lost a client and he's not happy with how he's playing.

I'm also really horny.

It's an unfortunate reality. Spicy romance books and my vibrator are not solving this problem.

Part of it might be because I keep thinking of Ford. We've spent a lot of time together lately and he's an attractive man and also, I find his care for his daughter very endearing and while I've always liked him... now I *like* him.

The team flies home late Thursday night. Rather than disturb Tilly in the middle of the night (although *she* disturbs *us* all the time) she and I stayed at Ford's place, and I put her down in her little cot in the bedroom. I watch TV for a while, yawning, trying to stay awake, and after Tilly wakes up around one-thirty and I feed her, I put her back down. I want to go to sleep, too.

I eye Ford's big bed. I could lie down there. Would that be weird? I sit on the edge and look around. Without a baby to distract me, I take in the details—a framed picture of his parents on the dresser, a pair of running shoes near the closet, a book on the nightstand. I reach for the soft throw blanket on the end of the bed and pull it up and over me as I lie down. I burrow my face into the pillow. It smells like Ford, that warm leather and spice scent. Oh God. It's turning me on. I squeeze my thighs together, close my eyes, and try not to think about his big hands and hard-packed abs.

I'm awakened by a low, husky voice saying my name. "Andi."

"Mmmm." I cuddle into the bed deeper. I don't want to wake up.

"Hey." My shoulder gets a gentle nudge. Then the bed moves as a heavy weight settles on it.

I blink my eyes open and my head jerks up.

Ford is next to me. On his bed.

I stare at him in the shadows. "Oh. Hi."

"Hi," he whispers. "You fell asleep."

"I did." Still disoriented, I ask, "Where am I?"

"In my bed." His low voice and those words make me quiver. Then he adds in an even deeper tone, "You're sleeping in my bed."

Those words... that tone of voice... are erotic as hell.

We gaze at each other. He has his head propped up on one elbow, his big body close enough for me to reach out and touch. The light coming through the door highlights his cheekbones and mouth. He watches me and it feels like he's burning me up with his eyes.

I inhale his scent again, deeper now he's here with me. Every nerve ending on my skin is electrified and a yearning ache blooms between my legs. My nipples tighten into hard nubs.

I want him so much. I've wanted him so much. It feels essential... unavoidable. I pull air into my lungs slowly.

His lips part as he gazes at me. My eyes linger there and my mouth opens slightly, too, with intense desire to taste him, to feel his lips, his beard stubble, his breath.

"Andi," he breathes.

"Yes." I blink slowly.

He lifts a hand and his fingertips touch my face. Am I still asleep? Am I dreaming?

"Ford..."

"Yeah." The corners of his mouth lift, his gaze moving from my mouth to my eyes. I look into those depths and see that he wants me too.

I lift my hand, curve my fingers around his hand at my cheek, and draw it slowly down. He pulls in a sharp inhale and then I press his hand to my breast.

"Jesus," he whispers, his eyelids going heavy.

My heart thuds against my ribs. My breast swells and pushes into his palm, and he cups it, gentle but firm. A small noise escapes my mouth. "I want this," I murmur.

"Fuck." His mouth is soft and vulnerable, his eyes dark, and he molds my breast again. I move my hands to his chest and lay them there, feeling his heartbeat as violent as mine. "Are you sure?"

"I'm sure."

His mouth moves closer to mine and I barely move my head so that our mouths meet.

My fingers curl into his dress shirt beneath the open suit jacket.

Our kiss deepens as he opens his mouth over mine and his tongue licks inside. His taste is heady, and I'm already sleep-addled. The room shifts around us and he moves, easing me onto my back, moving over me, one hand sliding into my hair, the other cupping my breast and squeezing, rubbing my nipple with his thumb through my T-shirt and bra. I ache to feel his weight on me.

"Wait."

He freezes.

I glance over at Tilly in her little bed and bite my lip.

He follows my gaze. "She's asleep."

"Yes. But..." I meet his eyes questioningly.

"Will we scar her for life if we have sex in the same room as her?"

I almost want to laugh. Or maybe cry. "I'm sure parents do it all the time."

"Yeah." He glances her way again. "If she wakes up, we can stop."

"Right." I wrap my arms around his neck while he kisses me again. And again. I'm on fire, heat burning from pussy into my belly, spreading over my entire body, and my pelvis lifts help-lessly against him. I want to part my thighs and welcome him between them and I'm moving ineffectually, wishfully.

Maybe he knows what I want... he moves over me, knees on either side of my hips, his mouth moving over my cheek, my jaw, my mouth again. His tongue slides deeper into my mouth and our mouths are feverish, frantic. He fondles my breast and I reach for his butt, cupping my hands around his tight ass and pulling him close. "Mmmm." I'm making needy sounds of excite-ment and want. "Oh God, I need to be quiet."

"Yeah," he whispers, then licks my bottom lip. "You taste good. And you feel so good." And he moves his legs so he's between my thighs now and presses his thick erection right to my center.

I give a soft cry at the sensation of having him right where I want him. I lift my knees and my hips roll against him, finding the pressure I crave on my clit. He meets my movements, and we're kissing and grinding together and panting.

He presses his face into the side of my neck, his breath warm and tickling, his mouth sucking gently, his tongue gliding over the spot. Heat surrounds me and tension coils inside me, tightening almost painfully and then shattering, consuming heat bursts low in my pelvis and spreads to my curling toes and fingertips. I whimper and make muffled, nonsensical noises as I shudder through my climax.

"Wow." He rubs his mouth over mine, inhales my short breaths. "Andi... you..."

I'm trembling, hands gripping his suit jacket. Jesus. We're still fully dressed and I just had an orgasm.

"Please," Ford murmurs against my lips, then brushes them over my cheek.

"Please what?"

"Please... can I rip your fucking clothes off?"

My belly flips, and a moan leaks from my lips. "Yes." I find his mouth and kiss him again. "I want yours off, too."

"Fuck, yeah." He rises onto his knees and, with his eyes fastened on mine, he removes his suit jacket and tosses it aside. His fingers move to the buttons of his shirt and I watch in fascination as he opens them one by one, excruciatingly slowly. I'm throbbing from my orgasm and from reawakening need. With the shirt gone, the pale light outlines his lean, athletic shape, the curves of muscles and angles of bone.

My T-shirt has ridden up and he grazes his fingers over the skin of my stomach. I shiver. His hands move higher, under the shirt, up to my breasts, and he cups them both through my lace bra. All the while, he's watching me closely, judging my reaction, which is to suck in a sharp breath. My nipples are painfully tight and my abs contract.

"Is this okay?" he whispers as he pushes my T-shirt higher, up over my breasts.

I swallow. "Yes."

He traces the scalloped edge of the bra cup, his gaze following his finger, down between my breasts, back up the other side. "This is so pretty. And look at your tits. Jesus." A low groan rises in his throat.

I can only stare up into his face, my entire body burning, my belly flipping at his attention. His admiration.

He slides a hand under my back and I shift to the side to give him access. His fingers snap open my bra with ease.

"You're good at that," I tease breathily.

"Good hands." He smiles. "Hockey player, remember?"

"Ah." A smile pulls at my lips. "Right." Our eyes meet with shared amusement that is hot and intimate.

"Still okay?"

"Oh, God, yes."

"Let's get you out of this." He grasps my sweater and I lift up so he can pull it off my arms and over my head. It joins his clothing somewhere on the floor. "And this. Although this black lace is sexy as hell." He draws the thin lace cups of my bra down, the straps falling off my arms, and his gaze is burning hot as he stares at my bare breasts.

"Perfect. Jesus." He leans in and presses a kiss between them, his mouth hot on my skin. "I've wanted this... wanted to see you... touch you..."

I sigh with pleasure and surrender.

He turns his head and kisses the inner curve of one breast,

then the other, slow open-mouthed kisses that have me sizzling and melting. His hands cup my flesh and he lifts his gaze to mine again. "I want to taste those sweet nipples."

I bob my head, no longer capable of speech, but I want him to know I'm totally with him on this.

When his lips close over one tip, my body jolts and my back arches, offering myself to him. He makes a rough noise and sucks gently, and the pull of his mouth sends a streamer of lovely sensation right between my legs. I can't stop the gasping, gulping sounds that spill from my lips.

"Oh God, that's so good. I love having my nipples sucked."

"Good." He licks one peak. "I love sucking them." And he moves to the other to sip that one, then suck harder. "I wanna know everything you like."

Pure desire sizzles over my skin, converging between my legs where I'm aching and wet.

Then he stretches out over me, skin to skin from chest to waist, crushing my breasts against his hard chest, and it feels so damn good my head is spinning. Electricity sparks every nerve ending in my body. He kisses me again, hands in my hair, and I clutch his shoulders and squeeze his hips with my thighs. I'm falling into sensation, his mouth owning mine in deep, thorough kisses.

His body burns against mine. "I'm losing patience," he mutters against my ear. "Need you naked."

19

ANDI

"Yes. You, too."

Once more he rises onto his knees between my legs and yanks at my leggings. They're very stretchy and go easily and he drags them off my legs. He gazes at my black lace panties. "They match."

My smile is shaky.

He rubs me through the fabric. "You're damp here."

"No kidding." I lift into his touch again shamelessly. "Ohhhh."

"Fuck." He grabs the sides of my panties and jerks them down. Now I'm naked, my breasts heavy, my pussy melting. He outlines the tattoo on my hip with his fingers. "This is nice, too."

"Th-thanks." A swirl of flowers and leaves trails over my left pelvic bone.

"I love it." And he bends to kiss it.

Oh, God. I blink up at the ceiling as delicious heat spreads from his lips through my body.

He shocks me then by sliding his arms under my pelvis and lifting me... to his mouth.

"Ohhhhh, God," I moan again. The touch of his lips on my skin there is luscious. He lays soft kisses up and down, presses his nose against me, then gently suckles the folds on either side of my opening. I can only make an unintelligible sound, my head tipping back, my fingers curling into the bed covers.

He plays with me there as if he can't get enough, long slow licks, lush sucks, soft kisses. The rough, greedy noises he makes inflame me even more, and I'm about to burst out of my over-sensitive skin when he focuses on my clit. "I'm gonna come again," I whisper. I let out a breath.

He lifts his head and peers up at me. His shiny mouth curves into a smile before he drags the back of his hand across it. "I wanna be inside you. Wanna feel that tight little pussy around me."

I hear the question. "Yes. But we need a condom."

He rolls off the bed and quickly strips off his suit pants and boxer briefs. I watch avidly as his cock is freed, jutting up and away from his body, long, solid, wet at the tip. I run my tongue over my bottom lip then catch it between my teeth as he moves to the nightstand, pulls open a drawer, and digs out a small package.

Watching him suit up is enthralling, his arms strong, his fingers long and lean on his heavy cock.

"I have to warn you," he says in a low, gravelly voice. "I'm about ready to blow. You are so fucking hot. This could be fast."

My belly flutters and I part my legs as he returns to the bed, moving between them on his knees. Oh... I look down at his thighs, thick and muscled and dusted with dark hair, and my pussy contracts hard. I take in his hand on his cock, the condom stretched thin around his girth.

He watches my face as he enters me, taking such sweet care

with me that my eyes sting. I ache with need. "Yeah," he murmurs. "So wet. Take it... just... like... that."

When he's fully seated inside me and I'm clenched around him, so close to an orgasm, he closes his hands around my waist and starts to move. His cheeks flushed, his eyes hungry, his mouth full and sensual, I throw my arms up over my head and lose myself in sensation. The wet sounds of our bodies joining fill the room along with the scent of him. "You feel so good."

"Ohhh... yeah... you too."

More than good... the fullness, the stretch of him on my body is sublime, tugging at pleasure points inside me, heating my blood even more. I'm burning.

"I've been thinking about this. So goddamn much."

I stare at him. "Me, too."

His strokes get harder and faster. My breasts bounce and he stares at them, then leans over to kiss me. His mouth is hard and demanding and I slide my hands around the back of his neck and kiss him back. I rarely come without touching my clit, but right now his pelvis is hard against me and I shift the angle of my hips so he's rubbing on just the right spot. His big cock inside me drags over sensitive nerve endings that twist up with the pleasure coiling inside me from the friction on my clit into a massive, exquisite helix of excitement. It tightens higher, higher, and I shatter, shudder, seized by hot, shocking ecstasy. My body clenches his as contractions rip through me, my abs and my thighs tightening, warm deliciousness sliding down my legs and making my toes curl.

His heart hammers against mine, his face buried in my neck as he murmurs, "Beautiful. Perfect. Can't stop... love fucking you."

I wrap my arms and legs around him and he comes, swelling and pulsing inside me, his body hard and solid and vibrating. His breath goes jagged, he groans, and I hold onto him all the way through it, moved and gratified and a little shaken.

* * *

A while later—five minutes? An hour? I don't even know—I whisper, "Good game."

After a startled beat, he cracks up laughing, then tries to muffle it. With an arm around my neck, he pulls me closer and kisses my forehead.

I'm smiling, too. "You do have great hands," I tell him.

"I do, for a goalie. My mouth is even better, though."

"Your mouth is definitely talented."

"You know another thing I'm good at because I'm a hockey player?"

"What?"

"I can score more than once a night."

"Oh, yeah?" I smirk at him. "I thought you were going to say you're fast..."

He gasps. "What?" And in a flash, with impressive strength, he rolls me onto my back and moves over me. "If you're implying I don't have stamina, I'll be happy to prove you wrong. I'm taking that as a challenge. And just so you know... I believe in ladies first."

Yes, he does. "I appreciate that." I kiss his jaw.

"Also... you're really beautiful."

"Oh." We gaze at each other, a connection between us thickening, wrapping around us.

"I also know when to play rough. And I always use protection."

I start giggling, one of those helpless laughs that you can't control, and we're both lying here in bed, our bodies shaking with mirth as we try to be quiet. Eventually I tilt my head back to look into his face. "One night I was watching one of your games and the announcers kept saying..." I dissolve into laughter again, struggling to get the words out, "D-dirty things.".

"Like what?"

"Like... you were down on your knees and you like to go down."

His smile is wicked. "I do like to go down... especially on you."

All my breath vacates my chest as he shifts on the bed, lower...

* * *

"I should go home." We just got Tilly up, fed, changed, and back to sleep. We're sitting on the side of his bed, him in a pair of boxer briefs, me in panties and my T-shirt.

His eyebrows tug together. "You don't have to."

I hesitate. "Um... should we talk about this?"

"I guess that would be the mature thing to do." He jerks his head toward the door, and I follow him out of the bedroom, We sit on his couch, one lamp still on.

"Obviously, I'm attracted to you," I begin.

He groans. "Fuck, me too."

"I think we've both been fighting it for a while. Because we knew it wasn't a good idea."

"We're friends," he says quietly. "I like being friends with you."

Is he saying that's all he wants?

"I also like kissing you. And fucking you."

A smile hovers on my lips.

"And I don't want to lose you as a friend."

I give a tiny nod. "I know. Me too."

"Because I'm not really made for relationships."

Yeah, he told me that.

And me... well, even if I no longer believe that the reason my marriage ended was because of my own shortcomings, I already made the mistake once of falling in love with a professional athlete who only cares about one thing—his career. So getting involved with Ford in a romantic way would just be heading for trouble.

"I don't think I am either," I say. "We talked about that."

"Phhht. There's nothing wrong with you."

"You say that now. But if we got involved, maybe you'd find out." He says nothing and I continue. "I haven't had sex in a while. I've been thinking about it a lot lately. So this was... good."

"Good?" He elevates an eyebrow. "You know it was better than that, Andi."

"Okay, yes, it was amazing and hot and..." And frankly, a little scary. "But my point is, I think we both needed that."

He regards me impassively. "Are you saying it's one and done? This is it?"

I nibble my bottom lip. "It could be. Or... we could keep doing this... just, you know, for the sex. But not get involved emotionally."

His lips quirk. "You bring the friendship and I'll bring the benefits."

I have to smile. "Yeah. No expectations. No commitment. It ends when it ends."

"And you think we can still be friends after that?"

"Sure." *No, I'm not sure.*

He goes silent for so long, I don't know what to think. Then he says, "Okay. I'd be an idiot to turn that down."

"Exactly!" I pause. "Would it help if we had rules?"

"I'm always in favor of rules."

"I know. Okay. Like I said, no expectations, no commitments."

He nods.

"Are we sleeping with other people, too? Or just each other?"

He scowls. "Fuck that. Just each other."

"Okay. But if we do want to date someone else, we have to be honest and open about it."

"Absolutely."

I hesitate. "Sleepovers. You're okay with that?"

One corner of his mouth lifts. "Sleeping alone is a waste of my sexual talent."

I laugh.

"But seriously, yeah, I'm okay with it." He stands and takes my hands, pulling me up with him. "Better than okay. Let me demonstrate that stamina."

He tugs me toward the bedroom and I go with him willingly, because holy hotness, this man knows how to kiss and how to make me come and it's spectacular, and I want this, so, so much, and I have to ignore that pesky little voice in the back of my mind that's whispering that this could be dangerous.

20

FORD

"Hi, niblet," I greet my daughter the next morning.

She looks up at me now, beams a big smile and says, "Badadaga!"

I turn to Andi. "I think she's trying to say daddy!"

She grins. "She could be."

I pick Tilly up and hold her in front of me. She babbles more and I kiss her cheeks, then cuddle her. "I missed you. Did you watch my games?"

"We did. Well, I did. Tilly watched parts of them."

"How did things go?"

"We survived." She makes a face. "Actually, things were fine. Elodie came and looked after her yesterday while I went to a meeting, so that was a big help. I just wish this little girl was sleeping through the night."

"I know. I'm going to get her sleeping. She's going to be on a schedule all day. Remember that app?"

She nods, but eyes me doubtfully. "How are you going to do that, with your own schedule? And my schedule?"

"Well, you'll have to help," I say with a beseeching expression.

"I've been tracking everything, and now I have a schedule. I'll write it all down. Or you could download the app, too."

"I guess I could do that."

"Do it now. I can show you everything."

She gets her phone and we sit next to each other on the couch while I explain things to her and tell her about full feedings, wake windows, and dream feeds.

"Wow, you've really been doing your research," she says.

I nod seriously. "Yes. So this is the schedule we have to follow."

"It seems very detailed." She still seems skeptical.

"It is. It has to be. Starting today. I have a day off so this is a good time to start."

"Okay. Let me know how it goes."

What? She's leaving? Okay, right. *She* doesn't have a day off. I shake my head. "Yeah. I will."

"Game tomorrow, right? So, the usual game day routine?"

"Right. The game's at six, so it'll be a bit of an earlier night." I smile. "I remember when I used to go out bar hopping after a Saturday night game. Good times."

"Yeah. I remember when I used to do the same on a Saturday night," she says dryly.

I tilt my head. "Shit. I'm sorry." Then I frown. "You want to go bar hopping?"

She thinks about it. "Not really. But we need to talk about that."

"About bar hopping?"

She lowers her chin. "About hiring a nanny for Tilly."

I exhale sharply. "I know."

"I like helping," she says gently. "And I'm kind of getting attached to the niblet. But it's getting really hard for both of us. I'm losing clients, you're uh..."

I scowl. "Playing like shit."

* * *

After our road trip, Coach calls me into his office.

"Are you sick?" he asks bluntly. "Hurt?"

"No." *Just tired.*

"Something's wrong."

I bow my head wearily. "My daughter isn't sleeping through the night. I only get a couple of hours' sleep at a time. I can't nap during the day because her schedule and my schedule don't line up. The other day when I got her up in the morning, I discovered she was wearing two diapers. In the middle of the night when I changed her I was so tired I just put a clean diaper over the dirty one."

"Who looks after her when you're here?" he asks.

"My neighbor. She's been great about helping out, but she has a business she runs so she's busy." She's also one of my distractions, dammit. "We've got my schedule covered, though, it's not a problem."

"It is a problem when you're playing like shit."

I close my eyes. I already know I've been playing like shit. He doesn't have to tell me. "Yeah."

"Do you need some time off?" he asks. "Guys have babies, sometimes they take some time to spend with the new baby. Obviously, you never did that."

"No. And no. I don't need time off."

"And the baby's mother? Where is she now?"

"Still with her parents in North Dakota. Apparently, they're having a slow recovery from their injuries and she's still helping them. She said she needs another month."

"Huh. Maybe you should try to get other childcare. This is your career, Ford."

"I know." I try not to sound snarly. I'm as frustrated as anyone about how I've been playing. Probably more so. "I know. Believe me, I'm trying. I worked hard all summer."

"I know you did. Look, we just want you at your best. If there's anything we can help with, say the word. You need to be healthy."

"I get it. Thanks. I appreciate the support."

I am so fucked.

* * *

Smitty's still hanging out in the player lounge, looking at his phone. Probably looking at Instagram images of that pop singer he smashed at the All-Star game. He's been obsessed with her ever since. I grab a bottle of water from the fridge and lean against the counter as I chug it.

He glances up at me. Takes in my expression. Looks back down at his phone.

I trudge over to one of the couches and sit.

"Everything okay?" Smitty asks.

"What do you think?" I lift the water bottle to my lips again.

"Is that a serious question? Or rhetorical?"

"It was rhetorical. You don't need to answer. Everything is not okay."

He gives me a sympathetic look.

"What happened to my life?" I lean my head back and close my eyes. "Everything was going according to plan."

"Life doesn't always go like we plan."

"I know." I exhale a sigh. "But I want it to. I like having a plan."

"Yeah."

"I didn't want kids. I like living my life just the way I want it. Free. My only responsibilities were to me and the team."

He grunts enigmatically and I lower my chin to peer at him. "What?"

"That sounds like a selfish existence."

"I *am* selfish."

"No, you're not."

I squint at him again. "Have you met me?"

He almost smiles. "Yeah. Okay, when you're single and committed to your career, you can be self-centered."

"See?"

"But that's not the same as selfish."

I squint at him. "What?"

"Selfish means..." He pauses, thinking. "You make your needs a priority over everyone else's."

I nod. "That's what I do."

"Is it though? Self-centered is more like being preoccupied with your own needs and wants but you can still care about other people. When you're single and alone, of course you're self-centered. There's nobody else to care about. But when you're self-ish, you pursue your own goals at the expense of others."

I still think the hockey skate fits. But I let that roll around in my tired brain.

So he's saying... when I'm alone it's okay to be self-centered because it's not hurting anyone else. Maybe? But when I'm not alone... which I no longer am, thanks to Tilly showing up... pursuing my goals at her expense is selfish. Is that what I've been doing?

I haven't exactly been pursuing my goal since she arrived. I've given up taekwondo, meditation sessions, time with my friends. A clean home. Ha. An orderly schedule. Sleep.

Dammit, I miss sleep.

I don't like it, but I've done it. Because... because she's my daughter and I have no choice.

But I do have a choice. I could have hired a nanny, dumped Tilly on her all day and night while I followed my dream. I didn't do that. Maybe there's hope for me?

"Maybe when things don't go the way you planned, the universe is trying to tell you something."

I give Smitty a skeptical look. "I didn't know you were into that woo-woo stuff."

He makes a face and shrugs.

"Ohhh. This is about whatshername... the singer... Nikki."

He rolls his eyes.

"You're still trying to hook up with her again?"

His shoulders slump. "It's not gonna happen. I'm busy traveling. She's busy traveling. Recording. Doing music videos. So... yeah, maybe the universe *is* trying to tell me something."

"Huh."

"But back to you," he says pointedly. "Sometimes we need to learn things. Get stronger. You don't get stronger taking it easy. You should know that."

Yeah. All those muscle-burning, mind-fucking workouts weren't exactly taking it easy. But I wanted to get stronger. Better.

"Life lesson," I murmur.

"Yeah. Maybe you need to change direction. Take a break." He shrugs.

"Shit. Coach just asked if I want to take some time off."

He purses his lips. "Might be an idea."

"I can't. I can't do that."

"Why not?"

"Because of my plan. My goal." The only one I've talked to about this is Andi.

"You think your hockey career will be trashed by taking a little time off?"

I stare across the room. "Yeah."

"But if you don't... you might be losing out on something else."

Tilly. Even... Andi. "They're going to leave anyway."

Smitty's forehead creases. "They?"

I sink my teeth into my bottom lip. "Er..."

Then his eyes widen. "Ohhhh. You caught feelings for your neighbor."

I meet his eyes briefly, then look away. "No, I haven't. But... we are sleeping together."

"Ah."

"Just friends," I add hastily. "No commitment. She feels the same. I'm not looking for long term."

He gives me a doubting look.

"I meant, Tilly's going to leave. When Willa comes back. Whenever the fuck that is." I rub my forehead. "She's going to leave anyway. So... I *need* to be selfish. I can't get all involved."

"That sounds really fucked up. But I think I get it. You've caught feelings for her, too."

"She's my daughter." Just saying those words gives me a chill of fear. Yeah, I'm afraid. When it comes to Tilly, I'm afraid of so many things. I'm afraid I'll mess up. I'm afraid I'll let her down. I'm afraid she'll get hurt. But most of all I'm afraid I've "caught feelings" for her when she's only here for a short time. And when she leaves, I'm going to be wrecked.

And when Tilly leaves... Andi leaves. There'll be no need for her to hang around with me anymore. And that... that's what I've always been afraid of. That I'm not worth being loved. Tilly will go back to her mom and yeah, I intend to fight that, but what if Willa doesn't want to share custody? It could get ugly, and in the meantime, Tilly won't remember me. She won't miss me.

And Andi will find some dude who's not selfish or self-centered or whatever, someone who puts her first. She deserves that.

And I'll be alone.

"I've always known I'm better off alone," I tell Smitty. "And that's okay. I don't need anyone."

"Oh, man." He shakes his head.

"So it's better if I keep playing. Keep myself in the game." And protect myself from the pain I know is coming.

"Remember Kosinski?" He's talking about our previous team captain, who got traded last year.

"Yeah?"

"You know what his problem was?"

"He was an asshole."

Smitty grins. "Yeah. But you know what the coaches thought of him?" He pauses. "He wasn't coachable."

"Ooookay." Where is this going?

"We all know what that means, when someone's uncoachable."

"Yeah. Not willing to learn. Not open to doing things differently. Doesn't listen to feedback or learn from it."

"Exactly. I think we can be like that in life, too."

"Oh. I see. You're dragging me. Got it."

He laughs and gets up. "Think about it. See you tomorrow."

21

ANDI

"I may have fucked up."

"How so?" Elodie lifts an eyebrow, sitting across from me in Josephine's Cocktail Lab. She lifts her guava daiquiri to sip it.

"I slept with Ford."

"Another man! Good for you."

I blink and pick up my espresso martini. "No, you don't understand. *Ford.*"

"Honey, since your divorce you've been sleeping your way through the state of New Jersey. And some of New York."

I choke on my martini. "Oh, come on!"

She laughs. "Okay, maybe a slight exaggeration. But that's what you wanted—to lose your second virginity."

Since Trevor was the only man I'd slept with prior to our divorce, I'd joked about losing my virginity again. "Yes, but... not with a friend. Someone I know." I rub my temple. "Someone I have to see again because I'm helping look after his kid."

"Oh." Her eyebrows pull down with sympathy. "Was it that bad?"

"Oh, God. No. It was... amazing." I blow out a breath and

resist the urge to fan myself. Just thinking about sex with Ford makes my girl parts flutter and heat up.

She brightens. "Ooooh, that's good!"

"Yes, but... sex always changes things. Even though we agreed it wouldn't be anything more than that."

"Hmmm. That is true."

"It wasn't a good idea. We're friends. We're both looking after Tilly. What if we mess this up?"

"You're both adults. You know the risks. If you want to keep your friendship, you have to *not* mess things up."

"Huh?"

"I mean... if you know the risks, you'll try harder to make things work with you two."

"No." I shake my head. "That is not the idea. We agreed this is just sex. We both needed it."

She studies me. "It's not just sex."

I roll my eyes. "Don't do that. Don't romanticize this. There is not going to be a happy ending."

"Uh huh." She gives me a sly look. "I bet there *was* a happy ending."

"Okay, yes, multiple, but that's not what I meant."

"I know. Why can't there be a happy ending?"

"He's focused on his career. Tilly showing up has set him back, but he's determined. And that doesn't leave room for any kind of romantic relationship. He's been very honest about that. And I made the mistake once of falling for a professional athlete whose goals took precedence over mine; I'm not doing that again."

Her expression sobers and she nods. "I get that. Trevor was a dick to you. But that doesn't mean Ford is the same."

"He's exactly the same. Okay, he says he doesn't cheat, but his whole life is hockey. Same as Trevor. I sacrificed so much for him and then he betrayed me."

"Hmmm. Well. I stand by my earlier statement: you two know the risks, so you'll try harder to make things work. Whatever 'work' means. If that means maintaining your friendship, fine." She takes a gulp of her drink. "It doesn't have to be a fuck up."

"Okay." I feel somewhat reassured. "That makes sense. I just have to be careful I don't get unrealistic ideas. Because I don't think I could handle falling in love and then losing it again."

"You can handle anything."

"That's not encouraging."

She sighs. "I don't think I'm expressing myself very well here. I'm trying to support you. If you get involved with Ford and things end, you're strong enough to handle it. You proved that last time."

"No, it's not you." I shake my head. "It's me. I'm being difficult. I'm just... trying to protect myself."

"I get that. But if things are really good with him in bed, enjoy! Live in the moment!"

I smile. "*That* is good advice."

"Sometimes I have words of wisdom. Not often, mind you. How's Tilly doing?"

I update her on the schedule we're now attempting to follow. "The problem is, every day is different for him. Some days he has a morning practice or a morning skate and a game; some days he doesn't. And sometimes she just doesn't cooperate. I was supposed to put her down for a nap from eleven till noon the other day and she wouldn't go to sleep, the little devil." I pause. "But she's awfully cute."

Elodie smiles.

The server arrives with our meals and sets my shrimp *fra diavolo* in front of me, and Elodie's rib eye in front of her.

I lean forward. "That looks good. Want a shrimp?"

She laughs. "Yes, and you can have a piece of steak."

We make the exchange and then I dig into my linguine. "The other thing that happens is we try to keep her awake after an evening feed and she just wants to go to sleep. I understand why a schedule is important though. After having her for a couple of nights while he was away, it would be great to get her sleeping through the night. Ford has to deal with that every night." I pout a little in sympathy for him.

"It's interesting that you're not annoyed by all this."

I wrinkle my nose. "Well, I am. A little. But she's a baby. She can't help it. We have to help her. And Ford is doing his best. Neither of us knew anything about babies. The good thing is, he's trying again to find a nanny. Hopefully he can find someone who can meet his high standards."

Elodie smiles again, looking smug.

"What?"

"Nothing."

"Have you heard anything from Haven after that scene at the awards dinner?"

"No! Thank God."

"It's kind of sad how jealous she is of you."

"I don't get why she's jealous. She got the man." I would have said that bitterly at one point, but now it just comes out neutrally.

"Maybe things aren't that great with them."

"They're having a baby."

"Yeah, but that's not always a good thing. Trevor didn't want kids. What if it was an accident?"

"Ohhh. I didn't think of that." I tip my head. "Oh, well!"

Elodie grins. "Not your problem."

"Nope! And my work for Mirabella Cosmetics is going great."

* * *

We're sliding into a routine that sort of works. Ford gets frustrated when Tilly won't go to sleep at the exact time he thinks she should, but I've talked him through it and even though it's not perfect, there have been a few nights she slept for eight hours. Progress!

I've been doing more research about sleep and milestones and things to do with her when she's in a wake window (look at me using this parental lingo) and I've been having fun playing games and making her smile and laugh. Her laughter is honestly the best thing ever. It totally banishes any stress or grumpiness.

"Watch this!" I say to Ford when he gets home one day. I drag him into the living room where Tilly's sitting with pillows all around her.

She sees him and gives him a big smile.

"She knows you!" I say. "But this... watch... Tilly!" I call to her. And she turns her head and looks at me.

"See? She knows her name!"

Ford is grinning hugely, and he crouches down on the floor near her. "Hi, baby girl. You know your name! Do you know who I am?"

"Gada."

"Close." He picks her up to give her a cuddle.

"And she's rolling!"

"Get out of here. Really? Can you roll over?"

"Show Daddy."

Ford lays her down on the floor on her back.

"Okay, she hasn't got back to tummy yet." I give her little nudges on her diapered bottom and she moves onto her side. Then I guide her thighs to gently turn her over. She straightens on her arms, looking at the toy in front of her. "God, she's cute! Look at her chubby little legs! Okay, roll over, Tilly."

She pushes her arms out, but doesn't move, and then... she does it! She rolls onto her back!

I clap. "Attagirl, Tilly! Look how strong you are!"

"That's amazing." Ford beams proudly. He looks up at me, both of us sitting on the floor, and our eyes meet. It's a shared moment of pure and simple joy. Something warm and tender passes between us.

We play with her for a while longer, but then I realize what time it is, and I have to start a business meeting. Ford picks her up to take her back to his place. "How long is your meeting? Do you have other meetings?"

"This'll probably be about an hour. Nothing else today. Why?"

"I'm meeting with a possible nanny at three. I want you to meet her, too."

I go very still. "Oh. I... okay. Sure."

"Great." He kisses me, softly, slowly, then pulls back with a smile, meeting my eyes. "Thanks. Okay, let's go, niblet."

I don't move from sitting on the floor after he's gone.

I don't know how I feel about this. He wants me to meet the possible nanny. I guess he wants my opinion? My blessing? I don't know. I'm... touched. And surprised. Also... pleased. I feel valued.

And a little worried. I'm not Tilly's mother. But dammit... I care about her. In fact, I might be a little in love with her. With her cute baby feet and chubby thighs and beautiful eyes. Her smile and baby babbling and her warm, round little body.

Oh, God. I was worried about what would happen between *Ford* and me when things end. But how am I going to survive losing *Tilly*?

I'm seized with unexpected anger at Willa. I wondered before how a mother could leave her child for months. But now I'm *pissed* that she did that. How could she do that to such a sweet little girl? She doesn't deserve Tilly!

I have to focus on business. I'll deal with this jumble of emotions later.

* * *

After I meet Lieve—a young Dutch woman working here after finishing college to spend time in the US—I stay and help Ford make dinner while we talk about her.

"She's young," I say.

"Very young. I don't like it."

I smile. "She seems responsible and mature, though. And she has experience caring for babies."

"True."

"You won't like anyone."

He grimaces. "You're right. Can you slice up those red peppers?"

"Yes, chef!"

He slides me a sideways look, then gives me a light swat on my butt.

I laugh and he squeezes my butt cheek and the next thing I know he has me against the counter kissing me breathless. When I draw back, I look into his eyes. "You have to do this," I say softly. "Most parents have to use childcare when they're working."

"I should just retire from hockey. Then there won't be a problem." He steps back to continue cooking the steak strips for our burrito bowls. "I could be a stay-at-home dad."

I laugh, then purse my lips at his serious expression. "You're not going to quit hockey."

"I could."

I lift my eyebrows.

"Okay, I probably won't."

"If it makes you feel any better, I'll be right next door. If Lieve needs anything, I'm usually there."

Okay, wait. Now *I'm* a little unhappy about someone else looking after Tilly when I'm right there. But I do need time to focus on work. And I'll still take care of her when Ford's on the road. "Have you heard from Willa?"

"No. She said she'd reach out around the end of the month."

"That's not very specific."

"I know." He goes silent as he lifts the steak slices onto a plate.

A terrible thought has invaded my head. "Is there any chance that you and Willa could..." I can't find the words.

But Ford knows. "No." He shakes his head.

"How do you know? You two haven't spent much time together." Other than enough time to make a baby. Ugh.

"I know because..." He halts, looking fixedly at the pan on the stove. "I just know."

I tip my head to the side. "Okay."

22

ANDI

"There's Daddy!" I hold Tilly at the glass while Ford skates up to us. Mask on top of his head, he grins at us.

"Hey, Tilly girl!" he calls to her. "Your first game!"

She smiles and babbles and bats at the glass. Ford makes faces at her and makes her laugh. It's so sweet.

She's wearing a tiny red Storm hoodie over black leggings. Ford wanted to get his name put on the back of it, but Archibald wouldn't fit across her body. She looks adorable though. I have little headphones for her to wear during the game when it's really loud.

People around us are smiling and pointing and I don't blame them because my ovaries are melting from the cuteness.

Ford skates back to his net to face warm-up shots from his teammates. We watch him stop puck after puck. A few get by him but that's because he's not trying that hard. Tilly seems fascinated by all the activity on the ice, her gaze following players around. She loves hockey!

After a while we go back up to our seats where the wives and girlfriends all sit. This scares the bejesus out of me.

I was a WAG before. I know what it means when a player invites someone to a game using his seats. Sure, there are women they're casually seeing that they invite, but not usually. The other Storm WAGs are going to see me here with Tilly and they're going to come to conclusions that aren't accurate.

I knew this would happen. When Ford suggested I bring Tilly to a game, I hesitated. I knew people would assume we're together. When I said that to Ford, he shrugged and said, "So what?"

I take my seat next to Mabel Smits, whose boyfriend and brother both play for the Storm. "Hi!" she greets me. We have met briefly before. "Who's this pretty girl?" She takes Tilly from me to bounce her on her lap and talk nonsense to her. Tilly has no fear of strangers, and happily beams at Mabel.

While she does that, I find the bottle I packed in the diaper bag, ready to feed Tilly before the game starts.

"So... you and Ford..." Mabel says to me with a gently inquisitive look.

"Me and Ford what?" I smile at her with equal inquisitiveness.

She smirks perceptively but doesn't push it.

I discovered the hockey Tumblr accounts and all the people who talk about hockey players and their marital or relationship status and rip apart the women who are dating players. And a lot of them are interested in Ford. They're going to freak out that Ford has a baby when they thought he didn't even have a girlfriend. Only, I'm not his girlfriend.

But it feels like I am.

We spend so much time together now, and not just because of Tilly. We have fun together. We watch TV and movies, talk about sports and politics, and laugh a lot. We hang out on his couch and eat popcorn and take Tilly shopping together. And yeah, we have sex together. And spend most nights together. And despite our rules and our understanding of what this is... I'm even more worried about my heart.

I point to Ford as he goes through his routine at the start of the game, skating loops in the crease, crouching down, sliding side to side, then a huge jump. He taps his pads then the goalposts and then knocks his forehead against the crossbar. "See, Daddy does the same thing every game," I tell her. "He's a little weird that way, but that's okay, he's a good goalie."

I hear Mabel's muffled giggle.

I knew about baseball stans but I didn't expect hockey to be so popular with women. But now that I'm sleeping with a hockey player, and I've met a lot of the team, I get it. I get all those thirst trap photos of him tossing his hair back and looking into the camera with his sexy, smoldering green eyes. Doing his stretches. Posing in a skintight compression shirt, muscles bulging.

I focus on the game, tensing whenever the puck is shot at Ford, cheering when he makes an amazing save. He's not actually being challenged that hard; the other team is not shooting the puck a lot. At one point, he leans on the goalpost casually, as if waiting for the play to come back to his end.

We laugh during a TV time out when he skates over to the boards and poses for selfies that kids are taking through glass with him. And again, when waiting for a faceoff in the other end, he starts dancing to the music. As soon as the puck is dropped and the music ends, he drops into a dramatic stance, ready for action.

"He's putting on his own show," I say to Mabel.

She laughs. "He is."

The Storm are up five-nothing in the third period but then Toronto scores. Ford is clearly pissed off, but when we watch the replay of the goal on the big screen, it was really fluky. The other team iced the puck. It bounced off the boards, not even hard, hit the back of Ford's skate, and ricocheted into the net.

Tilly's asleep in my arms so she doesn't see this moment of shame for Ford. She doesn't see him hang his head, then swing his stick at the goalpost. But he really doesn't have anything to be ashamed of. I guess he could have been tighter to the goalpost, but the puck wasn't even moving fast, it looked harmless.

"He's not going to be happy about that," I say.

"Oh, well. No shutout. But they're still going to win." Mabel shrugs.

"I didn't say the words. I did not say shutout. I didn't even think it!" I turn to Mabel. "You have to tell him that."

She eyes me. "Okay."

"He's really superstitious about that."

"Most hockey players are."

* * *

There are pictures everywhere online of Ford, Tilly, and me—me holding her up to the glass, waving her little hand at her dad, smiling at Ford with such open enjoyment. Oh, boy. I know better than to pay attention to that stuff, but I look at those pictures for longer than I should, smiling at the expressions on our faces. We look so happy.

I am happy.

But I'm also a little afraid to let myself be happy. Like this is a real relationship.

I should follow Ford's advice: Don't pay any attention to that shit.

I'm at Ford's place carrying Tilly from the kitchen after giving her a first taste of a wedge of well-cooked carrot when there's a knock at his door.

He lifts his eyebrows. "Who the hell is that? You're the only one who knocks on my door." He walks over and yanks it open. "Mom. Dad."

Whaaat?

"What are you doing here? I thought you were in Amsterdam."

"We cut the trip short. Only by a few days."

"Why? I mean... come in."

Oh, boy. I straighten.

"There's that baby!" Ford's mom holds out her arms and rushes at Tilly and me. "That's why!"

Ford lets out a low groan and covers his eyes.

My heart kicks against my ribs. My mouth goes dry and my eyes dart from Mrs. Archibald to Mr. Archibald following behind his wife, to Ford, who looks like aliens with weapons just walked into his condo. I attempt to school my features into a pleasant smile as Tilly is scooped up.

"Hello!" Mrs. Archibald says to Tilly, holding her in front of her. "Aren't you beautiful!"

Mrs. Archibald's ash-brown hair with a big white streak in the front is worn in a mass of messy curls around her face. She's wearing a long russet-colored dress with a teal-colored... thing... over it. I don't know whether to describe it as a cardigan? A jacket? A coverup? Her expression is genuinely elated, though.

She turns to Ford. "Why didn't you tell us about this? I have a serious bone to pick with you, young man."

Ford closes his eyes.

Now I see Mr. Archibald is carrying a suitcase. Holy crap. Are they here to stay? I blink over at Ford again.

"Come see her!" Mrs. Archibald says to her husband.

He's... astonishingly good-looking. He has the same square-jawed face as Ford, his skin more tanned and weathered. His mustache and beard are also similar, and even his hair—although his is longer than Ford's. Longer than his wife's.

I snap my mouth closed and swallow.

Mr. Archibald takes Tilly. "Hello, little miss. I'm your grandpa. You can call me Grandpa Archie." His eyes go misty and he looks at his wife. "We're grandparents, Dolly."

"Yes." She mists back at him. Then she looks at me. "I'm so sorry! We were just overcome with our granddaughter!" She rushes at me and throws her arms around me in a big hug. "I can't believe Ford didn't tell us about you *or* our granddaughter! Ford, I am *really* going to have words with you."

"Mom..."

"You're very pretty," Mrs. Archibald says to me, studying me with a smile. "I'm so happy to have a daughter."

"Mom!" Ford winces. "She's not your daughter."

"I mean daughter-in-law, of course."

"Not that either."

"Oh. You're not married." She lifts one shoulder. "That's no big deal. Are you going to get married?"

Omigod, omigod, omigod. She thinks I'm Tilly's mom and that Ford and I are a couple. My jaw slackens and I send Ford a panicked look.

"Mom." Ford's voice is tight, his jaw clenched. "This is my friend Andi."

Friend. That's right. I nod.

"She's been helping me with Tilly. She's not Tilly's mom."

Mrs. Archibald's head tilts. "Oh." Her eyebrows snug together. "Well, where is Tilly's mom?"

Ford scratches his cheek. "In North Dakota."

"This is sounding complicated," Mr. Archibald says. He bounces Tilly on his knee. She gnaws on her fist. "Sit down, son. You too, Andi."

Ford lowers himself onto the couch and I sit beside him.

Ford's mom takes another chair. "Start at the beginning, Ford."

Ford takes a breath. "Okay." He starts at the beginning and tells them what's happened. I give his parents credit for listening and not interrupting, only making comments like *oh my*, and *holy crap*.

The one thing he doesn't tell them is that we're sleeping together. Understandable, I guess.

"I need a gummie," Mrs. Archibald finally says, getting up to retrieve her purse. She pulls out a package and takes one then hands it to her husband. He also takes one and offers the pack to us. Ford and I shake our heads, though I am sorely tempted.

"Well." Mrs. Archibald sits again. She seems at a loss for words.

"I know, it's wild," Ford says. "But that's what's going on."

"Why didn't you let us know sooner?" She fixes a chiding gaze on him. "We could have come helped!"

"You were on your trip. You've been waiting your whole life to go on that trip."

"We would have cut it short. Family is important."

"I didn't want you to do that. I wanted you to enjoy yourselves. You've done enough for me."

She lowers her chin. "Ford. There's no such thing as enough when it comes to family. Yes, we supported you, but just because you're an adult doesn't mean that stops. We'll always be here for you."

I smile. Mrs. Archibald may be a free spirit, but she has a good heart.

"Okay." Ford nods, looking a little emotional. "We managed. And I have a nanny now. I'm not sure what's happening with Willa and her parents, though."

"I don't know how a mother could leave her child that long."
Mrs. Archibald shakes her head. "Her parents must have been
seriously injured."

I look over at Tilly. She's staring off to the side and yawning. I
give Ford a nudge.

"Yeah, she said it was serious." He looks at his phone. "It's
time for Tilly's nap."

"Oh, she can stay awake a while longer! I haven't gotten to
hold her much."

"No," Ford says firmly. "We've just gotten her on a schedule.
Well, sort of." He makes a face. "She doesn't always agree with
the schedule. But it's helped with her sleeping at night, so we're
not going to mess with it." He stands and takes Tilly from
his dad.

"She's tired," I say. "She needs a nap before she gets overtired.
Want me to put her down?" I stand, too.

Ford meets my eyes and his crinkle up at the corners.
"Thanks." He hands her off and I take her to his bedroom. I hear
Ford and his parents continuing to talk while I get her in her bed.
She's pretty good at settling herself if we get her here before she's
overtired. That's when we get reminded of her healthy lungs and
spicy temper. That makes me smile as I look down on her. I
admire the perfect curve of her cheeks, the tiny rosebud of her
mouth, the arc of her long lashes on her cheeks.

I turn on the monitor and quietly leave the room to rejoin the
others.

"Can I get anyone something to drink?" I ask.

"I'd love a whiskey," Mr. Archibald says.

"Sorry, Dad, I don't have any," Ford answers. "Coke? Water?
Gatorade?"

"There's herbal tea, also," I say.

"Herbal tea would be perfect," Mrs. Archibald says.

I go into the kitchen to make it. Ford's parents are telling him about their trip, which sounds amazing. Clearly, they had the time of their lives.

They've switched to asking Ford about his game when I carry mugs of tea into the living room. "Here you go, Mrs. Archibald." I set a cup on the coffee table.

"Oh, please call me Dahlia," she says. "And thank you."

"And you can call me Holden," Ford's dad says.

"You seem very at home here," Dahlia says. Her tone and expression are neutral, but I have a feeling the comment *isn't* neutral.

I smile. "I stayed here quite a bit looking after Tilly when Ford was at practices or games. Sometimes I took her to my place so I could get work done."

"And what is it you do, Andi?" Holden asks me.

I tell them about my job, my business that I've started.

"She's doing really well," Ford tells them. "She has more business than she can handle."

I turn to smile at him, touched by his compliment. He actually looks proud of me.

I catch Dahlia's knowing smirk.

Uh oh.

23

FORD

My parents have been here a few days, but I haven't seen much of them. The team practiced on Friday, then had a game on Long Island Saturday night, which isn't an overnight trip, but then a home game the very next day. Finally, I have a day off on Monday. The worst thing about this is not seeing Andi much. Andi and Tilly and my parents did come to the Sunday game, so *she* got to spend time with them. Which freaked her the fuck out.

I listened to her apprehension and reluctance, then set my hands on her shoulders, kissed her to shut her up, and said, "I want you there."

Mom and Dad take Tilly and me shopping and buy a bunch of gifts for Tilly—toys, books, weird little clothes. I'm not even kidding—a pink onesie and flowered bell-bottom pants—she can't even walk!—a one-piece furry outfit with ears that looks like a bear, and a set of footie rompers in navy, brown, and beige.

"These are gender-neutral colors," Mom says. "Pink is cute, but she doesn't *have* to wear pink."

I hold back my smile. "True."

We have lunch at a family-type restaurant. While we try to keep Tilly amused, Mom says, "So tell me the truth about Andi."

I blink over at her. "The truth?"

"Yes." One corner of her mouth lifts in a half-smile. "You said she's a friend, but she's clearly much more than that."

"Uh..."

"The way you both look at each other. The way you talk to each other. The care you take with each other." She tilts her head and lifts her eyebrows.

I glance at Dad. He, too, waits expectantly.

Huh. "Okay." I rub the back of my neck. "We're more than friends. But it's not... neither of us wants to get involved seriously. She just got out of a marriage where her husband cheated on her."

"Oh, no!" Mom's hand flies to her mouth. "That poor girl."

"And you know I don't have time for a relationship. I'm focused on hockey."

She regards me thoughtfully. "Yes. You always have been."

"Don't worry. I know how much you did for me and what you sacrificed so I could play. I won't let you down by not doing my best." I pause. "I owe you that."

Once again, she's silent and I give Tilly another toy.

"That's wrong," she finally says.

"What's wrong?"

"You don't owe us anything."

I stare blankly at her. "I feel like I do."

"You shouldn't feel like that. Is that what motivates you to work so hard?"

"Yeah." I pause. "Some."

She shakes her head. "You shouldn't want to work hard for us. We don't expect that. Children don't owe their parents anything. Even gratitude. Although I'm glad you feel gratitude. That's important for a happy life. But we did everything we did because we love you. Not because we expect anything from you in return. You've been very generous to us and we appreciate that. I hope you don't do that because you think we expect it."

"Uh. No. No, I did those things because... I love you, too."

"Exactly." She smiles. "And you should play hockey because you love it. Not because you owe us."

"I do love it."

"Good." She squeezes my hand. "I have a poem by Khalil Gibran that I love that I'll send you about having children."

Khalil Gibran. That is so Mom.

"Now. Back to Andi. She's a lovely young woman. So bright! So cheerful and positive. And she loves Tilly."

"Yeah."

"And I think she cares a lot about you."

I don't reply to that. What's happening between Andi and me has changed for sure, but I keep telling myself that when it ends, it ends, just like we said.

"I worry she could get hurt," Mom says softly.

"We agreed what this is." No commitment, no expectations, no catching feelings. We've been sticking to that.

"That's good. I feel like you two have gotten involved, though. So whatever you agreed to in the beginning might not fit anymore."

Ugh. I clear my throat and shift in my chair. She's nailed what I've been thinking. Talking to my mom about this is weird. "I understand."

"Okay. We're going home this afternoon. We've been away for so long, I'll be happy to get home. But I hope you'll invite us to come visit and spend time with Tilly again."

"I don't know what's going to happen when Willa comes back."

"I know." Her forehead creases. "I hate that for you. But we're here if you need us, for advice, or anything."

"You need a lawyer," Dad says gruffly.

"I've thought of that," I admit. "It's so weird because when she first left Tilly with us, I was so mad, I couldn't wait to get rid of her. I don't feel like that anymore."

"Us."

I blink at Mom. "What?"

"You said 'us.' When Willa first left Tilly with us." She smiles. "You *are* an us. You just haven't accepted it yet."

Oh, hell. That's not true.

Is it?

* * *

"I didn't go to the Halloween party this year because of having Tilly. It's a big thing. Everyone gets really dressed up."

"Like what?" Andi grins. "What did you go as last year?"

"I went as Colonel Sanders. And Smitty went as a chicken. Here, I'll show you." I swipe my phone to find the pics from last year.

She cracks up. "That's amazing."

"Yeah." I smile. "Anyway, I want to go to the Thanksgiving party. And you should come."

We don't get a lot of time off for Thanksgiving, so there's no time for guys to go home. Usually, a few people host a get-together so we can be with our hockey family for the holiday. This year it's Ben and Mabel hosting.

"Okay. Sure." She nods.

I can see she's hesitant. But everybody knows about us now. Everybody who has access to the internet. Including my parents.

I move closer and cup her face in my hands. Looking into her eyes, I murmur, "It'll be fine." I kiss her forehead.

I feel her soften. Her eyes close. She nods.

***

We arrive at Ben's place with a big pot of Andi's beer meatballs, along with wine and beer. I convinced Andi to make the meatballs with Pig Porter and they're fucking delicious. And of course we have Tilly in her car seat. I set her on the floor. She fell asleep on the way over and stays asleep.

"I'll take that food off your hands," Smitty says, greeting us at the door.

"Haha. Make sure it gets to the kitchen." I hand over the pot and Andi sets the bag of beverages on the floor while we take off our jackets.

"You can put your jackets in the spare bedroom," Mabel calls from the kitchen.

I take Andi's and drop both on the bed, then join her at the big kitchen counter where Mabel is pouring Andi a glass of rosé wine. Tilly snoozes on the floor at Andi's feet.

"Thanks," Andi says.

I grab a beer and crack it open. "Do you think there's enough food?"

Mabel grins and surveys the many dishes on the counter. "You guys really came through."

There's a football game on the big TV in the living room where a bunch of the guys lounge with snacks and drinks.

"Anything I can help with?" Andi asks Mabel.

"I think we're okay at the moment. I made the turkey yesterday, and Ben carved it."

"Butchered it, more like," Ben mutters. "I don't know how to carve a fucking turkey."

I laugh. "It can't be that hard."

"We watched on YouTube," Mabel says. "I don't know if it helped."

"YouTube's been very helpful for learning about baby things," Andi says, smiling. "Since neither Ford nor I had a clue. Although all those videos about burping the baby turn out to be untrue. Apparently studies have shown that babies who aren't burped don't cry more or have more spit ups. You have to do your research."

"What!" Mabel's mouth drops open. "Everyone does that!"

"I know!" Andi nods.

"And I was so diligent about that," I say sadly. "I was always so proud when I got a good belch."

Andi laughs. "You still do it."

I shrug. "I know it apparently doesn't help, but it doesn't hurt either."

Mabel and Andi get into a conversation about their jobs. Mabel's a librarian and Andi's interested in that.

"The other day I was reading to some little kids and I was showing them pictures of animal feet and asking what animal they belong to," Mabel says. "I showed them a picture of a squirrel foot, all skinny and hairy with long claws, and one kid said, 'That's my dad's feet.'"

"Oh my God!" Andi cracks up, as do the rest of us listening. "Dad needs a pedicure."

"Right?" Mabel giggles. "Kids are so fun. Do you know what the world's smallest mammal is?"

I grin at Mabel's random question.

"No," Andi says, smiling. "Tell me."

"The butterfly bat. It weighs less than an ounce!"

"Where do you find these bats?" Andi asks warily.

"Thailand." Mabel makes a face. "I'd love to see them."

"I don't really like bats," Andi confesses.

"They're so small though! And bats are important. They pollinate fruits and eat mosquitoes."

Andi nods doubtfully.

"That's why Batman chose the name Batman," I say.

Mabel and Andi both turn big eyes on me.

"What? Why?" Andi says.

"Because most people are afraid of bats. He wanted his enemies to be afraid of him."

"Whoa." Mabel seems impressed. "I did not know that."

"What weird conversation are you having over here?" Benny asks, walking around the counter and up to Mabel. He slides an arm around her waist and pulls her close with an affectionate smile. "Are you pestering them with weird questions?"

"Of course I am. But I'm learning things!"

"Amazing. I thought you knew everything."

Mabel swats his chest gently at his teasing and they share a smile that's so warm and devoted it gives me a pang in my chest.

"Okay!" Mabel claps her hands. "We're going to play a game. For anyone who's not watching football."

"Oh, boy. What game?" Benny asks.

Mabel holds up her phone. "It's called Head to Head. It's an app. Sort of like charades, except we can talk. We split into teams, and one team holds the phone up to their forehead." She demonstrates, the screen facing out. "And the app gives a phrase or a word or whatever. The other team has to give me clues so I can guess what it is."

I exchange a look with Andi. She smiles and shrugs, apparently game.

"You can't say the word, spell it out, or use a word that

rhymes," she adds. "Okay let's make teams. I want Andi on my team."

"Girls against guys?" Benny says dryly.

"No, that would not be fair to you guys," Mabel says seriously, eliciting a rumble of protest from the men. She winks. "We'll mix it up."

We're in teams of four—Andi, Mabel, Dilly and Crusher, versus me, Benny, Smitty, and his date, Bristol. Looks like maybe he's over Nikki Sullivan, the pop star he had that crush on.

"Who wants to go first?" Mabel asks.

"You go," we all say.

"Okay. There are different categories," Mabel adds. "Let's do Pop Culture. Okay. Gather around!" She starts the game and holds the phone up to her forehead.

We all crack up to see "ice skating."

"What's so funny?" She frowns.

"Hmmm. Can I act it out?" I ask.

"Yes!"

I start "skating," swinging my arms and pushing out my feet.

She stares blankly at me.

"There are blades on his feet," Benny says.

"Oh! Skating!"

"Too easy." I shake my head.

Mabel passes the phone to Andi. She makes a face but goes with it.

I screw up my face seeing the name, and look at my teammates.

"It's a name. First and last name," I say.

Benny holds out his left hand and points at his ring finger.

"Ring? Diamond?" Andi guesses.

"Close," Benny says. "A really big diamond."

"Rock?"

"Yeah! Okay, second name."

"Another name for penis," Bristol says.

Andi laughs. "Oh, boy. Cock? Dick?"

"No, no."

"Member? Dong? Wang?"

We're shaking our heads but also dying of laughter.

"Oh! Prick!"

"No!"

"Tool? Joystick?"

I almost fall down laughing.

"One-eyed trouser snake!"

"It's also a name," Bristol says, trying to breathe.

Andi's brows join above her nose. "I said Dick already."

"That's not it."

She thinks. "Oh! Johnson!" She frowns. "Rock?" I can't believe she does it, but just under the wire she cries, "Dwayne Johnson!"

Okay. My teammates and I are super competitive and we're losing, so we get a little intense. We mime putting on makeup when it's Sephora and sing "This ain't Texas" but Dilly doesn't get that it's Beyoncé.

It's our turn and we start getting pissy when we miss three in a row.

"This is a stupid game," Smitty says.

Everyone laughs.

"Oh, come on, it's fun," Mabel says.

We lose that first round.

"Let's go again," I say challengingly. "We're getting the hang of this." But then I realize what time it is. "Oh wait, I have to wake up Tilly."

"Just let her sleep," Benny says.

"No can do. We're on a schedule."

"Ford..." Andi murmurs.

"What?"

"You can let the schedule go for today. You're at a party."

I purse my lips. "I guess."

She moves closer and whispers in my ear. "Remember? Don't let your need for control and perfection cause you to miss out on things."

She said that when the guys threw the baby shower. And she's right.

"Okay." I smile down at her.

But then Tilly wakes up anyway and squawks. So much for that. I meet Andi's eyes and we both shrug.

I crouch down to lift Tilly from her seat. She's surly, too. "Need a diaper change?" I ask her. "Yes, you do. And you're probably hungry."

"Want me to do it?" Andi offers.

"Nah, I got this. Who wants to take my place?" I call out.

Alfie heads over and I carry Tilly and her diaper bag into the room where we left our coats. I'm on the floor changing her diaper when Mabel peeks in. "Hey."

"Hi." I smile at her. "That was fun."

"Yeah. How's Tilly doing?" She advances into the room with her glass of wine and perches on the bed. I like Mabel. She and I have a connection, I think because we're both a little different. She's bubbly and fun and says whatever she's thinking, which sometimes causes people to think she's a flake. But she's definitely not.

"Good." I tape the diaper closed. Tilly kicks her little legs and grins up at me. "Let's get your pants back on, niblet." I pick up the little blue jeans and shake them out, then work them onto her.

"You look so natural doing that," Mabel says.

I grin at her. "It didn't feel very natural at first. I'm still terrified I don't know what I'm doing." I tug Tilly's beige cashmere sweater down over her tummy. Yes, I splurged. It's super soft.

"I think all parents feel that way. It's so weird, isn't it? A few months ago, you were swearing you'd never have kids. And then this happens."

"Weird," I agree.

"And I told you maybe one day you'd meet a woman you want to have a family with."

I tilt my head to one side, not sure where this is going.

"Is that Andi?" she asks softly.

My head snaps up to look at her.

"She came to the game," Mabel says. "With Tilly. And they looked so cute together. Natural. Like you." She nods. "And I saw the way you looked at them."

"Aaaabababaga," Tilly says.

I pick her up. "Yeah."

"You're obviously more than friends."

Jesus. What is it? My mom said the same thing. We must look like we constantly want to jump each other and ball our brains out. "Yeah, we are."

Mabel gives a tiny squeal. "I knew it. I'm so happy for you."

"That doesn't mean it's serious," I object, but it's weak. Very weak. Because I'm feeling kind of serious about Andi. Like, I hate it when she's not around. My day feels brighter when she is. I love just talking to her.

Mabel cocks her head. "Okay." She pauses. "You're not taking advantage of her, are you?"

I scowl. "What does that mean?"

"It would be shitty if you were sleeping with her to keep her around to help with Tilly."

My jaw drops and nearly smacks Tilly's head. "What! That's bullshit."

"I'm just saying." She lifts one shoulder.

"That is not what's happening," I growl. "Not even close."

"Does she know that?"

I narrow my eyes at her. "Of course she does."

"Okay." She smiles. "I just know how single minded you can be. Especially about hockey."

I dip my chin in agreement.

"I would hate for you to be so inflexible that you would miss out on something great."

I gaze back at her. Just what Andi said—*don't let your need for control and perfection cause you to miss out on things.* "I get it."

She studies my face. "Okay, good." She stands. "If you ever want me to babysit while you two go out on a date, I'd be happy to. I love that baby."

I stand, too. "Um, thanks."

24

ANDI

Ford and I take turns with Tilly, although others at the party want to hold her and play with her, which is a nice break, too. We eat, drink, and play games. And laugh a lot.

I like these people. Mabel is a hoot, and the guys are so down to earth for professional athletes. I'm having fun.

Seeing Ford with his "hockey family" makes something flutter in my chest. I can't stop watching him, seeing how easy he is with them, and how much they respect him. Although you'd never know it from the chirping.

"Why are you wearing a mullet?" Eddy asks him.

Ford looks at him in horror. "This is not a mullet."

"Yes, it is."

Ford runs a hand through his hair. "This is the finest lettuce in the Metropolitan Division."

"You still losing hair?" Crusher asks.

"I'm not losing hair."

"You ever thought of going Mark Messier?" Eddy regards him thoughtfully. "I mean, if you're worried about losing hair you might as well shave it all off."

"No, but I could rock that look. My head is perfectly shaped."

This is apparently part of hockey. But underneath the put-downs and friendly insults, there's a strong sense of trust and affection among all of them.

* * *

The next Friday morning, around eleven o'clock, I've just finished my morning meeting. I sit back in my chair. What's in store for me tonight? Ford asked me earlier this week to keep Friday night open. But why? I have nothing planned, so it's not a problem, but it makes me curious.

Then he and Tilly show up at my door. My hair's in a messy bun with a pen stuck in it, I'm wearing old yoga pants and a sweatshirt... but they've seen me looking worse. "Come in. What's up?"

He strolls in with the baby. She reaches out to me. "Bama!"

Oh, no. Is she saying mama? Oh, God. My heart.

I take her from him, because she's happy to see me and I'm happy to see her and I want to squeeze her chubby little body. "Hi, baby." I give her smacking kisses all over her face and she laughs. I look back at Ford, pretending that never happened. "Hi."

"Hi." He smiles at both of us. "Tonight. We're going out."

"Oh." I blink and carry Tilly into my living room. "Where?"

"That's a surprise."

I squint at him. "Okay. Like... are we having dinner?"

"Yes."

"A child-friendly place," I say, nodding.

"No. Definitely not child friendly."

I tilt my head. "But... Tilly..."

"She's not coming with us."

My eyes widen.

"I've got a babysitter lined up," he continues. He moves closer to me. "And we are going on a date."

I blink a few times. "A... date?"

"Yeah." Now his confidence seems to falter, his eyebrows lowering a bit. "Andi, will you go out with me tonight?"

I gaze back at him. We've never gone on a date. Our relationship isn't like that. My heart is pumping at an uncomfortable speed. What does this mean? "I..."

He waits, his eyes flickering.

"I'm not hesitating because I don't want to," I say. "I'm just not sure why..."

His beautiful mouth softens and he tucks a piece of hair that's hanging in my face behind my ear with gentle familiarity. "I want to take you on a date. I want to have alone, adult time with you."

I smirk. "We have that all the time." Although even in bed, when Tilly's asleep, we're not really alone.

He laughs. "Okay, true. And it's hot as fuck."

"Ack! Language!"

"Right, right. Anyway. I want to go out with you. I want to wine you and dine you. And then sixty-nine you."

"Noooo." I start laughing.

"Sorry, I couldn't help it. I want this to be a romantic date."

Still choked up with laughter, I say, "Offering a sixty-nine is romantic?"

He collapses into laughter, too. "Sure, why not."

"But... why?"

"Because I love eating your pussy."

"Ford! Why are we going on a date?"

He's obviously using his dirty flirting to keep things light. But I push him.

"Because..." He takes a breath. "I like you. I like being with you, and not just in bed. I like talking to you and laughing with you."

My heart is now a ball of gooey goo. I swallow. We eye each other for a long moment. I want to analyze the shit out of this so I know what's happening, but right now I see the warmth in his eyes and the affectionate curve of his mouth, and... I want to go on a date with him. "Okay. I'll go out with you."

"Great."

"Who's babysitting? Lieve?"

"No. Mabel and Benny."

"What?"

"She offered, actually. At the party last week, she said we need some alone time. And I thought about it and... she's right." He strokes my cheek with his fingertips. I resist the urge to close my eyes and melt into him. "I'm going over there now to drop her off."

I pull in a slow, steadying breath. I knew people would get the wrong idea about us. But I don't say it. "That's so nice of her."

"Yeah." He pauses. "It really is. So we'll be staying overnight. Pack a bag."

"Ooooh, really?"

"And bring something nice to wear for dinner."

I look down at my faded, stretched-out shirt and grin. "Okay."

I zip to my closet after he leaves. I guess I don't need a new dress, since I have those three I bought with Elodie before the awards dinner. I've never even worn the blue one.

But what I'd really like? Some sexy lingerie.

I hold a quick debate with myself about whether I should reschedule a meeting this afternoon to go shopping. That's not exactly responsible. But what the hell! I'm my own boss, there have to be some benefits to it.

I head into Manhattan. There's a little place in Chelsea I

shopped at years ago called Blush. They had beautiful things. And I can afford to splurge now.

Everything in the city is decorated for Christmas, which makes me realize neither Ford nor I have a Christmas tree and I haven't done any Christmas shopping, other than the gifts I ordered online and shipped to my parents in Springfield. But first I'm going to take care of myself.

I browse leisurely through the shop, stroking silk and lace, admiring colors, picking up a few items to study them. There's a whole holiday-themed display with red items. Ford's favorite color. Yes. It will be red.

I look at a bustier trimmed with white fur. That might be a bit much.

I try on a few things. I end up buying a bias-cut silk slip in a luminous red, edged with French lace, and a matching thong panty. My belly flutters with excitement as I survey my image in the mirror. Will he like it?

I like it. So I'm buying it.

And since I'm here, I also purchase a silk robe in a delicate shade of blush pink that Elodie will love.

Out on the sidewalk, snowflakes are falling—soft, lazy ones. I smile and stroll up the street. I pause outside a children's book-store, then step inside. I'm overwhelmed by the selection, but a sales associate directs me to the section for infants and toddlers. Kids need books! Tilly needs books.

I could go crazy here, but I limit my purchase to four cute picture books, including *My First Book of Sharks*. I grin. Ford will love reading that to her.

And I should buy something for Ford.

Oh, sure, I'm going to buy the rich hockey player something he can't buy himself.

Oh, wait. I saw something in one of the books at the store... I'll check into that later, at home.

There's a toy store right around the corner, and I can't resist going in. I want to buy everything for Tilly! I end up with a teething toy—she'll need it soon!—the cutest little soft unicorn booties with rattles, and some soft blocks.

I pause in front of a display of books called *The Story of You*. I love that idea, but Ford can't fill in any information from Tilly's first four months. That makes me sad.

But I'm happy with the things I got.

Time to head home. I need to do some serious waxing to prep for my big date tonight.

25

FORD

The limo picks us up at five and delivers us to the Plaza Hotel. Andi looks around in amazement as we enter the chateau-like building. It's decorated for Christmas and the elegant interior is even more stunning than usual.

"I came here once for afternoon tea," she whispers as we walk through the lobby. "Years ago."

"It's nice."

She slants me an amused look. "Yes. Very nice."

We take in about a gazillion tiny white lights on trees, with oversized gifts and shiny red ball ornaments arranged around them. The glittering chandeliers above, French doors, and gleaming stone floor create a magical glow.

"It's so beautiful." Andi gazes raptly at a display of trees.

I've already checked in and left some goodies in the room, so I have the room keys. Yes, I've planned every detail of this date.

Why am I doing this? Andi asked the question and I got nervous.

After my little talk with Mabel at the Thanksgiving party, I was confused. Does Mabel think I'm using Andi? Because I'm not.

More importantly, does *Andi* think I'm using Andi?

I need her, yes. But it's not like that. That's not me. Sure, I'm committed to my career. And yeah, I can be selfish or self-centered or whatever. But I'm honest about that. I don't play games or hide ulterior motives. What you see is what you get. Like it or leave it.

I need Andi for more than looking after Tilly. Or for sex, although that is fucking hot and amazing. But I'd never use someone.

Does Andi think that?

That made me feel a little like throwing up.

Then Mabel offered to babysit so we could go out, and I realized... I've never taken Andi on a date. And shame intensified that nauseous feeling.

I have to rectify that. I have to show her that I value her as more than a sex partner or a babysitter for my daughter. I value her as a woman, a smart, hard-working, woman who's patient and kind and has never let me down, not once. A friend who makes me laugh, a lover who turns me on, a woman I consider a partner in caring for Tilly. She deserves to be spoiled. Pampered. I don't know... honored. I want to worship her like the goddess she is.

That's why I'm doing this.

We go straight to the eighteenth floor. I carry both our bags and Andi walks into our room ahead of me.

"Whoa. This is beautiful." She pauses. "A little old-fashioned, but still beautiful."

"Not my style of décor," I agree. "But this is just one night."

"It's very ritzy." She walks to the window flanked with long drapes and peers out at the view of Central Park. "Amazing." She turns to study the king-size bed with an ornate headboard and luxurious white bedding, a small sitting area with two chairs and a table, and marble and gilt furniture. "There's even a chandelier in here." The crystals sparkle above us.

I toss the key cards onto the dresser. "Okay, take off your clothes."

She bursts out laughing and saunters toward me. "I expected a *little* more romance than that."

I grin. "I'm kidding. We have an appointment in the spa in fifteen minutes."

"The spa." She slides her fingers around the back of my neck under my collar. Shivers slide down my spine. "That sounds lovely."

"We're having a couples massage." I set my hands on her waist and pull her closer.

"So decadent."

"Right?" I brush a kiss over her mouth.

"This is... incredible." She turns her head slightly as I move my mouth over her cheek. "Indulgent. I feel spoiled."

"Good. That's how I want you to feel." I nuzzle her ear, breathing in her scent. "You've been doing so much for me. And for Tilly. And growing your business. I want you to be pampered. I want you to relax and let me look after you."

"'Look after me.'" Her lips quirk. "I hope that means lots of orgasms."

"As many as you can handle and still walk out of here tomorrow." I kiss her mouth again, giving just a hint of tongue and a nibble on the bottom lip.

"That sounds... definitely spoiled." Her tone has gone breathy and low.

I open my mouth on her throat. "I want to spoil you rotten. Also fuck you senseless."

She lets out a soft laugh. "Perfect."

Great. I'm hard as a goalpost and have to lie down on a massage table. I'll try to think about sharks.

"Those are for you." I point to a big bouquet of orange roses on the dresser.

Her lips part and she walks over to them, brushing the petals with her fingertips. She plucks out the card that says *Orange is for passion, desire, energy, and fascination*. She gazes at it for a long moment. "They're beautiful. Thank you."

"You're welcome." I'm not sure if she likes them or not. Maybe I'm overdoing it.

She heads into the bathroom. "Whoa."

I follow her and peer over her shoulder at mosaic floors and walls with a gilded floral motif and gold-plated fixtures. "Wow."

She gives me a look over her shoulder that's both excited and fascinated. "Look. The toilet is in a separate room."

I grin and she disappears into the water closet. When she comes out, I say, "Did you see the tub?" I gesture at the soaker tub.

"Ohhhh, that's nice."

"We can make use of it later." I kiss the back of her neck and fondle her sweet ass. I can't keep my hands off her. That's pretty much what this date is going to be—me molesting her non-stop.

"I can't wait."

We make our way to the spa for our appointment. It, too, is plush and elegant. As we sit in the waiting room, she leans over to me. "I'm intimidated."

"Yeah?"

She nods, eyes wide. "Do you do stuff like this often? I know you're a rich hockey player, I just never imagined..."

"All the time." I wave a hand. "This is nothing."

She gazes back at me.

"I'm kidding. But don't worry. Don't be intimidated. You deserve this."

"Okay."

Two attendants arrive to show us in. We meet up again in another waiting area, now dressed in thick white robes and slippers.

"Oooh, you look good," she says to me. "Like Hugh Hefner."

I choke on a laugh. "Please. No. Not him."

"You know what I mean."

The massage is different than what I'm used to. The team massage therapist, Trey, is usually trying to fix something and it's often painful. This is slow and sensuous and relaxing. Piano music drifts peacefully and soothingly through the room. Surrounded by a scent that makes me think of dark velvet nights and exotic spices, I occasionally lift my head to look over at Andi, taking in her bare back in the soft light. She looks at me too and we share a smile.

We're there for an hour, but it's over too soon. The attendants leave us alone and we climb off the tables, both of us naked. Seeing Andi like this, her smooth skin glossy from the massage oil, her face flushed, hair messy, makes me instantly hard again. As I walk toward her, her gaze drops to my massive erection.

"Ford!"

I smile and slide my arms around her, prodding her with my swollen dick. "I want you."

"Not here!"

"I just want a kiss." I give her one. "We'll do more later."

She moans. "Don't tease me unless you're going to please me."

"Oh, I will definitely please you. I will please you all night long." I give her a long, deep kiss then let her go so we can go get dressed.

"What are we doing next?" she asks in the elevator. "What's the plan?"

"Maybe I don't have a plan. Maybe I'm just winging it."

She gives me a look. "I know you. There's a plan."

I grin. "Okay, there is. We have dinner reservations at Pascal."

"No!"

"Yes."

"Ooooh. Amazing! I've heard good things about it."

"I hope it's good. We can walk there."

"Perfect."

She goes into the bathroom to get ready. I pour a glass of wine and carry it in for her. She's standing in front of the vanity in a strapless bra and a tiny pair of panties, both in the exact color of her skin, giving the effect that she's naked. I stop and stare for a moment then set down the glass for her.

"Aw, thank you."

"I see your underwear matches." I move up behind her and close my hands over her hips. Heat runs down my belly into my groin. "Jesus, you're sexy."

Her expression turns sultry. She's wearing her contact lenses, her eyes all shadowy, her cheeks glowy.

I press against her, enjoying the feel of her ass against me. I slide my hands around to her front, over her smooth stomach, then up to her bra. It's easy to tug it down and let her tits spill free, round and tipped with perfect caramel-colored nipples. I watch as those little buds pucker.

"Ford…"

"Mmm?" I kiss her shoulder and cup her tits.

"Do we have time…?"

I smile against her skin. "Time for what?" My dick is hard and my balls are pulled up tight, aching.

"Time for you to fuck me."

"I always have time for that." I suck on the side of her neck, inhaling her scent, then drag my tongue over it. "Right here." I slide a hand down under her panties, then between her legs, and she widens her stance to accommodate me.

I pinch her nipple while fingering her, slicking up her wetness, circling her clit. Her arousal stokes mine, and my balls tighten. "You're wet. Ready."

"I'm always ready when I'm with you." Her cheeks flush even pinker. She pushes her round little ass into me.

My dick gets even harder. I flick open the button of my jeans and yank the zipper down, then pull out my aching cock. "I'm always ready when I'm with you, too," I say roughly. I bend to kiss her shoulder again, and urgency has me opening my mouth and setting my teeth on her skin.

She draws in a sharp breath, her lips parting, eyes going hazy.

"I love watching you when I touch you." I tug aside the string of her thong, then go still. "Shit. Need a condom." I stretch to reach my toiletry bag sitting on the counter and fumble in it for a rubber. I have it on in seconds and then I'm back in place, sliding her panties aside, sliding the head of my cock up and down through her slit, letting out a groan. "Feels so good."

"Mmmm." She grips the edge of the vanity, arching her back, thrusting out that sweet ass, and I nudge the head of my cock at her entrance. I have to bend my knees, and she goes onto her tip toes with a breathy cry. "Yessss..."

I grip her hips and press into her. She's all liquid heat. "Such a tight little kitty," I mutter. "So slippery. And so fucking hot."

She moans, leaning forward. I watch her in the mirror, the way her soft mouth opens, her eyes dark and smoky.

"There. I'm in." I hold myself there for a few seconds, fighting for control. Our eyes meet and she mewls. "You want it, honey? Oh, yeah. You want it bad."

"Yes. I love it. I love being filled like this." Her eyes drift closed and she presses a hand to her abdomen. "So deep."

"Wanna fuck you so deep." I pull out and thrust in again.

"Oh!"

And again. And again. "Look at your pretty tits jiggling." I bend over her, cupping both breasts in my hands, my ass clenching as I push into her. Then I move a hand to her shoulder to and another to her hip to steady her as I bang her harder, plunging into her again and again. I delve into her panties again and find that swollen bud. She jolts and whimpers and I circle over it, fucking into her tight pussy.

I'm addicted to her. To her silky, hot pussy, her soft mouth, her sweet tits. Also her sharp mind, her kindness, her big heart. To all of her. Every inch, inside and out. A groan climbs my throat as pressure builds in my belly and my balls.

Her abs contract and her body stiffens. Her head falls back against me and she's coming, contracting around me, making little cries of pleasure. Or pain. Or both. I want to watch her face but my vision is blurring. Darkening. And I'm there, too, growling as I pump my release into her in hot, weighty pulses.

26

ANDI

I can barely walk out of the bathroom to collapse onto the bed. "Holy shit, that was hot."

Ford follows me, his jeans undone but his junk tucked back inside. *He's* hot. What am I doing with this gorgeous man? Here in the Plaza fucking Hotel, for fuck's sake.

He walks over to the window and draws the curtains closed. "In case of peeping Toms," he says as he turns.

My heart trips. "Thank you."

He walks up to the bed, leans down and kisses me. "Don't be late."

I manage a lazy smile. "You just destroyed me."

He smirks. "You're welcome."

I take a few long breaths while my heart slows and strength returns to my limbs. "Okay." I sit up on the side of the bed. "I'll finish getting ready now."

My makeup was done. My hair is a disaster. I fluff it. Oh, well.

I move to the closet where I hung my dress earlier. I step into it and pull up the side zipper. It's the other dress I bought before the awards dinner—midnight-blue, one-shouldered, with a big bow and trailing fabric on that shoulder.

Ford watches me. "Wow. That is hot."

"Thank you." I move to the full-length mirror to check my appearance, turning in front of it.

"Yes, your ass looks spectacular." He walks up behind me, cups my butt, and lays a kiss on my shoulder. "The night we went to that awards dinner and you were wearing that red dress... I thought you were the hottest thing I'd ever seen."

My lips curve up.

"Until now," he says, meeting my eyes in the mirror. "You're so beautiful."

My heart expands. "Thank you."

He drops another kiss on my bare shoulder. "Are we ready to go?"

"I am. I just need my shoes." My sexy slingbacks with the sharpest pointed toe.

Outside on the sidewalk, he says, "This way." He takes my hand and leads the way to Sixth Avenue and around the corner. It's a couple of blocks to the restaurant through busy Friday-night sidewalks, the city glittering and glamorous around us.

Pascal is a French bistro, a small place, with supposedly incredible food. We're seated at a table for two, me taking the seat on the red velvet banquette. I look around in the low golden lighting, surveying the brass fixtures, white tablecloths, and lots of ornate mirrors on the wall.

"Very French," I murmur, settling into my seat. I look at Ford to see him staring at me I intently. "What?" I smile.

"Just admiring you. You're gorgeous. And..." He leans forward. "You look freshly fucked."

I drop my gaze, heat sliding into my cheeks. "I wonder why."

He chuckles.

"You know what was really hot?"

One eyebrow goes skyward.

"We could be as noisy as we wanted."

His lips kick up in a smile. "That is very true." He leans closer. "I can't wait to make you scream later."

I sink my teeth into my bottom lip and resist the urge to fan myself with the menu. "This place is so elegant." I pick up a thick folder which contains the wine list. "We could be sitting in Paris."

"You fit right in."

"Aw. Thank you."

"I'd like to go to Paris."

"Me, too. Holy crap, there are three pages of champagnes!" I look up at Ford. "I don't even know where to start with this."

"We'll get advice."

We start with foie gras. Ford requests the filet mignon au poivre, and I order braised beef in red wine. He also orders a Ladoix premier cru burgundy recommended by the sommelier. I almost choke at the price. "You are going all out tonight."

Ford laughs. "Yeah. I calculated how much I would have spent if we'd been dating for the last three months and decided to spend it all tonight."

My mouth drops open. "Really?"

"No."

We both laugh.

"But I like that idea," he adds.

Before our food arrives, Ford takes out his phone, then hesitates.

I lift my eyebrows and restrain my smile. "Go ahead."

He gives me an innocent look. "What?"

"Check on Tilly. I know you want to."

"Sorry. This is supposed to be romantic."

"It's fine. If you don't do it, I will."

He grins and unlocks his phone. But before he can do anything, he sees photos. He holds the phone up to show me pics of Tilly being cuddled by Mabel, sitting on the floor with pillows, playing with a soft lamb stuffy I don't recognize, and then holding a beer bottle. Ford makes a strangled noise. "I hope that's Benny's idea of a joke."

I laugh. "I'm sure it is. She seems to be okay."

"Yeah." He sends a quick text message anyway and they confirm all is fine.

We talk our way through dinner, sharing tastes, drinking the delicious wine. We talk about travel and movies and TV shows, finding some things in common.

"What's something you're really bad at but you enjoy doing anyway?" I ask him, picking up my glass of wine.

"Hmmm. I'd say... bowling."

I laugh. "I can't believe you're not good at bowling."

"I suck at it. I'm not that great at axe throwing, either."

"Axe throwing! Ack!"

"We did it once last year, a bunch of us. Mabel almost got taken out by a wild throw."

I make a face. "I don't think I'd be good at that either."

"It's kind of satisfying. Mabel was imagining throwing the axe at her ex-boyfriend."

"Ah." I purse my lips. "I could definitely do that."

"Trevor doesn't deserve you."

"Thank you." He's being so sweet tonight, with all these romantic gestures and compliments. Although the sex in the bathroom was not sweet—it was dirty and hot and so, so good...

"I agree."

"I'm glad you know that. So what's something *you* suck at but like doing anyway?"

"Cooking," I say immediately.

"You help me cook all the time."

"Help is the key word there. I just follow your orders."

"Hey. Are you implying I'm bossy?"

I lean forward. "You do like to be in control."

"Can't argue with that." He meets my eyes and sparks crackle between us.

"Perfectionism and control issues," I say lightly.

He contemplates me for a long moment, then picks up his glass of wine and takes a sip. "Yep," he agrees. "But I'm working on it."

I tilt my head, smiling slightly. "Yeah?"

"Yeah. I've gone for therapy. I still go, sometimes."

I nod. I told him that I went for therapy after the divorce. It's not something to be ashamed or embarrassed about. Sometimes we all need help with our health—mental or physical. "That's good."

"I was developing some unhealthy coping mechanisms. Mainly my superstitions. They were starting to rule my life."

"Oh. That sounds like a problem."

"Yeah. Sometimes superstitions help us, but if they start interfering in our ability to function, that's not good. My therapist pointed out that if you think your successes are lucky because of the things you do, or don't do, it negates all your skill and hard work."

I consider that. "That's interesting."

He nods. "And you can't rely on luck to be successful."

"Absolutely."

"Also..." He drops his gaze. "When it gets compulsive, it's usually because you're trying to avoid something. In my case, it was anxiety. I had a lot of thought distortions. Obviously. About what would happen if I didn't drive the exact same route to the game every time, or if I didn't park in the same spot every game."

He looks up at me, his expression guarded. "My shrink actually put me on antidepressants to help with it."

I make a face. "I know. I saw them in your bathroom. I wasn't snooping!" I hold up a hand.

One corner of his mouth lifts. "You can snoop all you want in my place."

"It's not a big deal," I say. "Medications for mental health are just as necessary as antibiotics or painkillers for physical health."

"Yeah." His expression slides into relief. "Exactly. Anyway. Therapy helped me understand the impact my parents' way of life had on me. Why I need to feel in control."

"Because things were out of control when you were a kid."

"Right." He pauses. "Tell me about your family. You've mentioned they live in Illinois."

"That's right. Springfield. That's where I grew up. There's not much to tell." I smile. "My parents are very nice and normal— they're both teachers, although my dad's a principal now—and my life was pretty average. I guess I was lucky."

"Yeah."

"My mom and I text all the time. She sends me cute dog videos because she knows I love dogs."

"You had a dog growing up?"

"Yes! We always had a dog. There were Barkley and Homer, and they still have Daisy. I'll show you a picture!" I pull out my phone and swipe through the photo gallery to find a recent pic of Daisy.

Leaning closer as I swipe, Ford says, "Are those all pictures of Tilly?"

"Oh. Yeah." I stop scrolling and give him a toothy smile. "I like taking pictures of her."

He grins.

I find a picture of Daisy and show him the camera.

"Oh, wow. She's beautiful."

"She's an Australian Shepherd."

"Look at those eyes."

Daisy's eyes are a pale blue. "I love them." I put away my phone. "We also had a few cats over the years. Rabbits. Guinea pigs. Mom drew the line at hamsters. They were too much like mice. I was always rescuing strays and injured animals. Once, a racoon."

His eyebrows shoot up.

"And a feral pig." I pout. "That didn't go well."

"Jesus."

"I wanted to keep him as a pet. He was young and small. And really cute! But they told me he was going to get huge and also could carry brucellosis or pseudorabies. And that if he got angry, he'd fight like a wild pig, not a domestic pig. It could be dangerous."

"I know you like animals, but a feral pig..." He shakes his head. "You're making me nervous."

I laugh. "You think I'll expose Tilly to brucellosis?"

"I don't even know what is."

"It's a bacterial infection. It can infect dogs, which was what convinced me to give up the pig." I pause. "Also, I didn't want to get it."

"Good decision. And no... I don't think you'd expose Tilly to that. Do you want a dog of your own?"

"I would love it. But pets aren't allowed in our building."

"Right." He nods, lips pursed.

"I tried to tell Trevor I wanted to live somewhere pet-friendly, but he really liked this place, so..." I shrug.

We finish our meal with crème caramel that we share, and then walk leisurely back to the hotel, this time going over to Fifth Avenue. The air is crisp, the city still vibrant and bright.

"How about a drink in the lounge?" Ford says as we enter the hotel. "The Champagne Bar."

I really want to get up to our room and jump him. I bite my lip and look at him through my eyelashes.

He leans down and murmurs in my ear, "If you keep looking at me like that we're fucking right on that table over there."

"Oh." My belly flip-flops and I blink rapidly at him. "I might let you do that."

He groans. "Champagne?" He nuzzles my hair. "Or sex. Hell, let's do both. Come on."

He leads me to the bar and when we're seated, orders a bottle of Louis Roederer—what is happening here?

"A whole bottle?" I ask. "We just had a bottle of wine at the restaurant."

"We can take it up to the room. Have a glass of champagne in the bathtub."

"Ohhhh, God." I shift in my seat, my inner muscles tightening low inside me. I press a hand to my chest. "I am dying. Like, I think I'm having a heart attack. I need to compose myself."

He laughs softly. "I don't want you to die. I want you to enjoy this."

"I am enjoying it. So much. I'm just... overwhelmed."

He kisses me softly. "Good."

The champagne is bubbly and bright. "I love it."

"I'm glad."

I walk into the bathroom carrying the bottle of champagne and two glasses. Andi's already stretched out in the tub, her tawny nipples peeking temptingly out of the soap bubbles. Her lips curve seductively.

I'm already half hard and seeing her like that has more blood flowing south.

I pour champagne then climb in to join her, handing her a glass. We sit face to face, legs stretched out, and the hot water sloshes warm and languid around us, steamy and scented with the same fragrance as the massage oil earlier.

I sip champagne, then lean forward to kiss her. "Mmm."

"That was an amazing dinner. Thank you."

"It was great. And you looked hot. Beautiful." I kiss her shoulder, then her collarbone.

Her eyes go shiny.

She's not going to cry, is she? "Am I doing this wrong?"

"No." She slides closer through the water, hooks an arm around my neck and kisses me hard. "You're doing this perfectly. I feel like I'm in a dream."

"Yeah, me too." I slide my mouth down over her jaw. Then I tip my glass above her chest.

She gasps as icy champagne hits her heated skin. Rivulets run down the upper slope of one breast and drip off her nipple. I lower my head and lick it up, slowly, sliding my tongue over the underside of her breast, the inside of it, the nipple, the top. She moans and hangs on to my shoulder, leaning back a bit to give me room.

"You taste delicious. Even better than the champagne."

I do it again on the other side, then take a mouthful of the wine and hold it there before swallowing. When I pull her nipple into my mouth I can feel the heat of her flesh against the cold of my tongue. She quivers.

"Oh, God. That's... so erotic."

"I know how much you like your nipples sucked."

"I do..."

I pour more bubbly over her and lick it off again and again, until she's trembling and whimpering and her hips are shifting in the water.

"Are you aching here?" I slide a hand between her legs.

"Yessss."

"Good." I set my glass on the edge of the tub and clasp her waist, then lift her.

"What are you doing?"

"Just turning you around."

We lose a little water over the side as we make the adjustments and I lean against the back of the tub with Andi settled in front of me between my legs, her back to my front. I glide my hands over wet skin to find her tits and cup them.

Yeah. Erotic. This is so goddamn erotic my dick is about to blow. My balls are pulled up tight, pressure building, electric prickles all over my skin.

She turns her head and shifts to the side so I can find her mouth with mine and kiss her. I lick into her mouth, nip at her plump bottom lip, trace her upper lip with my tongue. Her breathing quickens. "I love kissing you. You taste delicious. Sweet. And sexy."

Another inarticulate noise escapes her lips.

I reach for the small bottle of body wash, pour it into one hand and suds it up all over her. Her skin is slippery and smooth and delectable. I kiss her again, hands on her soapy tits. I play with her nipples and her legs shift as her arousal builds. My hand glides over her stomach, over her smooth, bare mound, and between her legs. "I can feel you pulsing," I whisper in her ear. "So hot."

I kiss her neck, her shoulder, then suck on the soft skin there, carefully, restraining my urge to devour her.

"I want to turn around again."

I smile and let her move. The ends of her hair are wet, her cheeks flushed an adorable pink. Her gaze drops to my dick, poking out of the water, ruddy and swollen. She licks her lips. My cock jumps. I fucking love how she looks at me like that... like she's ravenous for my dick.

I lift my hips, flaunting myself at her. Her eyes go hazy, her lips shiny and parted. My heart is pounding and I'm so turned on I hurt.

She slides her hands over my thighs in the water. Excitement builds, heat rushing through my body. "You're beautiful, too," she says quietly. She takes her time admiring me and then, sweet Jesus, she leans forward to take me in her mouth.

I make a helpless, needy sound, hips lifting. I push into her mouth before I can stop myself, then go still, my heart racing, breathing suspended. *Easy, man. Go easy*.

It's a fucking battle. Thank God I've practiced self-control because right now I want to fuck up into her hot little mouth and take and take and take. But I don't want to hurt her or scare her.

I've never had tender, protective feelings like this during sex. What is happening to me?

I push myself up and brace my ass against the edge of the tub, and watch her suck on me, her lips stretched around my girth, and it's so fucking filthy and beautiful it makes my breath tighten in my chest. Tremors run down my thighs and throbbing need builds in my body.

She slides her mouth off me, but keeps her hand wrapped around me as she kisses my abs, my chest, then sucks my nipples. I gasp as sensation flashes right to my balls, then I growl. Then she's licking my dick again, long slides of her tongue up and down, slowly like she's savoring me. I fucking love that.

"Okay," I gasp. "That's it. We're fucking. Right now." I grab a bottle of lube I left in here earlier. Water is not conducive to natural lubrication and I want this to be good for her. With a smile, she takes it from me and slicks up my cock, nearly undoing me. Then I lube up her pussy, enjoying the feel of my fingers sliding through her softness. I turn her to face away from me, on her knees, hands on the side of the tub. What a view of her perfect ass. And that tattoo scrolling up her spine.

She arches her back and pushes her ass out, taunting me, and I'm lost. I drive into her, hard.

"Yes," she wheezes, her hands tightening on the edge of the tub. "Do that. Hard."

"Christ, yeah."

She reaches between her legs and I feel the tension build in her, her pussy clamping around me. She cries out, her head falling forward.

She feels so fucking incredible, and... Wait. I don't have a condom on. I know she's on birth control, but...

Fuck, I can't stop it now, my orgasm is bearing down on me, the pressure intense and fiery and inexorable. I grit my teeth, close my eyes and grab my cock, pulling it out of her. I pump once and I'm coming, a line of fire sizzling down my spine, my balls squeezing, and I explode in hot rushes onto her lower back. Sensation pours through me in exquisite, agonizing waves until I'm spent, panting, leaning over her to growl into her ear. "Jesus. Jesus Christ. Andi... you're fucking killing me."

When I can move, I say, "Let me clean you up. I'm so sorry. I forgot a condom." I gently wash her back and she slides down into the water to turn and face me.

"You know I'm on birth control. Are you worried about STIs?"

Her frank question startles me. "No! Are you?"

"I don't know." She searches my face. "No. I trust you."

I blow out a breath. "I've been tested."

"I went after the first time we slept together. So I'm okay, too."

"Okay. So..." I cock my head. "Does that mean no more condoms?"

She smiles. "I'm good with that."

I kiss her smile. "Fucking you bare felt incredible. Let's do it again."

* * *

After more sex, this time in the bed, making more use of the lube and the champagne, and sleep, we enjoy morning sex. Instead of getting dressed and going downstairs, we order room service and have French toast and fruit in bed, talking and flirting and kissing. She's wearing a sexy little red slip that I fucking love.

The limo takes us home, but we get in my car and drive over to Benny's place to pick up Tilly. I only texted two more times last night, and once this morning to make sure everything was okay.

"She was a little fussy last night." Mabel hands her over to me. "When she realized you'd left, I think. She got a little sad. But we played with her and she settled down. She's so cute! We had fun."

"Thank you so much for this," I say. "We had a great time."

"I'm happy to look after her!"

"Did she sleep all night?" Andi asks, petting Tilly's hair.

"No." Benny makes a face. "But we gave her a bottle and she wasn't awake for long."

"I'm sorry," I say. "It's hard getting up in the night."

"I think we can handle it for one night," he says dryly. "We're fine. We can go back to bed now."

I grin. "Yeah, you can."

We get Tilly into her little jacket and a hat and then into her car seat and head home.

"I wish *I* could go back to bed," Andi says with a yawn.

I slant her a glance. "You can."

After a short pause, she says, "Yeah. I guess I could. I have a lot of work to do though."

"You always have a lot of work to do."

This time her silence turns sticky. "What does that mean?"

"It means just what I said—you always have a lot of work to do." Oh, shit. I remember what she said about being afraid her working so much is what led to Trevor cheating on her. "That's all I mean, truly. I wasn't complaining."

She nods without looking at me. "Okay."

"If I did think you work too much, it would only be because I want you to have time for fun, too."

"I do have time for fun."

"Okay, good."

The air in the car feels frosty. Shit. After such a fantastic night, I don't want it to end like this. But I'm not sure what's wrong.

28

ANDI

When I made that stupid comment about wishing I could go back to bed, it was because I was thinking that I have a child to look after. And then Ford reminded me that I *don't* have a child to look after, and I *could* go back to bed. It felt like a slap.

And I was already confused. We just had an amazing overnight date where Ford went all out. But what does it really mean? I still don't know. I wanted to think it meant something important, that Ford's feelings for me are changing.

Because *my* feelings for *him* are changing.

I'm falling in love with him.

And I'm terrified.

He never said anything, though. Through the romantic dinner and his vulnerability in telling me about his therapy, all during the bubble bath and champagne and the kisses and orgasms, I started hoping. And then he said that, and splat, I was back down to earth.

I need to be careful.

I have to keep telling myself that when I bring home a small

Christmas tree. I should put it in my apartment, but I want it for Tilly. She's too young to know what it is, but I want her to have that experience, so I haul it into Ford's place while he's at a practice. Lieve is there and admires the tree, helping me put it up.

Back at my place, I dig out the ornaments that Trevor and I used to decorate our tree with. I haven't put up a tree since the divorce. After studying them, I carry them to the trash and toss them in.

Then I go shopping for new ones.

Ford has a late day because they're shooting photos and videos for social media for Christmas, wearing ugly sweaters and posing in awkward photos, so I spend the afternoon working.

Around five o'clock I get a text.

> **FORD**
> We have a problem.

Is it about the tree? Is he joking or does he hate it?

> **ANDI**
> What is it?

> **FORD**
> Come over here.

> **ANDI**
> Come over here...?

> **FORD**
> (eye roll emoji) Please

I grin and save what I'm working on, then go next door. I walk in and breathe in the fresh evergreen aroma, and then I see my little tree... and another huge one. My mouth drops open and I look over at Ford, who laughs. "See?"

I tilt my head and walk closer. "Did you get a tree, too?"

"Yeah. The social media guy was asking us who puts their tree up first, and I realized I don't even have a tree, or ornaments. I've never bothered. So I picked up a tree on the way home."

I bite my lip. "Great minds think alike."

"Apparently."

"I can take my tree to my place."

"Okay. Then you can have one there, too."

"I bought ornaments but not enough for that tree." It's a six-foot Douglas fir.

"We can get more. Let's go shopping."

"I just did that!" I protest, but I'm laughing.

So we make another trip back to the garden center where he bought the tree. Tilly's in the sling on his front as he shows her ornaments and adds them to the cart which is soon full of all kinds of décor for the tree, including a "Baby's First Christmas" ornament that makes my throat clog with emotion. I hide one ornament from him, and pay for it myself on the way out.

Then we go home to decorate.

Home. To *his* home. Not *our* home. I'm getting all sentimental and soft again. I have to be careful. How much longer do we have? It's been three months since Willa left Tilly here, and she has to be coming back soon. And then what? When Tilly's gone, Ford won't need me anymore. Our arrangement will end. We'll go back to being friends. Or maybe not even that.

Tilly seems entranced by the lights and sparkly things, bouncing in her seat as we decorate, and Ford helps her "hang" a few things. We lose one ornament when she grabs it off the tree before he can stop her and hurls it to the floor.

We look at each other with "yikes" faces, then burst out laughing.

It's hard not to feel the spirit of the season, a sense of togetherness and shared traditions and new traditions. Joy.

But I have to be careful.

That's why I go home to sleep in my own bed tonight.

29

FORD

I get the text from Willa just as I'm going on the ice for a morning skate before we leave for Columbus. I don't have time to reply, so I chuck my phone in my locker. Is she going to put off coming back for Tilly again? I don't know if that's what I want or what I don't want. What I do know is that I'm kind of pissed off at her. But I put that aside as I jump onto the ice and focus on Pete, our goalie coach. He has me and Bender together at one end of the ice. Pete's in the net demonstrating what he wants us to do.

"Now we're going east–west on our feet. Then back in, down to the goal line, and right out again... and east–west, this time at the top of the paint."

I nod, taking in everything he says. I respect him as a goalie coach and he's been a great mentor to me, even talking to Victor about his training plans for me. I go into the net and go through the motions he described. I'm quick on picking up things like that, maybe because of all the taekwondo patterns I've learned. Then I watch Bender do the same, helping him.

Then Pete starts shooting pucks at us, so the patterns become real as we try to stop the frozen rubber from getting past us.

I'm sweaty and pleasantly tired by the end of practice and Bender and I joke around as we skate off. "You must have taped your ankles up good today, Bender," I say. "They weren't even collapsing." His nickname comes from his name, Bendik, but it's also a derogatory name for someone who thinks they can skate but can't.

"Fuck you," he says with a laugh. "I've heard better chirps from a dead bird."

"Haha."

We're leaving shortly for the airport for a five-day road trip to Columbus, St. Louis, and Charlotte. This is the longest I've left Tilly (and Andi) and I'm feeling out of sorts about it. Lieve is working out fine and I totally trust Andi, so I don't know why I'm bothered. I'll need to stay focused on the trip. I'm starting tonight, but I don't know how many of the games I'll get to play. I hope it's all three. Things are going better lately, but I still feel a need to prove myself.

We board the bus in business casual clothes for the half hour or so ride to the airport in Teterboro. I grab a seat next to Smitty who's engrossed in his phone. Oh, shit. That reminds me...

I pull out my own phone to look at Willa's message.

I stare at it. She's back and she wants to talk.

What does that mean? She wants Tilly back? Well, obviously she does. Shit.

My gut tightens into a rock. I knew this was coming. I have to deal with it.

I text her back with numb fingers.

FORD

> Just leaving on a road trip. I'll be back Sunday morning. I can come see you then.

She agrees to that. I'm antsy. I wish I could go see her right now and get this done. How the hell am I going to play hockey over the next five days with this hanging over my head?

I glance over at Smitty's phone and see an image of a woman, so I lean closer. "Oh, man... is that Nikki Sullivan?"

He jumps. "Uh. Yeah."

"I thought you were over her. What about Bristol?"

"It was just a casual thing."

"That's hot." The singer is posed in a skimpy silver-sequined outfit.

He closes Instagram and scowls.

"So you're still obsessed with Nikki. Still stalking her."

"I'm not stalking her."

I laugh. "Yeah, you are. Online."

He growls.

"You're really hung up on her."

"No, I'm not." He opens a game app and starts playing.

Okay. Fine.

For the rest of the bus ride I contemplate the things I'll say to Willa and what she might say to me. This is supposed to prepare me and ease my anxiety but instead only reinforces how much this is beyond my control. And I fucking hate that.

When we get to the hotel in Columbus, I sit on the bed in my room and send another text, this time to Andi.

> FORD
>
> I heard from Willa. She's back.

> ANDI
>
> Oh.

> FORD
>
> I'll get this all sorted when I'm home. Finally.

> ANDI
>
> Okay.

The little dots jump around as she types, then stop. Then start again, then stop. And I don't hear from her again.

The other night, when we decorated the tree, it felt so normal and comfortable and... like we were a family. And then she left, and went home to sleep in her own bed.

She probably knows that Willa won't be gone much longer. She's probably eager to get back to her normal life. I don't blame her.

I exhale sharply. It's time to go to the arena.

* * *

This is a test of my self-discipline. *Discipline is the bridge between goals and success.* I do all my usual routines. I've got this.

But on the ice, when play is up at the other end, instead of thinking about sharks, I'm thinking about Willa. And Tilly. And Andi.

My chest is tight and I have a faint headache. After a whistle, I squeeze water over my head and give it a shake to try to regain focus.

It's so fucking frustrating that I don't know what's going on. I feel like my life is out of my control, and that's one of my worst fears.

Or... is it? It used to be. But now... when I think of losing Tilly and Andi, I think that might have changed. Control and rules are great. I love 'em. But Tilly is teaching me that I'm not always going to have control of her, even at this age. And I might be okay with that. Or learning to be okay with that.

I always told myself I don't need anyone else. People pushed me around as a kid. Fine. Who needs them? Even playing hockey —yeah, it's a team sport, but I'm on my own here in the net.

Except when I think of my life going back to the way it was

before—which, honestly, was all I wanted for a while after Tilly arrived—it makes me want to vomit. It seems bleak. Empty. Lonely.

Maybe... now my biggest fear is losing them.

With the score tied one all, I'm suddenly aware of a two-on-one happening in front of me, with two Columbus players coming in on net and only Crusher trying to stop them. Hakim is desperately trying to catch up. Columbus winger Heinonen is a right-handed shooter and he's coming up on the left. He's dangerous. Crusher comes in on the strong side post, trying to stop him from cutting to the middle. He's got his stick out to take away the pass to the other winger, which I would have a hard time stopping. But it's also harder for that winger to shoot from his backhand.

I take all this in in seconds. I know the decision Crusher made on how to play this, but there's risk and reward to any decision. And I'm still trying to figure out how this happened.

Heinonen passes it. I slide to my left. But in a lightning-fast move, the winger passes it back to Heinonen. I move again but Crusher has not only failed to stop the pass, he's failed to stop Heinonen from cutting to the middle and shooting. I throw out my glove hand and spread my legs, but not fast enough. And he scores.

"Fuck!" I'm spreadeagled on the ice while Columbus celebrates around me.

I get up and hurl my stick across the ice.

Fuck, fuck, fuck. It's not Crusher's fault he was left all alone. My job is to stop the puck. And I didn't do it.

And it was a tied fucking game! Jesus!

I'm fucking pissed. And not just at myself. One of their other players, Ouellette, was pulling shit earlier, in a scrum in front of my net he fucking chopped my stick out of my hands. I got it back and the play moved away but he can't fucking do that.

Deep breaths. In. Out. In. Out. It doesn't matter what just happened, I have to be ready for the next time. Not fucking head tripping about what my life will be like without Tilly and Andi.

I'm a professional. I have to do this.

I fish the puck out of the net and shoot it toward the linesman. Then I go for a bit of a skate, centering myself. I've got this.

I still have that tightness in my chest. And my head throbs.

I've got this.

Moments later, Columbus controls the puck.

Ouellette is right in front of me, screening me, waiting for the puck. I'm still pissed about that goal, not to mention the other ten times Ouellette slashed me and the refs ignored it, and I whack the back of his legs with my stick.

Bad idea. Baaaad idea.

Ouellette turns around and crosschecks me. "What the fuck, asshole!"

"Fuck you!" I bellow. We both throw some wild punches and I take him to the ice, going down on top of him.

Mayhem ensues. Every player and every ref on the ice gather around us. I want to punch Ouellette, but he's down on the ice and I just can't do it. Fuck me.

A fight breaks out between Crusher and a Columbus player, and the refs immediately step in. Other guys are paired up, shoving and dancing and chirping.

Eventually, one of the refs drags me off Ouellette. I get to my feet. My mask is off. Sweat drips into my eyes. I grab my water bottle and squirt it in my face, breathing heavily.

Dilly skates up and taps my pad with his stick. "You okay?"

"Yeah." I set my jaw.

"He's been slashing you all night."

"Yep."

I have time to compose myself as the refs gather to confer on penalties. I end up with a slashing penalty and Ouellette gets two for crosschecking.

I have to be better. I need to be a machine. I can't let my emotions get the best of me.

I see every puck clearly. I am on angle, square, with perfect depth. My hands and feet move with speed and accuracy.

We're down by one goal. Coach pulls me near the end of the game for the extra attacker. I hustle to the bench and watch the guys control the play in the O zone.

I lean over the boards. "Come on, guys! Let's fucking go!"

Passing, passing, passing, waiting for a lane. And then a Columbus player intercepts a pass and he's off toward our empty net. Our guys make desperate attempts to stop him, but he shoots the puck and scores into the empty net.

I drop my head forward. Shiiiiit.

I drop onto the bench, sweaty and grouchy. Yeah, I'm definitely in Coach's bad books as we return to the dressing room. I'm in my own bad books, for Chrissake.

30

ANDI

Oh, boy. What does it mean?

I sit for a long time at my desk with my phone in my hand, thinking about Ford's message. Willa is back. Things will be sorted out. That's good.

Then why do I feel so gloomy? My limbs feel heavy. I just want to go to bed.

I don't know what Willa's going to want now. Will she just take Tilly and disappear again?

My heart hurts for Ford if that happens. He loves his daughter and he wants to be a father to her. Willa has to recognize that.

But I don't know her at all. She left her child with a stranger (albeit with a biological link), so I'm not convinced she has her child's best interests in mind. Or anyone else's for that matter. It's admirable that she went to care for her parents, but she was gone *months*. It wasn't fair to Ford to do that. Or to Tilly. So it won't be a surprise if she takes Tilly and goes.

And that will mean I no longer have a reason to help Ford.

I drop my phone and lean my head on my desk on folded

arms. I feel like the world is slowly spinning around me, and heaviness lodges in my stomach.

Things will go back to the way they were before. That's what Ford and I agreed on. He'll be my neighbor. My friend. I'll ask him to fix a leaky tap. He'll... well, he's never needed much from me before Tilly arrived.

I abandon any pretense of working and trudge to my bedroom. I lie down on the bed.

I think about my life before. I worked my ass off to get my consulting business going. I saw Elodie and my other friends sometimes. I went home with men sometimes. But holy crap, does that existence ever seem lonely now. Kind of like right after my divorce, when I was bereft and depressed and broken. Elodie said I can survive anything, because I survived that.

But right now, the excruciating emotions make me not so sure of that. It's crazy. Tilly is not my daughter. Ford is not my husband or even boyfriend, really. It should be *easier* to recover from losing them. So why does it hurt so much?

Hot tears slide from the corners of my eyes and into my hair. I let them flow. I let myself wallow in misery for a little while. But I can't do it for long, because Lieve is looking after Tilly and it's time to pick her up.

I wash my face with cold water and brush my hair, then go over to Ford's place.

"Hi!" I call to Lieve as I enter.

"Hi, Andi!"

"How's my girl?" I ask her, walking over to where Tilly is lying on her playmat with the little gym above her. She's batting at colorful plastic flowers and babbling away. Adorable.

"She's good today. Very happy." She gives me an update on feeds and diaper changes and sleep.

Tilly sees me and her babbles change and her arms reach out.

A hot softness fills my chest. "Hi, baby girl." I get down on the floor and reach for her. She knows now when we're going to pick her up. "Hi! Are you having fun?" I give her kisses and a little squeeze.

I look at Lieve. "I'll stay here for a bit, since she's having fun with this."

"Sounds good." Lieve stands and goes to get her coat and purse. "I'll see you tomorrow."

I play with Tilly, admiring her, trying to imprint her little features into my memory in case I don't have much time left with her. I'll probably see her again—Ford does live next door to me— but... I don't know how that's going to go. Ford and I might not even be friends anymore. I know we talked about it and said we could do that, but I didn't expect to fall in love with him. And I can't imagine seeing him on the reg as just a friend. What if he meets someone else? I don't think I could bear that.

I shake a rattling toy for Tilly and she grabs it away from me.

Maybe, if Ford and I are done with whatever this is, I should move away. A knife twists in my heart at that thought, but I also think about how hard it will be to see him, to see Tilly, if we're not even friends anymore. I'll look into real estate listings later and see what's out there.

When Tilly grows fussy, I pick her up. I was going to take her to my place for the night, but it's easier to just stay here. And I might only have a few nights left in Ford's bed. I change her and get her settled in her little cot. Then I slump on Ford's couch with my phone. The game doesn't start for a few hours yet. I shouldn't even watch it.

But I do.

It's a train wreck.

Mostly for Ford. What is up with him?

He jumps a guy! Everyone ends up fighting and Ford gets a penalty!

Does that mean he has to sit in the penalty box?

No, apparently not. Oh, another player sits there for him. He stays in goal. I don't know if that's fair but those are the rules.

Tilly wakes up and I'm pulled away from the game for a few minutes to change her diaper and get a bottle ready, but I settle on the couch to feed her and watch more. After that, I sit with her on the floor, making faces at her and playing peekaboo with her. And I watch the team lose when the other team scores into the empty net at the end of the game.

"Your daddy is not going to be happy about this," I say to Tilly, making her do little bicycle legs.

She squawks.

"I know." I make a face. "He lost his temper. I guess I understand it. He's probably as upset as I am." I look down at Tilly's face. She smiles.

I smile back. "I love you, niblet." My heart squeezes up so tight I can't breathe, and I blink back tears.

I search the TV screen for a glimpse of Ford, but the Storm disappear off the ice and the bench pretty damn quick. Will they interview him? I bet the media wants to ask him about that fight. So I keep watching.

It takes a little while but sure enough Ford does come out of the dressing room to talk to the media.

"Is that the kind of game you want to play?" one reporter asks.

"Are you fucking kidding me?" I shout at the TV. "Dumbass."

"Oh sure," Ford drawls. "I love getting penalties."

Oh, he's pissed.

The reporters don't seem to get it, though.

"I also love getting slashed ten times in a game," Ford adds.

Ohhhh.

"Is that one of your worst games this season?" another guy asks.

Ford pierces him with a glare. "I let in two goals," he snarls. "So, no."

Ouch.

"We're told you have a pretty strict regimen before every game. Did you deviate from that tonight?"

"What is this? Ask Me Anything? Look, this is the last place I want to be right now, talking to you. Next question."

I wince and watch the rest of the mercifully short interview with my bottom lip caught between my teeth.

"Don't worry, baby, he'll never talk to you that way." I cuddle Tilly. Or me, hopefully.

* * *

The next day I volunteer at Bright Side Animal Shelter. That's a good thing because the animals distract me from my morose mood. There's nothing better than puppy hugs and kisses to cheer you up.

On my way there, I stop at Bagelicious for caffeine and carbs. It's just around the corner from my place and I often pop down here to grab coffee. The barista hands me my flat white and I step aside to wait for my bagel to be toasted.

"Andi."

I turn at hearing my name. I blink. It's Trevor.

"Uh... hi."

He gives a tentative smile. "Hi. How are you?"

"I'm good..." I don't smile back at him. What's he doing here?

"You look great. I didn't get to tell you that night at the awards dinner, but I like the new hair."

"Uh... thanks." The cut and balayage highlights were done so long ago it doesn't seem new to me anymore.

"And congratulations, by the way. I'm sorry about how things went down that night."

"You're sorry?" I shake my head, confused.

"Yeah. Haven was..." He stops and rubs a hand over his mouth. "I guess I don't need to apologize on her behalf."

"I guess that's true."

My bagel's up so I move to the counter and take it from the girl with a smile. "Thanks."

When I turn back around, Trevor's still there, with a coffee in his hand. "Could we talk?" He indicates one of the small tables that's empty.

I'd rather scoop out my own eyeballs with a grapefruit spoon. "Why?"

His lips twist wryly. "I get it. You don't want to talk to me. But I have some things I'd like to talk to you about. If you'll listen."

I purse my lips. I should just walk out. But I say grudgingly, "Okay."

We sit and I unwrap my bagel. I study him as I take a bite and chew. He's still good-looking—deep brown eyes, perfect beard stubble, boyish smile. Once upon a time I was attracted to him. Now I just feel like he's... dishonest. Disloyal. Two-faced. "I guess you're not playing now."

"Nope. But only a few months until spring training."

"Right."

"I saw pictures of you at a hockey game with... is that Ford's baby?"

My head jerks back. Not what I expected. "Yes," I say slowly. "It's his baby."

"What were you doing there? What's going on?"

Answers flood my mind. But I want to be careful what I say.

Then again, it's Trevor. I certainly don't need to be concerned about his feelings. I might as well be honest. "You know Ford and I are friends."

He makes a face, with a little head shake, like *yeah, but that's ridiculous.*

I lower my chin and look up at him over my glasses. "He has a daughter he never knew about and I've been helping him look after her."

"Whoa. Weird."

"And... we've..." We... I've fallen in love. Ford hasn't. And Willa is back. So there's no point in telling Trevor that we've become more than friends. Because that's ending now. "Well, he needed some help, and I owed him."

His forehead puckers. "Wow." He sits back in his chair, holding his coffee cup in both hands on the table. His lip curls. "That is wild. You don't even like kids."

I just smile at that. "So wild," I say lightly. "Is that what you came here to talk to me about? Because—"

"Haven and I broke up."

Huh. I gulp my coffee. After I swallow, I say. "That's what you wanted to tell me? Why would you think I care?" My question is genuine—I don't care.

He sits back in his chair. "I... I don't know. I thought you might." He keeps his gaze focused on me.

Oh, no. No, no, no.

I exhale, take another sip of coffee, and say, "What happened with you and Haven?"

"She got pregnant."

My eyes widen. "Are you serious?"

"You must have noticed at the dinner that she was pregnant."

"Of course I did. I mean, are you serious that you broke up

with her because she's pregnant?" Incredulity makes my voice rise.

"You know I never wanted kids."

"I know, but... it happened. You're going to be a father, whether you like it or not." I gape at him. Would he renege on his parental responsibilities? Surely he's not *that* despicable?

"Yeah, I know. Don't worry, I'll support her and the kid. I just don't want to live that kind of life."

"What kind of life?" I ask slowly.

"You know. We talked about it. We always wanted our freedom. We were both focused on our careers."

I dip my chin in agreement.

"And babies cry a lot."

Was that a joke?

"They do," I agree, now with firsthand experience. But now... that doesn't really seem like enough of a reason to turn your back on your own child. I let out a breath and push the remainder of my bagel away. "I'm... surprised by this."

"I wanted you to know. In case... maybe..."

I stare at him. Holy shit. He wants to get back together. Are you fucking kidding me?

I may have wanted this, after we broke up. I may have fantasized about him coming to me and saying he made a terrible mistake and I'm the one he really wants. I could have that life I lost, the life I mourned after the divorce.

The one I now realize was hollow.

But now... I've lost again. I imagined myself with Ford and Tilly, the three of us a team, and now that's never going to happen. The ache in my chest is so profound I have to press the heel of my hand there.

I could go back to Trevor and try again.

"Trevor."

He nods.

"You are a jerkbag."

His mouth opens.

"A douchewagon. A dickweasel."

"Hey..."

I hold up a hand again. I never had a chance to let loose on him. "You used me. You betrayed me. You cheated on me with a friend. Who I worked with. That was a great job and I had to leave it. You're a self-absorbed, self-centered, lying, cheating bastard, and now I see on top of all that you're an irresponsible deadbeat. I would rather roll around naked in dog poop than get back together with you."

He regards me with narrowed eyes.

"And you know that's all true." I move my head slowly from side to side. "Now I know what it's like to be with a good man."

"You *are* fucking him, aren't you?" He curls his lip.

I ignore that and lean forward. "I don't know what happened with you and Haven, how that started, how it ended, what happened in between, but *you* got her pregnant and *you* have to deal with that. Man up, for God's sake. If you two can't work things out, fine, it's probably for the best, but you have responsi-bilities to her and to that child and you need to live up to them."

Apparently, he's speechless.

"It's true, I never wanted kids." My disgust with him ebbs. "It's true, I felt the same way—I wanted freedom. Freedom to have fun, to work hard, to do whatever I wanted whenever I wanted. Babies cry a lot, and they poop and puke and make life hard. And I totally understand anyone who makes the decision to not have children. It's personal and private and valid." Then I think of Tilly and her sweet little face, her infectious baby laugh, her joy when she sees me, and my heart swells so big in my chest I almost can't breathe. "But please, please, please, I beg you, get to know your child. Take responsibility. Give yourself the chance to fall in love with her. Or him. Maybe you can't. Maybe you really are too self-centered for that. But maybe you can. And maybe having that baby will teach you what love really is."

He stares at me.

I stand and pick up my uneaten bagel in the wrapper, then my coffee. "I don't want to see you ever again. Good luck."

I march out of the coffee shop. On the street, I pause. Holy shit. That was good!

I'm proud of myself. But I'm also alone. Again.

At the shelter, I take Atticus and Diva for a walk, bundled up against the chilly wind that's blowing today. I help Joe give another dog a bath, and I spend some time brushing Diego. Or attempting to. He's not thrilled about it, but the idea is to get him used to it, so I try.

And I think.

Thoughts keep cycling through my head and I'm not getting any clarity on how I should be handling this. I need to talk to my best friend.

* * *

Elodie comes over since I'm looking after Tilly tonight, arriving with a bottle of wine and a large pizza.

"Amazing," I say gratefully, taking the pizza box from her.

"Where's Tilly?"

"She's asleep right now." I check the time. "I'll wake her up in about half an hour."

"How's the sleep, wake, food schedule going?"

I laugh. "Eat, wake, sleep cycle."

"Whatever." She grins, following me to my kitchen. She pulls two wine glasses out of the cupboard, familiar with where they are, while I grab plates for our pizza.

"It's going really well, actually. She's less fussy because she doesn't sleep too long or stay awake too long and she's sleeping better at night, which is fantastic."

"I never thought I'd see you like this." She pours the wine.

"Me either." I make a face.

We take our pizza and wine into the living room to eat. After a couple of bites, I say, "I have some... news."

"What is it?"

I take a breath. "Tilly's mom is back."

Elodie's eyes widen and she lowers her pizza back to the plate. "What? Holy mother of cake."

"I know." I close my eyes briefly.

"What happened? Did you see her? Did Ford?"

"No. She wants to meet, but he's away until Sunday." I swallow thickly. "We don't know what she's going to say."

Elodie gets the dilemma quickly. "Oh, man. I'm sorry."

I give a quick nod. I relate Ford's message, which basically said nothing, and all my spiraling thoughts and emotions since then.

"I don't know if he'll want a relationship with me now that Willa is back and he won't likely have Tilly, at least full-time."

She eyes me. "You said you could do this."

"I thought I could." I scrunch up my face. "But I want more."

"Are you in love with him?"

I hesitate, then drop my head forward. "Yes."

"Oh, Andi." She reaches over and squeezes my hand.

"I should have known better. My judgment about men is flawed. Professional athletes are only concerned with themselves —with their careers and getting ahead."

"Like Trevor."

"Oh! I almost forgot! I ran into him today."

Her head jerks back. "Shut the front door. Really? Where?"

"At Bagelicious. I... think he was looking for me. He wanted to talk."

"He better not be fucking stalking you." She scowls.

"Yikes. I don't think so. I told him I never want to see him again."

"Whoa."

"Get this! He and Haven broke up!"

Her jaw drops.

I related the conversation I had with him.

"Wow," she says slowly. "That's wild. Didn't I say that, though? He's such a shithead. It's karma."

"Right?"

She takes a gulp of her wine. "You think Ford is like that, too."

"He's been very clear his priority is his career."

"It sounds like that's changed, though."

Then I tell her about the game last night. "If he was distracted about Tilly, that's really bad. He can't be happy about that."

"Hmmm."

"I have to admit, he's really made Tilly the priority."

Elodie shakes her head. "You should see the look on your face."

I blink. "What?"

"Like you're in love."

I drop my head forward.

"Andi. Think about it. Is Ford really like Trevor?"

I know the answer immediately. I don't have to think about it. Ford is nothing like Trevor. They are both professional athletes and dedicated to their sport. But that's it. Ford was there for me as a friend, even before we started sleeping together. He went to the awards dinner with me. He went for a beer with a friend so he could talk about his grief. His teammates love him and respect him. He changed his whole life for his daughter, rather than reneging on his responsibilities to her—unlike Trevor.

He's a good man.

"No." I screw up my face. "No, he's not like Trevor at all. But it's probably best if things end between us once Tilly's gone. He won't need me anymore. I can get back to normal. It's been tough running a business and looking after a baby."

"Many people do it," Elodie says dryly.

"I know, I know. We got through it." I tell her about my misgivings about seeing Ford and being "just friends" and maybe seeing Tilly once in a while in passing. As I talk, my voice catches and I try to breathe around the emotion swelling from my chest into my throat. "I don't think I can stand that."

She looks at me with sympathy. "I get that."

"I think I'll move."

"Whaaat!"

I nod. "Oh. I have to wake up Tilly." I wipe my fingers on a paper napkin. "I'll be right back."

I hurry into her room and gently rouse her. When she beams a smile up at me, I almost burst into tears. This is killing me.

I talk and sing to her as I change her diaper, and she watches my face intently in that wise way she has. When she's dressed again, I carry her out to the kitchen to get her a bottle and then rejoin Elodie. "Here she is! The big girl's awake."

"Hi, Tilly." Elodie leans over. "Remember me? No? That's okay." She sighs as if deeply offended.

As I feed Tilly, we resume our conversation. "So, yeah, I looked at condos for sale last night. I found a few things I like. And they're pet friendly! I could adopt a dog from the shelter."

"Are you sure Ford isn't going to want to continue things with you?"

"No." I drop my gaze to Tilly. "But I'm afraid to hope for that."

"That amazing date he took you on had to mean something."

"I thought so, too. But he never said anything. I keep thinking maybe this will be a relief for him—to get more time back, to get his focus back. He's worked so hard to improve his game. He hasn't been playing his best and I know it bothers him."

"Right."

"But then I think about how much he loves Tilly now. He doesn't want to lose her entirely. His dad told him to talk to a lawyer about it, and he has that positive DNA test, so it seems likely he'd be able to get at least partial custody."

We hash things out until we're going over the same stuff again. And there's no point in talking about it anymore. I won't know what's going on until Ford comes home. But I'm going to be prepared. I'll have a plan for moving on with my life.

I'm stronger than I was before. I can handle this. I can be sad and heartbroken and also proud of myself and confident that I can still live my best life, however it turns out.

I just might need a little time to get over the heartbroken part of that.

I pat Tilly's back until she burps because I can't break that practice and then we play with her on the floor.

"How's your Christmas shopping coming along?" I ask Elodie. "Are you going to your parents?"

"Yeah. On the 24th. What about you?"

"I hadn't planned to go home for Christmas," I say slowly. "I don't know why. But now, I kind of want to. I want to see Mom and Dad and Daisy. I can go for as long as I want, since I'll be unencumbered. If I have to do some work while there, that's fine." I remember my own shopping the other day. "I already bought Ford and Tilly Christmas presents," I say sadly. "I think they'll like them."

Not surprisingly, Bender gets the start in the next game. And we win. At the end of the game I go onto the ice and follow the other guys as they line up to bump helmets with Bender to celebrate the win. I throw my arms out and give him a hug. "Fantastic game. Way to pump up the guys and turn things around."

"Thanks, man."

I'm hoping to start the third game of our road trip but that doesn't happen. I'm pissed, but resigned. I don't deserve it after that game in Columbus. And I'm happy when we get another win and Bender gets a shutout.

This isn't what I planned for this year, though.

Well, none of it is. Did I plan to have a daughter? Did I plan to fall in love?

Sitting on the bus in the dark going back to the hotel, I go very still. What? *Love?*

My heart starts knocking in my chest, fast enough to steal my breath. My head goes empty. I shove a hand through my hair and look out the window.

Holy shit. I feel like the bus is closing in on me. I need to get off. My head whips around in a panic.

"What?" Dilly, sitting beside me, gives me a weird look. "Are you okay?"

"No. I'm fucked."

"Yeah." He sighs.

He has no idea what's going on.

As we get off the bus at the hotel, some of the guys are making a plan to go out. We don't fly home until morning. "Coming, Archie?" Crusher calls to me.

Fuck it. I need a drink. Or ten. So I tag along with them to Atlas, an EMD club on George Street.

It's Saturday night and the place is jumping. Pumping music, light shows, a full-wall video screen, packed with people. We get shown to a private booth in the back where it's quieter. We order drinks and take in the high-tech ambience.

I sit back in my chair and down my drink, then order another. I'm well into the second before Crusher says to me, "You're quiet."

"Yeah." I shrug.

"You sulking?"

I scowl at him. "Sulking? Fuck off. I don't sulk."

"What's wrong, then?"

After a beat, I say, "I'm the only one who doesn't have a goal song."

Every player on the team picks a goal song that's played in our home arena when they score.

The others stare back at me, then start laughing.

"I want a goal song," I add, sounding like a cranky kid being told he can't have candy before dinner.

"You're a goalie," Benny says.

"Thank you, Captain Obvious."

He narrows his eyes at me.

"Start scoring goals and we'll get you your own goal song," Smitty jokes.

I've never scored a goal. But it happens. I'd like to score a goal. Goalie goals are cool. "If I ever get to play again, I'll try that."

"You *are* sulking." Crusher shakes his head.

I give him a black look.

"Bruh," Dilly says. "Get it all the way together."

"It's not like you to be so emo over a loss." Benny watches me.

"It's not just the loss. I fucked up. And I didn't play, two games in a row."

"That's happened before," Benny points out.

"Yeah, well..." I don't know where I'm going with this. I flag our server and order another drink.

"It's also not like you to drink this much." Smitty's eyebrows shoot up.

He's right. I shrug, lifting my empty glass. "Let's get fucked up."

They all exchange glances.

"What is going on with you?" Smitty asks. "For real."

I rub my forehead. "I heard from Willa."

"Oh, shit." Benny stares at me. "What did she say? Is she back?"

"Yeah. She's back. I'm going to see her... fuck... tomorrow."

"Jesus." Benny makes a face. "So is she going to take Tilly back?"

"I don't know. But yeah, I expect so." A corkscrew twists into my chest. Oh, fuck me sideways with a cheese grater, I can't cry in front of these guys. I grab Crusher's drink and swallow another mouthful of bourbon.

"Okay, you have rights," Smitty says. "You're her father."

"I know. I talked to a lawyer about it."

"So you want to keep her?" Crusher asks.

"Hell, yeah." I glare at him. Then I slump. "But, obviously, I won't be able to keep her full-time. I don't know how this is going to go. And then..." I stop.

"What?" Benny prompts.

"Never mind."

"Hell, no, tell us what you were going to say," Crusher pushes me. "How can we help you if we don't know what's bugging you?"

"I don't need help."

They all make derisive noises. "Dude. You definitely need help. You were not yourself in that game in Columbus and you've been moping this whole trip," Smitty says.

"We know you have a temper, but that was extra," Dilly adds.

"And you usually don't let things get you down once you've smashed a stick or whatever," Crusher puts in.

I stare into the amber liquid in the glass. "I miss them."

"Miss... who?" Crusher asks.

"Tilly and Andi."

"Andi," Crusher replies. "We're getting somewhere."

"You two are obviously more than friends now," Benny says. "I saw you after that date. You could have set my condo on fire with the heat you two were generating."

"You took her on a date?" Crusher asks. "Okay." He rubs his hands together. "Now we're cooking with gas."

I scowl at him.

"This can't be just because you miss them," Smitty says.

"I miss Mabel and *I'm* not crying into my bourbon," Benny adds.

"That's my bourbon," Crusher corrects him.

I roll my eyes. "It's not that exactly. It's the fact that I miss them that makes me realize how fucked I am."

"Explain," Dilly says.

I don't know if I can. I was already confused and my head's feeling a little woolly. I heave a sigh. "Willa's going to want Tilly back. Even if I tell her I want partial custody, she doesn't have to agree to that right now. So Tilly's gone. But I'll fight for her." I set my jaw and look up at my friends. "And I'll get her back. Even just part-time. I'm not letting her go now that I know her. Know of her."

They all nod.

"But Andi..." I drop my head again, shaking it.

They all wait.

"Here's the problem." I look up at them. "She doesn't want kids."

I get perplexed looks from all of them.

"I..." I point at my own chest. "...have a kid."

"Right."

"So you think she doesn't want anything long term with you because you have a kid?" Benny asks.

"Obviously." I nod, pain building behind my ribs. "She doesn't want kids. Why would she want to be with a guy who has a kid?"

"Dude. She's been helping you look after Tilly for months," Benny says. "She loves Tilly."

Yeah. She does. She couldn't take care of her and interact with her with such tenderness and affection and thoughtfulness if she didn't love her. "But that's not her kid. She can leave Tilly and go home and not worry about her." Like she did the other night. "I think she's ready to get back to her normal life. And I get that."

"So... if you didn't have a kid, would you still want Andi in your life?" Smitty asks.

I gape at him. "Fuck, yeah."

One corner of Smitty's mouth lifts. "That didn't take long."

"Not just as a babysitter," Benny adds.

"Fuck, no!" I scowl.

"And not just a fuck buddy?" Dilly asks.

"No!" My heart is banging against my sternum. "But..."

"Another but," Dilly says with a longsuffering exhalation. "Tell us."

"Even if she's okay with me having a kid, which I guess... I don't know, I think she does love Tilly, but... we agreed we would just be bang buddies. No commitment."

"She went on that date with you," Benny points out.

"True." I wanted to show her she's special and important to me. "But on the way home she got weird. Quiet."

"Huh."

"I probably went overboard with the date," I say glumly. "Since we're supposed to be fuck buddies."

"Hmmm." Benny shrugs.

"I know I'm an oddball." I turn my glass in my hand. "Relationships aren't for people like me. I'm wrapped up in my own life. Hockey takes a lot of time and commitment."

"Oh, yeah, that's why all hockey players are single," Benny says.

"Sarcasm." I lift my glass to him. "Point taken."

"You're not that wrapped up in your own life." Smitty's forehead furrows. "You took on a baby. You didn't have to do that."

"I didn't have much choice."

"Sure, you did. You could've given Willa a pile of money and sent her on her way."

"I never even thought of doing that."

"See?"

"Even so, I'm better off alone."

"You're not alone, man." Benny shakes his head. "You have us. We're a team."

"I'm alone in that net."

They all give me incredulous looks.

"What the fuck?" Benny demands. "What does that mean?"

"It's true. It's the life of a goalie. Nobody else to blame when I screw up."

"How the *fuck* did you make it this far in hockey without knowing you have a whole team backing you up?" Benny nearly shouts.

My eyes shift. "Uh…"

"Sure, you may be alone in net. But what you face depends a lot on how we play in front of you," Smitty says. "When we play shitty, *we* let *you* down."

"And you're not always alone. The other night when you were out of position and they got the puck, *I* made a save," Crusher says. "I got your back. That's my job."

"Also, you and Bender are a team," Dilly points out. "You always congratulate him on a win, and when he plays well. You always help him during practices. And he supports you, too. You two challenge each other and make each other better."

Another valid argument. I'm starting to feel like an idiot.

"I'm set in my ways," I mumble. "Too regimented. I like routine."

They all nod.

"But you're not uncoachable," Smitty says, reminding me of that conversation we had. "On the ice, anyway. Off the ice… maybe you are."

I rub my forehead, thinking. *Open to doing things differently… changing up a routine… willing to learn…* "It pissed me off at first, when Tilly came. I couldn't stick to my schedule. I couldn't go to taekwondo classes, or meditate. I felt like I was losing control of my life. But after a while... she was more important than that."

"There you go." Smitty nods. "If you're trying to use that as a reason why Andi wouldn't want to be with you, fuck that."

I toss back another swallow of bourbon, and I'm silent for a few minutes. Finally, I say, "So what am I supposed to do? Just give them both up and... and..." My throat clogs and my jaw aches from grinding my back teeth together.

"Hell, no." Smitty nods. "You're going to fight for Tilly. You have to fight for Andi, too."

"How?"

"Just tell her how you feel." Smitty waves a hand.

"I'd rather remove my own spleen with a hockey skate," I mumble.

"I never said it was easy." He grimaces. "But you have to. Otherwise you'll never really know how she feels."

"That seems... logical." But this idea strikes terror into my heart. Because it's becoming even more clear what my biggest fear really is. Yeah, I'm afraid of losing them. But I'm terrified of putting myself out there... admitting I need someone. I'm terrified she'll reject me. Because I'm not worth loving.

But these guys... they've tried to show me that maybe I am worth it. That I'm not too selfish for someone to love. That I don't have to be alone.

Be the shark.

"What?"

Oh, shit. I guess I said that out loud? I swallow. "You can be the shark and rule the ocean, or you can be a goldfish and wait for fish food in the fishbowl."

They all regard me with bewildered expressions again.

Then Benny laughs. "That's brilliant. There you go. Be the fucking shark. The great white. Go after what you want."

"Yeah." I lift my chin and push my shoulders back. I'm wasted, but determination calms me. Focuses me. I've spent my whole life going after what I want. I'm not stopping now. Not when the most important thing in my life is on the line...

Love.

32

ANDI

I'm in Ford's kitchen, getting things ready for his week. I've checked his schedule and know what days he has games and practices. I've looked at his planner and know he has a visit to a children's hospital on Wednesday afternoon. I've texted all that to Lieve. I've cooked a big batch of quinoa that he can use for meals, and I've cut up a lot of healthy veggies for roasting, for game days.

All the while, there's a hard pulse in my stomach and a massive fissure in my chest.

Tilly's on the floor nearby, sitting in her baby seat, playing with toys and squealing at a high pitch. She's dressed in a little blue dress so she looks nice for her dad when he gets home. I look over at her. I don't know what's happening. Should I pack up her things?

The pressure behind my eyes intensifies as I move across the room and look at all her toys and books. I pick up one of several diaper bags and begin filling it with her favorite toys. Then I move to the bedroom to gather some of her lotions and shampoos, wipes and diaper rash cream. I pick up her little hair-brush... and that's when I break down.

I sit on the bed with the hairbrush in my hands, tears running down my cheeks. I have to get a grip. I have to be strong.

"I'm going to miss you so much," I sob aloud, swiping at tears.

I know this has to happen. It's Tilly's mother. I was angry for Tilly when Willa left her here. She needs her mother. I'll miss her, but I'll survive. I have to let her go so she can have what she really needs. I need to be strong and handle this like a big girl.

But God, it *hurts*.

Images churn through my mind, so many of Tilly: her laughing, smiling, babbling—the adorable way she grabs the toes of both feet. Her splashing in the tub, trying to roll over and then doing it, falling over when she first started sitting. Ford with his hand under her butt holding her up in the air with one hand to stop her crying. Wrapping her in a blanket by rolling her over rather than wrapping the blanket around her. Singing "Baby Shark" to her in a completely off-tone, high-pitched voice and her cracking up.

Another sob escapes my lips.

But I have those memories. I will always have them and I'll always be grateful for the time I had with her. Getting to know Tilly has changed me. And the most important thing is for her to be happy and healthy and loved.

Tilly is getting louder and protesting being alone, so I get up and go back to the living room. I sit down on the floor in front of her and smile through my tears. "I love you, Tilly. I'll miss you so much. But I want you to be happy. I want that most of all."

The door opens and closes.

My head whips around. It's too early for Ford to be back.

But it's him. He walks in, handsome as always—other than the lines of strain on his face—stylish in black pants and a black and white tweed coat. When he sees Tilly and me, his strained expression softens, and his lips quirk. "Hi."

Then he notices my wet face. The smile disappears, his forehead creasing, his eyes shadowing, and he strides toward us and crouches down.

"What's wrong?" he demands. "Why are you crying?"

I slide the back of my hand across my cheek. "I'm sorry. I don't know. I just started crying and I c-can't stop."

"What's wrong?" He sets his hands on my shoulders.

I cry harder.

"Badadadaba!" Tilly cries.

With a frustrated smile, he turns and reaches for her, lifting her out of the seat. "Hi, baby girl. Did you miss me?" He stands, holding her up in front of his face. She babbles happily. Then he cuddles her against him and closes his eyes. "I love you, Tilly. More than I ever thought I could."

Heat and light expand in my chest, a glowing fullness.

"Gabadada aaaaaayeeee."

"I missed you, too. Can I talk to Andi for a minute?"

She makes a gurgling noise.

"Thanks."

I push to my feet. Ford sits on the couch, Tilly on his lap, and I sit next to them, trying to act like I haven't just bawled my eyes out.

"I've never seen you cry," he says to me, appearing distressed. "I don't like it."

"I'm sorry."

"Tell me what's wrong."

"What do you *think* is wrong?" I cry.

"Jesus." He swallows. "Okay. I know."

He doesn't know all the reasons I'm crying.

"I just..." I hiccup. "I just was thinking about what's going to happen and... I..."

"What?" He smooths his thumb along my wet cheekbone. "Tell me. Please."

"I don't know what's going to happen, but I know I'm going to miss Tilly." And I sob again.

He stares at me. "Yeah?"

I bob my head, feeling my lips push out. "I started packing some of her things. I don't know if you'll take her with you? Or take her things? Or... have you already seen Willa?"

"No. I haven't seen her. Andi..." He stops. "You really care about her."

"Of course I care about her!" My voice rises as my emotions surge. Does he not know that? I lift my gaze to his face and he watches me closely, an anxious expression on his face. But also... his eyes light up with... something.

"Andi..."

Fuck it. I'm just going to tell him. "I know I have n-no right, but... but I love Tilly. And I love you."

His eyes widen.

My heart is galloping faster than a racehorse and my hands are shaking. "I thought I could do it. I thought I could be friends with bennies. But I fell in love with you." And I sob again.

Tilly stretches an arm out to me, wiggling her fingers, her forehead creased.

I take her hand and smile at her. "I'm okay, honey bunny." I kiss her fingers.

Ford's mouth opens and that light in his eyes glow brighter. "Did you say... you love me?" He gazes into my eyes and I stare back, sinking into that clear green almost as if I'm falling through cool sea water.

"Yes," I whisper. "I'm sorry. I know that wasn't our agreement... but I fell in love with you. Both of you."

"Don't apologize." He closes his eyes, his mouth tightening briefly. "Do not apologize for that." He opens his eyes and focuses on me. "Because I'm in love with you, too."

My heart is beating so loud I can't hear anything but that. Did he really just say that?

"I love you," he says again, a rough edge to his voice, and as I search his face, I see the hint of strain in the corners of his eyes. His hand on my cheek trembles ever so slightly.

"Oh." My pulse races, my head helium-light. "Oh."

The corners of his mouth lift. "Yeah." Now a thumb brushes over my lips. "But..." His Adam's apple rises and falls. "But Andi... I have Tilly. I'm not going to let her go. Are you okay with that?"

My eyebrows slope down and my mouth opens but nothing comes out. Finally, I manage to whisper, "I don't understand that. I love you. And I love Tilly."

"You said you didn't want kids. You and Trevor agreed to that. But I have a kid."

Ohhhhh. My heart expands. "Ford." I hold the eye contact. "I love you. And I love her. I know she has to be with her mother and I want her to be happy and loved. But she needs her dad just like she needs her mom. I'll support you whatever you want to do. I'll help you fight for her."

He nods, still looking apprehensive. "I would understand if you wanted to go back to your regular life."

I tilt my head, pressure building behind my eyes again. "I don't want that."

The relief that flows over his face is incandescent. His eyes blaze and his mouth curves into a smile. "You are so fucking perfect."

One corner of my mouth lifts. "Hardly."

"Perfect for me." He lowers his head to kiss me. When his lips touch mine, I open for him. The kiss is long and deep and achingly sweet.

This is really happening. He loves me, too. Joy pours through me, lightening my limbs, warming my soul.

We draw apart, but only inches. I can see the darker green ring around his irises, his thick eyelashes, the tiny mole at the outer corner of his left eye. We sit like that for a moment, just looking. I touch my fingertips to his face and he cups my jaw with one hand.

"I haven't seen Willa," he finally says. "I wanted to come here first, because I wanted to tell you how I feel about you. Because I wanted you to know that before I go see Willa. Because whatever happens... even if Willa wants full custody of Tilly and I have to give her back and fight for her... I love you and I want you in my life."

A smile quivers on my lips. "I was so afraid... I was sure that without Tilly here, we had no future together. You wouldn't need me."

"I need you," he says in a low voice. "I need *you*. Not to look after Tilly. I need you for me. I need your optimism. Your wisdom. Your sense of humor and how you never give up. Don't ever change that." He holds my gaze steadily. "Once you said your optimism might be a weakness, but I disagree. It's a strength. And your loyalty. I love that about you."

My heart nearly explodes in my chest.

"I need you in my life to open my eyes to the whole world outside of hockey. I always told myself I didn't need anyone else. But you and Tilly both showed me I do. I never knew how much I could love someone. Sometimes it hurts, I love you so much."

I blink wet eyelashes at him, nodding. "I kept thinking about our agreement. You said you didn't want a relationship. I was afraid to admit I wanted more than just screwing around."

He closes his eyes as if in pain. "I've always been on my own. I didn't want to rely on anyone else. I was a selfish dick."

I make a noise in my throat and shake my head.

"Yeah, I was. Still am. But I'm working on it." He holds my gaze steadily. "I was so focused on being a better goaltender. But now I want to be a better man. For you. And a better father. For Tilly."

My heart turns over in my chest and the corners of my eyes sting. I don't want to cry again. I'm already a mess.

"I have so much more to tell you. But I have to go see Willa. We'll talk later."

"Okay." I'm still scared about what's going to happen. But Ford and I will be together no matter what. We can do it— together. "Are you taking Tilly?"

"Yeah. Willa asked me to bring her."

My stomach plunges all the way to my toes. "Will you leave her with Willa?"

"We didn't discuss that. But no. Not today." His jaw hardens. "We'll figure out a plan for that."

"Okay. Let's get her ready. She probably needs a diaper change."

"Yeah. I'll do it. Come on, little girl."

He carries her into her room and I almost lose it, but I have to keep it together. I yank stuff out of the diaper bag and then repack it with things they'll need for the afternoon. I pick up her favorite bunny stuffy and add it into the bag.

When Ford comes back, he hands Tilly to me. I smile down at her. Thank God for all those pictures on my phone. She's so beautiful and perfect. She smiles back at me. "I love you, Tilly. So much." I give her a gentle squeeze. "You go see your mom. She loves you, too."

We get her into her jacket and a hat, buckle her into the car seat, and Ford picks it up.

My eyes are wet, but I'm keeping my head up and my spine straight. "Good luck."

"Thanks. I love you." He kisses me again, soft and warm and heartening.

"I love you, too." I want to say it over and over. Later I'll do that. "I'm here for you."

Because as much as I'm devastated by the thought of losing her... it has to be way worse for Ford. He's her father. This could destroy him.

When they're gone, I wrap my arms around my middle and turn in a circle, lost.

Rise above the storm and you will find the sunshine.

I believe in those words. I try to live those words. But right now, it's fucking hard.

33

FORD

Willa sent me her address and my GPS guides me to Newark. As I'm driving slowly down Broadway, I'm not sure if I'm in the right place. This is a hospital. I don't see the number I'm looking for, so I have to go around the block, and the second time around I realize there's a smaller building on the hospital grounds. I pull into a parking lot.

I'm not getting a good feeling.

A sign on the building says *Dorothy's House*. Whoever Dorothy is.

I walk into a foyer with a reception desk. "Hi. I'm here to see Willa Callahan."

The woman nods. "Ford?"

"Yes."

"Willa's in room E10. That's in the east wing." She gestures at double doors and I walk through them into a big lounge that feels like an expensive ski lodge—lots of wood, a big brick fireplace, and different arrangements of comfortable furniture. A few people are gathered together, and voices come from a room on one side that appears to be a dining room. I follow the sign for the east wing and carry Tilly down the carpeted hallway to yet another lounge, smaller but with the same ambience—comfortable and homelike. A kitchenette takes up one wall, a big TV another, and several doors open off it.

My eyes pass over the woman sitting at a table without recognition, but then it sinks in, and I jerk my gaze back to her. Willa.

Jesus.

I'm frozen. I can't move. I can't think.

She's wearing a scarf on her head, clearly because she has no hair. Her face is different—cheeks hollowed, her skin pale, almost translucent. She's so thin and fragile looking.

"Ford." She smiles. "Come here. I want to see my baby."

I force my feet to move. I set the baby carrier on the table and unfasten Tilly. She's asleep and her little lips pout as I disturb her. "Wake up, Tilly," I say gently.

"Tilly?"

"Yeah." I cough. "That what we've... I've... been calling her."

"It's cute. Hi, honey." Her voice rises and she reaches for Tilly. "Oh my God, I've missed you so much."

Tilly fusses and lets out a squawk as Willa cuddles her.

"It's okay, Tilly." I reach over and rub her back. "This is your mom."

Willa holds Tilly away from her to study her, still smiling. "Are you still a grouch when you wake up?"

"She can be, yeah."

I pull out another chair at the table and sit. My stomach is hard as a rock and my heart is thudding rapidly.

"Look how big you are!" Willa sets Tilly on the table in front of her, still holding her. Tilly eyes her, at first with a small notch between her eyebrows, then with a less skeptical look. "Tell me about her. What things is she doing?"

I fill Willa in on Tilly's milestones. When Willa wipes some drool from Tilly's chin, I add, "And she's teething."

"Are you getting teeth? Are you?" Willa coos and smiles at her.

This is surreal, watching Willa with her baby, me telling her about milestones. My brain is still reeling from this whole situation.

Willa glances up at me. "I guess you have questions."

I make a helpless gesture.

"I know." She makes a face. "This all really, really sucks." Her voice catches. "Obviously you can see I'm sick."

I nod, a hockey puck now stuck in my throat.

"I'm not going to get better," she continues softly. "This is a palliative care facility. There's nothing more they can do for me other than manage my pain. I might still have months left... but we don't know... and I didn't want to leave it too long." She pauses and clears her throat. "I wanted to see Matilda one more time and also explain everything to you."

"God, Willa. I'm so sorry."

She nods. "I've come to terms with it. It's been a really long haul. I fought so hard. For Matilda." She stops again and looks at Tilly, getting control. "I'm sorry, baby. I tried really hard for you."

My nose stings and my eyes burn. Jesus.

"I'm sorry for how I handled this," she says. "I lied to you."

"Your parents...?"

"My mom passed away years ago from Covid. My dad... I never really knew. He lives in California. They were an excuse. I couldn't deal with the treatment I was having and look after Tilly. I thought you would be the best one to take her. I did plan to tell you about her... but my life got off course. And I hoped that I'd get through this and come back for her." She looks up at me, her eyes full of anguish. "I know we didn't know each other well, but I liked you. My gut told me that you would look after her."

"I didn't want her," I say hoarsely. "At first. I'm ashamed of that now. Willa... I want you to know that I love her so much."

"I'm so glad." Her smile is sad. "But how could you not?"

I attempt a smile, too. "Right?"

"I saw pictures of you and Tilly online. At one of your games. It was so cute seeing you and Tilly at the glass. Was that your girlfriend with her?"

"Yes. Andi."

"You all looked so happy. When I saw that, I knew... I made the right decision."

Jesus. I cough. "Andi loves Tilly, too."

"Thank you for telling me that."

I'm disintegrating. Unraveling. I pull in a deep breath, trying to hold it together.

"I have some things to go over with you," Willa says, gesturing to a box and some papers on the table. "Some legal things. I've taken care of everything."

"Okay." I slide the box over closer to us with shaking hands.

* * *

A few hours later, I walk out with Tilly. And yeah... there are tears on my face. I cannot imagine the strength it must have taken Willa to do all this. Her story ripped a huge hole in my gut.

I get Tilly buckled in and I sit in the driver's seat for a long time, staring sightlessly out of the window. My hands clench into fists and I close my eyes, everything inside me burning and raw.

Tilly's annoyed cries penetrate my fog of misery.

I turn around. "What's wrong, niblet? You want to get home?"

Willa just gave her a bottle and I changed her diaper before we left. I think she's just antsy sitting in the stationary car. I start the engine.

I'll have to tell Andi about this. It's not going to be easy. But fuck... again, Willa had the guts to do it. So can I. We're doing it for Tilly.

I'll do anything for Tilly. And I'm in awe of Willa's love that she took these steps, in her situation. My annoyance with her and how she showed up out of the blue has evaporated. I can only imagine the agony she went through coming to that decision.

I'll do anything for Tilly... and for Andi. The knowledge that Andi loves me and is waiting for me gives me strength.

I think about these things all the way home. Dread forms a knot in my stomach as I carry Tilly and the box of items Willa gave me up the elevator to my place. I assume Andi's still here, and she is, cleaning in the kitchen.

She looks up as we walk in, then drops the kitchen towel on the counter and moves toward us, wide-eyed. "Are you okay?"

I must look like a ghoul. I set sleeping Tilly on the floor in her car seat, lower the box to the floor next to her, and step into Andi's embrace. I bury my face against her hair, closing my eyes against the smart of tears, the agony of a knife turning in my gut. Sobs overtake me and I shake against Andi. We cling to each other for endless moments.

"Shhh." She runs her hands over me, holds me tighter. "It's okay. You're here. I'm here. Tilly's here."

I give a mute nod, embarrassed but helpless.

"I love you," she whispers, kissing my jaw. "I love you. I've got you."

My chest shudders. I try to breathe, holding Andi tighter.

I thought I didn't need anyone else. But I was so, so wrong.

"We need to sit down," I say, my voice husky. "And I really need a drink."

When we're seated in the living room with glasses of bourbon in hand, Andi says, "We should wake up Tilly. This'll throw her off schedule."

I look at her and give her an unhappy smile. "You know what? There are worse things than getting off schedule. Let her sleep."

Andi's eyes are soft and warm as she nods. "Okay."

I tell her about Willa, choking out the words, dashing a couple more tears from my face. Andi listens, covering her mouth at one point, closing her eyes at another.

"She postponed some of her cancer treatment because she was pregnant." I can barely say the words through the gravel in my throat. "I... she was worried about how it could affect Tilly."

"Oh no." She covers her mouth, eyes big and shiny. "What if that..."

"She didn't say that made a difference in her recovery. I didn't want to ask. But holy shit."

Andi is silent for a moment, then says, "She has no other family?"

"She said a few cousins that she doesn't know."

Andi nods.

"She gave me these things." I rise and retrieve the box from the foyer. I set it on the coffee table and lift the lid. "These are legal papers, giving me full custody. Tilly's birth certificate."

"Ohhhh." Andi sighs out the word. "Oh my God."

"This..." I pick up a sealed envelope. "This is for Tilly. It's a letter from Willa. She said she leaves it up to me to decide the right time she should have it."

Now Andi's eyes are wet. She snags a tissue from a box nearby.

"And she wants Tilly to have these things. I didn't look at what's in here."

I pull out a small teddy bear, a simple one for a newborn.

Then a smaller box. When I open it, there's jewelry there—some gold necklaces, a birthstone ring, a pair of diamond earrings. It's not much, but that makes it even sadder.

There's a book called *Your Story*, and when I open it, there are pictures of Tilly, and Willa has written in her weight and length at birth, one month, two months, and little stories about Tilly. Jesus, this is killing me.

There are baby clothes, again tiny newborn ones—a couple of dresses, a onesie, a pair of impossibly small socks. I hold up a thumb drive and meet Andi's eyes.

"We can see what's on it," she says. "I'll get your laptop."

As she does that, I lift out a photo album. I open it to see pictures carefully labeled with names and dates. When Andi sits down again, she peers at it too. "That's Willa's mother."

"Yes." I flip the page. There are pictures of Willa as a child, a teenager, an adult, some with friends, some alone.

"This will be wonderful for Tilly to have," Andi says softly.

"Yeah."

We check out the thumb drive and find more pictures—baby pictures of Tilly, taken with Willa's phone—in the hospital when she was born, when she was weeks old, then months. And then they stop.

Andi sniffles, then blows her nose into the tissue.

This is fucking torture.

34

ANDI

It's too much.

My chest burns, anguish squeezing my lungs as I listen to Ford tell me about Tilly's mother. I've never met this woman but I am gutted by what she has gone through. Is still going through. I can't even imagine the pain she endured today, seeing her baby again and knowing it's for the last time. I am wrecked for Tilly and how she knew her mother for such a short time, for how she will never see her again. And then looking at the things she saved for Tilly and the pictures and the letter she wrote—clearly Willa wants Tilly to know her.

There's a book like the one I saw in the store that day, with the missing pieces from Tilly's first months. And it's all packed into a pretty storage box with pink flowers on it, like the ones you buy at Michael's.

It's all too much.

The tears keep flowing and I can't stop them. Pressing a hand to my stomach, I rise to my feet.

I look at Tilly's sweet, round face, her perfect lips, the tiny blue veins on her eyelids. I'm swamped with such a fierce, protective love it's painful. "I'm so sorry, baby." I swipe ineffectually at my wet face.

I turn to Ford. His eyes are red, his misery evident on his face. "I can't do this," I sob.

"I know. It's so fucked up."

"I mean, I really can't do this."

His eyebrows pull together. "Andi..."

I shake my head, my heart lodged painfully in my throat, making it difficult to squeeze air into my lungs. "It's too much. I can't handle it. I have to go."

His mouth falls open. "Andi—"

But I'm fleeing, my feet carrying my numb legs across the room. I almost leave without my key, and I pause to scoop it up from the table at the door, then dash out.

I just have to make it to my own apartment. Then I can fall apart. Then I can hate myself and hate this fucking world that allows such horrible things to happen to people who don't deserve it. Like innocent babies. And mothers.

I slam the door shut behind me, stumble to my bedroom, and plant myself face down on the bed. I let out the sobs that I've been trying to hold back, crying until I'm exhausted and limp. I know I'm freaking out. I can't help it. I was trying to be strong for Tilly but I guess I'm not that strong.

I fall asleep for a while.

I wake up in the dark. My eyes are gritty. I feel like I've been run over by a Zamboni.

I roll onto my back and stare up at the ceiling to think about everything.

The sick feeling in my stomach is guilt. So much guilt.

I judged Willa so harshly and unfairly. I thought she abandoned her baby. I was angry at her. I thought she didn't deserve Tilly.

I hate myself for that.

She made the biggest sacrifice possible for her daughter. And made sure her daughter was going to be looked after when she was gone. The selflessness of her love for Tilly overwhelms me.

I don't have that in me. I told Ford I'd be there for him no matter what, but now he's going to be a full-time father, forever. And I hate myself even more when I think about how I wished that Tilly could stay with Ford forever because he loves her and doesn't want to lose her. "This is not what I wanted," I sob out loud.

The guilt of wishing for something that came true, but at such cost to others, has my stomach swirling to the point I think I might vomit. If only I could go back and change those thoughts! I am the worst person in the world.

I drag myself off the bed and trudge to the bathroom to wash my face. I peer at my reflection in the mirror, my face red, my eyes swollen.

I'm not Tilly's mother. I don't deserve to be. But I love that tiny little human.

There's no biological connection. How can I love her so much?

But I also love Ford. And Elodie. In different ways, of course, but there's no biological connection there either. Clearly there doesn't have to be, to love someone. You love them for who they are.

My love for Tilly didn't happen immediately. It grew over time. There were challenges and frustrations. But it grew, fierce and strong and boundless.

Making myself take deep, slow breaths, I dry my hands. The reality that Tilly is not leaving is sinking in. I want to be happy, but how can I? Willa is dying. *Tilly's mom* is dying. It's such a massive conflict inside me, I don't know how to deal with it.

I told Ford I'd be there for him no matter what. Am I really ready for this new future? Can I be a mother figure to Tilly? What will that mean for me and Ford? How much will my life change?

My head aches and I swallow an Advil capsule, then wander back to my bed. I'm so tired. Drained.

I take off my clothes and pull on my softest pajamas, then curl up in a ball under the covers. I feel hollow and cold. Freezing. My thoughts are blurry and floating. I can't catch any one of them before it drifts away. And I sleep again.

* * *

In the morning, I'm stiff and sore and queasy. I guzzle a glass of water and make myself a piece of toast so I have something in my stomach.

I had a dream. It was crazy. But it's stuck in my head. It's something I need to do.

I find my phone, amazed it's not dead. As my stomach churns at what I'm contemplating, I'm not sure if the toast was a good idea.

I unlock my phone and see all the messages from Ford. My bottom lip pushes out unhappily. I just took off, freaking out, cowardly. I close my eyes and take a deep breath. I have to do this.

It takes some doing, but finally I get her on the phone. I swallow the excess saliva in my mouth. "Willa? My name is Andi Marsh."

Silence.

"I'm Ford Archibald's girlfriend." I *almost* hesitate on the word girlfriend.

"I know who you are." Her voice is soft. "I saw pictures of you online with Matilda."

I sink my teeth briefly into my bottom lip. "Yes." I pull air into my lungs, lost for a moment. "Ford mentioned where you are. I hope I'm not... I don't want to..." *Fuck.* I close my eyes and tip my head back. "This is probably nuts, but I felt like I needed to talk to you."

"Okay."

"I don't know where to start." I rub at the ache in my throat and swallow once. Twice. "I want you to know that I love Tilly. Matilda. I love her so much. I never thought I wanted children, and honestly, I was afraid of her at first." I choke out a laugh. "But she made me fall in love with her and now I would do anything for her. Anything. That's what I want you to know."

"Thank you."

"I can't imagine being in your situation. I am so, so sorry. I admire you so much, though, for your love for your daughter and your selflessness. Your sacrifice." My voice is trembling. "It won't be in vain. Ford and I will take care of her and love her. And we'll make sure that when she's old enough to understand, she knows you and your love for her."

"Oh." I can't see Willa, but I hear her choked voice. For a moment, she says nothing, then, "Thank you. I appreciate that. This is so hard."

"Yeah. I'm sure it is." I'm trying not to lose my shit again, like I did yesterday.

"I love her so much. More than anything. That's the hardest part. But knowing she's loved... that means so much."

Relief floods my body, weakening my legs, and I sink onto a stool at my kitchen counter. "I didn't want to make things worse. Or hurt you."

"No, no. You haven't." She sniffs, and I brush tears from my eyes. "Can you tell me more about yourself?"

I blink. And swallow. Rub my wet face. "Um. Sure. What do you want to know?"

"Just... who you are."

"Well. I love coffee. And cocktails." Ack. "Like, not for breakfast or anything."

Willa laughs softly.

I don't know what to say. "I have a tattoo on my back that says *Rise above the storm and you will find the sunshine.* I try to remember that when things are tough. My mom always told me nobody ever damaged their eyesight by looking at the bright side. Sometimes..." I clear my throat. "Sometimes it's really hard, though. But it helps."

"I love that."

We talk for nearly an hour, which is bonkers because we don't even know each other. I tell her about Ford and me. I tell her what I've learned from Tilly. She talks about Tilly, too.

"Our children never really belong to us," Willa says.

"I think that's true. Tilly is her own person."

"Yes, exactly."

When we finally end the conversation, knowing we won't speak again, I dig deep for my optimism and faith.

"Thank you for this, Andi," Willa says. "You didn't make things worse. You made them easier."

"I doubt that," I croak.

"A little easier. It's still hard. But I feel some peace of mind now, knowing you a bit, and knowing Ford, and that you two love Matilda. So thank you."

I don't cry. I feel more peaceful, too. That was so hard. But not as hard as it is for Willa.

Life is hard. Sometimes it's great. Sometimes it's fucked up.

But it's also short. Too damn short. And sometimes a lot shorter than it should be.

I can't be a coward anymore. I have to be as brave as Willa, although what I'm going through is nothing compared to what she's experiencing.

Life is short, so we have to live it. And I'm going to do that. For Ford. For Tilly. For Willa. And for me.

35

FORD

Since Andi bolted out of my place in tears, I've been freaking the fuck out myself.

I know this is hard. I fucking *know* it. I'm *living* it, for fuck's sake.

But we need to get through this together. I thought we agreed on that. We love each other.

I thought we did, anyway.

Of course this stirs up my doubts again.

I wanted to chase her down the hall and force her to listen to me. I can't stand seeing her so heartbroken. I can't handle her tears.

It's too much. I can't handle it. I have to go.

What does that mean? Is she gone forever? Is she being a coward? Is she dumping me, just like I was afraid of?

Jesus hula-hooping Christ.

I have a little person to attend to, though, and somehow, I know that chasing after Andi isn't the best idea right now.

So I leave her be, hoping she's figuring things out and that what she's figuring out still includes me. I take Tilly for a walk.

Give her a bath. I make myself eat dinner. And I get us both to bed. Tonight, she's the one sleeping and I'm not.

There's a lot to think about. Willa. Tilly. Andi.

Weirdly, I don't think about hockey. Maybe I should.

In the morning, Lieve arrives because I have a goddamn practice. How in the cinnamon toast fuck am I supposed to focus on hockey right now? All I can think about is Andi down the hall, doing what I don't know.

I'm so fucking afraid that what she said meant, *I'm out, forever, have a nice life.*

But also... Andi's not that cowardly. She said she loves me and I believe her. And I know she loves Tilly. I have to have faith in her strength and courage and positivity. Yeah.

Focusing on hockey is the easy part, though. The hard part is the guys asking me questions about what happened with Andi. Did I tell her how I feel? What happened with Willa? What's going to happen with Tilly?

"I don't want to talk about it," I snarl at them. "Let's focus on hockey."

I see the surprise and concern on their faces. I suck in a deep breath. "It's been rough," I tell them in a muted tone. "I'll tell you all. Just not today."

They all give me space, thank fuck.

I throw myself into the practice, giving it my all. It does distract me from all the other shit that happened. Burning some adrenaline helps. Being physically spent helps. After I shower and get dressed, I check my phone for messages or calls from Andi. There's nothing. Shit.

I leave right away to get home, hoping Andi's working through things. Trying to stay positive.

Mid-afternoon, I'm sitting on the couch with Tilly, giving her a bottle. She's holding it in her little hands, using the handles on the new bottle we got her. She's growing up.

There's a soft knock on the door, then it opens and Andi walks in.

My heart fucking stops.

We stare at each other. She's so goddamn beautiful, even though she looks tired and sad.

Tilly sees her, takes the nipple out of her mouth, and says happily, "Amamagabama."

Andi smiles at her. "Hi to you, too."

She looks back at me. I hold her gaze steadily, no doubt all my questions showing on my face as I extend a hand to her.

She walks over and sits beside me and takes my hand, curling her fingers around mine and leaning her head on my shoulder. "I'm sorry," she whispers. "I lost it."

"Are you okay now?"

"Not entirely. But I will be."

"It's hard."

"It is. It's huge. I felt overwhelmed. Doubtful. Scared."

"I get it."

She tells me how terrible she feels about Willa and how guilty she feels—I get that too—and how sad she is for Tilly.

"I know, sweetheart. I know. This is so fu—, I mean effed up."

"Yes."

"I'm going to put Tilly down for a nap. We can talk more."

"She really is off schedule."

"Yeah."

"But you're right—there are some things more important than that. Especially right now."

I take Tilly into the bedroom and talk to her while I settle her into her cot, trying not show her how fucked up I am. Then I close the bedroom door behind me and turn on the monitor.

I return to the couch and pick up my phone and send a quick text, then toss it back to the coffee table. In response to Andi's inquiring look, I say, "I just told Mabel not to come after all."

She tilts her head. "She was coming here?"

"Yeah. I asked if she could look after Tilly for a while so I could come talk to you." I'd run out of patience. I eye her uncertainly.

She pulls in a deep breath and lets it out. "Thank you. And I'm sorry."

Relief slides through me. "C'mere." I sit and pull her into my arms, lifting her legs to stretch them across my lap. With one arm around her, I take her hand with my other and lift it to my lips.

"I thought a lot," she says. "And... I talked to Willa."

My head jerks in surprise. "Really?"

"Yeah. We talked for a long time, actually. About a lot of things. Mostly Tilly." She slips her arm around my shoulders. "I wasn't sure if it was the right thing to do, but in the end, she said it made things a little easier. For her to know us, that we love Tilly and will take care of her."

I lean my forehead against hers. "Wow." That took guts. Holy shit. And I thought she was being cowardly. Her inner strength blows me away.

"Yeah. And it made me feel more at peace, too." She tells me more about the conversation with Willa, and I listen intently. "In the end, I realized that sometimes life sucks. But we need to live it and make the best of it while we're here. Because it's short."

I close my eyes, my chest squeezing painfully. "Yeah," I rasp out.

"Do you think we can really do this?"

I lift my head and meet her eyes. "I had my doubts," I say honestly.

She nods. "You *are* a good father," she whispers. "You love her. You can be a good parent if you love your child and try hard."

With a knuckle beneath her chin, I make her hold my gaze. "That means, you, too."

She goes very still. Her lips quiver. "Yeah. Even me. I had my doubts, too. How can I do this? Am I really ready for a whole different life? Can I be a mother figure to Tilly?"

I kiss her temple. "You can." I pause. When I speak, my throat feels full of sand. "But I understand if you don't want to sign on for that."

"That's not what I'm saying. At all. I love you. I love Tilly."

A champagne bottle of relief bursts in my core, sending effervescence sparkling through my veins. "Then you can do it. We both can. Knowing you believe in me gives me courage."

She lowers her chin, then lifts her head and gazes into my eyes. "Me too."

I stamp my mouth on hers, holding her in a long kiss, full of relief and gratitude, strength and adoration. When I slowly draw back, I say, "I'm sorry, too."

"For what?" She touches my face.

"For putting you through this."

"None of this is your fault."

"I know. But this whole mess is part of the package."

"I know that," she says softly. "So is your rigid attachment to schedules and plans. Your ten-step hair-care routine. Your dirty jokes and your personal eating utensils and weird eye exercises."

Our eyes meet. One corner of my mouth kicks up. "And you still love me."

"I do. I love you for all of that. And for the great father you are."

I close my eyes on another rush of emotion. "I never thought

I would meet someone who would love me like that. I was afraid to tell you I was falling in love with you."

"You took me on that date. That amazing date. Everything you did made me think you loved me. But you never said it, and I was so confused."

"I guess I hoped you'd get it without me having to say it."

She huffs out a laugh. "Chicken."

"Oh, hell, yeah. And then on our way home after we picked up Tilly, you got all quiet. And I figured the date didn't mean anything to you."

"I'm sorry. It meant a lot to me. I was so hopeful that it meant as much to you, and then you made that comment about how I could have a nap—remember? And it felt like a smack. Because I was thinking of myself as Tilly's parent and you were still thinking of me as your neighbor who was helping with her."

"No." My eyebrows pull down. "No. Christ, I'm sorry. That's not how I thought of you at all. When I said that, I just meant... there are two of us. You could have a nap if you wanted, and I would look after Tilly."

"Oh."

"And then I stuck my skate in my mouth with that comment that you work a lot." I shake my head. "I respect you for how hard you work. I love that about you."

Her expression goes soft. "Thank you."

"That night after we decorated the tree... you went back to your place. I figured you wanted some space. So you could get back to your normal life."

"Oh. No." She pauses, searching for words. "I was scared. That was such a couple thing to do. A family thing. And I had to remind myself that we weren't a family and Tilly would be leaving soon and I wanted space, but it was because I was trying to protect myself. I was so scared of everything I was going to lose."

"Fuck."

"We have to talk about these things," she says quietly. "When they happen."

"They won't happen."

"Yes, they will. Communication is hard. It's hard to admit we're hurt. We're going to screw up. But we have to always try."

"You're right. The guys smacked some sense into me the other night in Charlotte. They made me see that I had to tell you how I felt. That's why I came straight home."

"They smacked some sense into you?" Her lips curve sweetly.

"Yeah." I rub my face. "I may have been a little hungover on top of depressed."

"Oh dear."

"I was trying to drown my fears in bourbon." I grimace. "They gave me hope that maybe you'd be willing to stick around with a jerk like me. And actually... they made me think maybe I'm not a total jerk."

She strokes her fingers down the side of my neck. "You are not a jerk. You've given up so much for Tilly. Willingly. Because you love her."

"Yeah." I swallow thickly. "They also made me realize I'm not alone. Even when I'm in net. We're a team. I *knew* that." I grunt at my own stupidity. "My stupid insecurities were fucking with me. And same thing with you. I was afraid you'd walk away when Tilly was gone." I pause. "I was *terrified* of that."

"Even though that's what we agreed on. That we'd walk away when it was over."

"Yeah."

"I was terrified, too. That you wouldn't want me anymore. That when Tilly was gone, we'd be done."

"No. I didn't want to lose you. We're a team, too." I slide my nose alongside hers and breathe in her sweet scent. "Right?"

"Right," she whispers. "Yes. Absolutely."

"Something you said also made me realize I had to talk to you."

"What did I say?"

"When the guys were throwing the baby shower for me, you said I shouldn't be so inflexible that I miss out on something great. And you... are something great."

She looks into my eyes, and I let it all show. My love. My devotion. My need for her. "Thank you. You are something great, too."

"When my parents were here, I told them I don't want to disappoint them, after all they did for me."

She nods, fingering the collar of my shirt.

"And Mom said I shouldn't feel like that. She said they did everything they did because they love me. Not because they ever expected anything from me in return. And now I understand that. Because I would do anything for Tilly. Because I love her."

"Yeah. I know. I feel the same."

"You were ready to let her go, so she could have her mom." That fucking killed me. I wished she didn't have to make that sacrifice. And then... she didn't. But it was hard to deal with.

"Yeah. I didn't have a choice, though. I had no claim on her at all. I just... love her and I only wanted her to be happy and have everything she needs. Even though it hurt." She takes a breath. "I don't know how I ended up feeling like this about her."

"Well, like Willa said... how could you not?"

Her eyes turn shiny. "Exactly."

I bend my head and kiss her again. Softly. Tenderly. With a promise. "My mom knew I was falling for you before I even did."

"She did?"

"Yeah. She noticed that I said, 'When Willa first left Tilly with *us*,' and she said, 'You *are* an us. You just haven't accepted it yet.'"

"Your mom is a little, uh…"

"Wacky?" My lips quirk.

She rolls her lips in on a smile. "But she's wise. I like her."

"Yeah. She can be. She likes you, too."

She lets that smile free and it's gorgeous.

"I love you."

A smile trembles on her lips. "I love you, too."

I lean in to kiss her, gentle brushes of my mouth on hers, then deeper kisses, licking inside, stroking and sucking. Heat builds as our hands move over each other. The kisses get hotter, consuming, long and deep. Excitement and desire coil inside me, my cock thickening. My blood is fire and I'm desperate for more… more… "Let's move to my room," I murmur.

"Mmmm."

And just as we both stand, a cry comes from the baby monitor.

We freeze in place. My body is pulsing with need. We look at each other.

"Jesus," I groan, grabbing my throbbing erection through my jeans. "Now? I could cry."

"Me too." She bites her lip on a smile. "Um… rain check?"

"Oh, fuck yeah." I kiss her hard one last time. "Be ready. I'm gonna strip you naked, lick your pussy until you scream, and then fuck your brains out."

36

FORD

"Finally."

"Finally I can collect on that rain check?"

"Hell, yeah." I flick on the lamp beside the bed, then back Andi up to the mattress and ease her onto the duvet, coming down beside her.

She turns her face so our mouths meet and surprises me by reaching for my hand. She pulls it up and presses it to her breast. I remember the first time we had sex, how she did that. But now it means more. My hand is over her heart. I hold it there, measuring the beat of her heart, watching her face. "You're so beautiful."

Her smile is luminous. I move over her, and she pushes her elbows into the mattress and lifts her head as I nuzzle her throat, her breasts. I nudge up her sweater, and she sits up so I can tug it off. I admire her pretty pink lace bra. "Matching panties?"

"What do you think?" Her eyelashes flicker with flirty seduction.

"I think we need to get this off you." I flick the bra open and drop it over the side of the bed, and for a moment I can only gaze at her, her beautiful breasts bare for me, emotion swelling in my chest, stealing my breath. Christ. This woman... is she really mine? "I love you."

Her mouth curves sweetly. "I love you, too."

I bend my head, lick and suck, loving the feel and taste of her nipples in my mouth, loving how she responds, her hands in my hair, her body tightening and arching. I fucking love doing this to her, setting her on fire, making her aching and eager. I lick her breasts, nipping at the soft curves, and slide a hand down between her thighs. I rub her, absorbing the damp heat of her through her leggings. "You're wet, honey."

"I know," she groans.

"Shhh. We need to be quiet."

"Right. Right." She pants a couple of soft breaths, then whispers, "I need you to touch me there."

"Oh, yeah." I move back between her thighs to drag her leggings off. Perfect. I study the tiny pink lace thong. "Have I ever told you how much I like your underwear?"

"Mmm. Yes, you have."

"These are so pretty. But they're coming off, too." I slide the lace down her legs and then study her, naked on the bed in front of me. "Christ, you're beautiful, Andi."

"So are you." She reaches for me and lays her palms on my chest, rubbing over my pecs. Heat slides down through me to my balls.

"I want to worship you. Show you everything you are to me." I shift back so I can kiss her mouth as I fondle her. I pet her folds with my fingertips, then slide deep inside. "Gorgeous." I brush my lips over the top of one breast. "So hot and slippery."

I slide an arm beneath her, lick and suck her breasts, grazing her with my teeth. She moans and writhes at my touch. Electricity sizzles over my nerve endings, tension growing in my spine. My balls ache, and sensation wraps around my cock, making me crazy for her.

I caress her stomach, the curve of her hip, and again between her legs, every touch full of adoration and awe and a desire to please her. Make her feel so good. Venturing lower, I lick the shallow indent of her navel and across her stomach, then ease her legs apart to move between them, dragging my tongue along her thighs, then to her center.

"Oh my God, Ford." She drops flat on her back. "Oh my God."

"You taste so sweet." I lick again. "I could do this forever." I pull back to study her. "Look at that pretty pussy. So soft and pink."

She whimpers, her hands sliding into my hair and twisting. "I want you inside me."

"Yeah. I will be. Believe me." I lift her knee with one hand and push it up and back. I slide my other arm under her hip to hug her other thigh and lap at her with slow, reverent strokes of my tongue. When I lick over her clit, her hips jerk and lift against me. I use one thumb to open her more to my tongue. "Smooth. Juicy." Damn, I need to be inside her now.

I unbutton my shirt and shrug it off, then strip off my pants, underwear, and socks. I move back between her thighs, on my knees, nudging her legs wider for me. I fist my stiff cock and stroke it up and down through her creamy center, brushing the head over her clit. My balls tighten even more at the root of my cock, sizzling pleasure licking over me like flames.

Trembling, she opens her eyes, and I hold her gaze steadily as I stroke her. Her stomach muscles tighten. "Fuck me," she whispers.

"You want this?" I stroke my cock.

Her gaze drops to my hand and watches. "Yes. I want you inside me." She reaches out again and grazes her fingertips over my chest and abs, all the way down to the hair at the base of my cock. My muscles twitch, and my skin burns.

I find her entrance and push inside, all the while holding her gaze. We stare into each other's eyes in a connection that makes my heart inflate with raw emotion. I can't look away as her body closes around me, almost unbearably hot and tight, skin to skin, and I push in slowly, watching her face closely. "Okay, beautiful?"

"Oh, yeah." Her hips move, changing the angle, taking me deeper. I reach for one of her hands, lace our fingers together, and lift her other leg higher. Her gaze returns to my face, and I fuck her hard, deep, joining us in the closest connection we can have. And it's still not enough. I want her so much it almost scares me.

She curls her fingers around mine and holds on tight. Her eyes hazy, her wet lips parted, she looks so goddamn beautiful it makes my chest hurt.

A groan climbs my throat as my heart fills with love, and pleasure twists in my body. Andi's eyes widen as her orgasm builds, then drift closed, her body tightening, squeezing me. Electricity shorts out my brain and fire explodes low in my belly, burning through me, my balls, my cock, streaking up my spine. I fall over her, burying my face in the side of her neck as wave after wave of hot pleasure rolls over me, pulsing through my veins. "Love you, Andi," I gasp into the soft skin of her neck.

"I love you, too, Ford." Her arms wrap tightly around me, and her mouth opens on my shoulder in a long kiss.

I shift to my side, keeping us joined, and hold her like the precious gift she is. "You make me better," I mumble into her hair.

She strokes my shoulder, my upper arm. "You make yourself better."

"I want to be better for you. And for Tilly."

"Ford, we love you as you are. I know you think you're messed up and weird, but I think you're amazing. Talented. Hard working. Protective."

"Nitpicky."

I sense her smile. "How about neat and organized?"

"Okay. You're right. Even at my worst, I'm fucking incredible."

She bursts out laughing, then slaps a hand over her mouth, her body shaking against mine, and I lift my head to smile into her eyes.

Love is scary and complicated. It's acceptance and intimacy, safety and friendship, painful and... fun. Especially with Andi... it's fun.

* * *

Tilly's still too young to know what Christmas is all about, but the rest of us know and we've bought a shit ton of gifts for her. My parents are here to celebrate with us, proud grandparents who are obviously going to spoil Tilly rotten.

It's a bittersweet Christmas, though. Willa passed away a few days ago. I fucking hate that Tilly has lost her mother. I'm also fiercely, sharply determined to look after Tilly the best I possibly can, and also to make sure she knows her mother as well as I can tell her.

We're gathered in the living room on Christmas morning. The first gift is one I bring out from the closet in the spare room —a huge bouquet of red roses for Andi.

She takes them with wonder, admiring the bright petals then lifting her eyes to mine. "Thank you."

"I screwed up last time with the flowers."

She looks up from the card, where I wrote *Red roses are for devotion, passion, romance, desire, and true love.* "The ones at the hotel?"

I bend my head closer to her. "Yeah. I was absolutely a coward. Everyone knows red roses are for love. I thought giving you red roses would be too much. So I went with... what was it? Passion, desire, fascination." I pause. "Those *are* all true, by the way. But red was what I felt. Love."

Her eyes get glossy. "You are such a romantic, Ford Archibald."

"Who knew?" I shrug. "I kind of enjoy it."

"Just like you enjoy being a girl dad."

"Oh, hey, hold on." Mom speaks up. "Let's be careful with that term."

I hike my eyebrows up and turn to her. "Girl dad?"

"Yes." Holding Tilly, she stands, passion animating her face.

Oh, boy. Here we go. I repress a smile.

"The idea of a 'girl dad' makes us go along with the gender binary."

I slid my gaze over to Andi, who's also listening and when she meets my eyes, hers are dancing.

"Girl dads are great if it means actually showing up for your daughter, not just doing something perceived as feminine, like doing her hair or playing with Barbies. And let's not feed the patriarchy. Men get praised for changing a diaper or taking their daughter for a walk. Come on! Praise for doing the bare minimum? That's bullshit."

"My mother, the feminist," I murmur.

"You bet your ass I am," she says, but she's smiling. "You just listen to Grandma, Tilly."

"Ignore the swearwords, though," I say. "And I'm a feminist, too."

Andi gives me side eye.

"I am! Hey, I know you could have fixed your bed yourself when it broke, I just wanted to help."

"You broke her bed?" Dad frowns.

"Much as I'm happy you're having energetic sex, that is a bit TMI, even for me," Mom says.

"I didn't break her bed! *She* broke it!"

"I was alone," Andi adds hastily. "Anyway, I can vouch for the fact that he's changed a lot of diapers. He was a single dad; there was nobody else to change them. He still does more than me."

Mom beams. "We raised you right."

I press my lips together. Yeah. Yeah, they did. Even though I wanted more from them in terms of boundaries and rules, there were things they taught me—empathy, loyalty, honesty. Love. Important things. Maybe I'm just now realizing how important.

"I love you, Mom."

She sends me a soft look of affection. "I love you, too."

"You too, Dad."

"Love you, son."

Andi and I exchange another glance that's loaded with emotion. God, I love her, too.

We get busy opening gifts in front of the big tree I'm so glad we have. I sit on the floor with Tilly between my legs, a pile of gifts in front of us. I pick up a gift with a tag that says *To Tilly, From Andi.*

"I bought those presents weeks ago," Andi says. "I wasn't sure I'd get to give them to you."

Fuck. I pause at the sharp jab to my heart.

Tilly's curious and I help her by ripping the paper a bit. She grabs the wrapping paper in her fist and yanks, pulling off a big chunk.

"Attagirl."

She waves the paper around then brings it in front of her to study it and crumple it, more interested in the paper than the gift. Then she starts to stuff it into her mouth and I swiftly pluck it away from her. Eventually we get the present open. "Books! Perfect." I hold the books to show her. "You love books."

"She'll be reading in no time," Mom says.

"She should probably learn to talk first," I say dryly. Then I see one of the books. *My First Book of Sharks*. I separate it from the others, then turn to Andi.

She smiles.

Christ. I love her.

With my chest full of emotion, I show the book to Tilly. She turns one of the stiff pages. She's brilliant.

"Look. That's a shark. A basking shark." I pause. What if talking about sharks makes her cry?

Nope. She's fascinated. That's my girl.

We next open gifts from Mom and Dad, and they open ones to and from each other.

Then Andi opens the one from me. It's in a gift bag since it's an odd shape.

She pulls out the stuffed animal with a puzzled expression. "Is this for me or for Tilly?"

"It's for you."

She turns the animal and realizes what it is. "Oh! It's Bailey!"

"No. Not Bailey."

"What?" Her forehead wrinkles.

"That's the dog I'm going to get you as soon as we live somewhere pets are allowed."

She stares back at me, lips parted. She's so beautiful, her cheeks peachy smooth, her eyes big and warm.

Am I jumping the gun? I lick my bottom lip, suddenly nervous. We haven't talked about living together. In a way, it seems soon. But also, it seems like we already are, at times, she spends so much time here.

"Ford." She presses her lips together and peers down at the soft toy. "Thank you."

"He's wearing something that's also for you."

She glances up, then down, and fingers the necklace around the dog's neck. "Oh!" She jerks her eyes back up to me. "Oh my God, Ford."

I'm nervous again.

She undoes the tiny clasp of the gold chain and holds up the necklace. A one-carat diamond sparkles in the lights. "This is beautiful."

I shift away from Tilly and move behind Andi to fasten the necklace at her nape. I bend and kiss the side of her neck. "I felt like it wasn't enough. The dog's not real. Yet. But I wanted you to have something real."

"I love it. I've never had anything so beautiful. Thank you." She turns her head and our mouths meet in a long, hot, emotional kiss.

Mom and Dad clear their throats.

We draw apart with smiles.

"Open yours now," Andi urges me. She hands me a gift bag.

I open it and pull out something wrapped in red tissue. It's a Christmas ornament. I hold it up. A shark. Wearing a Santa hat. I grin. "This is awesome. Thank you."

She hands me a small box wrapped in silver paper. "And this."

I fumble open the paper, then lift the lid off the box. Inside is a bracelet—rustic black beads with one silver bead. I look closer. The silver bead is a shark. Grinning, I pull out the bracelet and slip it onto my left wrist. "Thanks. This is cool."

"There's more."

I go back to the box and find a folded paper. I open it and read it. Then I look up at Andi again. "Each bracelet comes with a shark?"

"Yes." She bites her lip. "There's information in there about your shark—a picture of it, and its name. You can track where he goes on a map and get information about his journey."

"Holy shit. Oops, I mean, holy shoot." Excitement rushes through my veins as I look down at the picture. "He's a good-looking shark. His name is Jawesome."

Mom's forehead creases. "His name is awesome?"

"No, Jawesome." I grin at Mom.

Dad laughs. "That's good. Let's see that."

I go over and show it to him. I think he's as excited as I am.

I look over at Andi, watching with a glow on her face. I have to kiss her again. "This is the best gift ever. Thank you."

"Be the shark," she whispers.

Yeah.

Later, after we've opened all the presents, eaten Christmas dinner, and Mom and Dad are playing with Tilly, I go up to the rooftop. I've been getting back to meditation and it's a good thing. My stress and anxiety and negative thoughts were spiraling, which is understandable, given everything that's been going on, but not as much as it could have.

What's helped? My trust in Andi. I trust her to be there for me. That's huge in quieting my anxiety.

But meditation is always good, and part of it is thinking about my goals and how I feel about them. Things have changed. How do I feel about my goals now? I still have hockey goals and I'm still determined to be the best I can be. But I also know that it won't be the end of the world if I don't achieve them. Because my other goals—to be a good father, a good partner to Andi, a good friend and teammate—are more important. And I can succeed in more ways than just playing the most games or stopping the most pucks.

Becoming a father has brought out a better version of myself. A version of me I didn't even know existed. I still work hard. But now I love even harder. I never knew love could feel like this... like the whole world is clutched in Tilly's tiny fist. You don't know what this type of love is before you have kids—and you're not meant to.

I never knew love could feel like what I feel for Andi. She, too, has also brought out a better version of me. The love I feel for her is different but just as powerful. I never thought anyone would love someone as screwed up as me. And yet she does. I want to live up to her love and trust and faith in me and be the man who deserves that. Because her love is everything to me.

Andi once asked me if I believe in soulmates. I told her I believed in them for other people because my soul is freaky. But I've found someone who loves my freak. Is that a soulmate? There's always been a sense of connection with Andi. It wasn't love at first sight; she was married. There was a physical attraction, yes. But as I got to know her better, she challenged me. She asked me questions about things I didn't want to talk about. The parts of me that are hurt and hidden. And when I talked about those things, she understood.

I've always felt like I'm on a journey. Becoming a father changed that journey. I feel like Andi is a partner on the journey. And I know I don't want to do it without her.

EPILOGUE
ANDI

August

The heat and humidity have been stifling all day. The overcast sky is gloomy. But it's not dampening the mood of our housewarming party.

We're in the back yard of our new house, which we moved into last month. It's a beautiful space, with a stone patio, flowerbeds full of perennials, and lots of comfortable chairs. Ford is over starting the barbecue, talking to Marek and Ben. More of their teammates are by the cooler. My parents and Ford's parents are seated around a table, talking away.

"Mama!" Tilly comes running across the patio, her steps still a little choppy. "Mama!"

When she first started calling me that, I thought my heart would burst. And I wasn't sure if it was the right thing to do. Ford and I talked about it. Of course she sees me as her mother, even though we've told her about Willa. We've told her how much Willa loved her. She's still pretty young to understand all that, though.

I crouch down to her level. "What, honey bun?"

"Kiki." She gestures.

"What's wrong with Kiki?"

"Baba ga met buh." She points, her expression serious.

"Oh." I have no idea what she's saying. At fifteen months old, she talks up a storm with facial expressions and gestures and we have entire conversations. She seems to know exactly what she's saying, even if nobody else does. It's adorable.

"Pay," she says, frowning.

"You want to play with Kiki?"

"Yuh!"

"Okay, where is she?" I take her hand.

At that moment, Kiki appears, gamboling across the patio toward us. We just got her a few weeks ago from Bright Side, where I still volunteer. She's a mix of something with a lot of Australian Shepherd so I fell in love with her. She's a year old, so she's still very puppyish.

Chasing her are Cain and Alec, Holly and Turks' two boys. And behind them is Elodie, looking frazzled.

"Kiki!" I crouch again and she runs to me. She's so pretty. I give her a rub. "Good girl."

"Googrrr," Tilly repeats.

"Yeah, that's it. Can you say dog?"

She gazes back at me.

"Dog."

Nope. She's not going to say it. Smiling, I shake my head.

"She was upset that the boys wouldn't let her play with the dog," Elodie says.

I make a face at her, then look at Tilly. "You have to share the puppy."

"Mine." She's developing a personality, including temper tantrums and mischievousness.

"Yes, she's yours, but you have her all the time and Cain and Alec don't."

"Let's get ice cream," Elodie says to the boys. They bounce across the patio with her.

"You can pet Kiki." I hold Kiki still.

"No." She shakes her head and points across the patio where the boys went. "Eyes."

"You want ice cream?"

"Yuh!"

"Of course you do."

After the playoffs ended, we looked at a short list of homes I'd put together and loved this one—a five-bedroom, three-and-a-half-bath Colonial in Essex County that's mostly been updated. It's not too far from the arena and practice facility for Ford, and I can work anywhere. This house has a beautiful office with French doors separating it from the living room and big windows looking into the back yard.

I freaked out at the price, but Ford talked me down. Not that I'm broke, but he has more money than I've ever imagined having.

Tilly and I follow Elodie and we get the kids ice cream.

"Are you having fun?" I ask Elodie with a smirk.

"I do like kids, but holy shit, the energy. Oops." She covers her mouth with her hand.

"I know, right?"

Ford joins us. "We'll be ready to cook in a few minutes."

"Okay. Let's bring the food out."

Elodie and Ford follow me inside, Holly keeping an eye on Tilly. The kitchen is bright and big, and I have hotdogs, hamburgers and chicken breasts ready to go on the grill. Ford picks up one tray and disappears outside again.

"How's business going?" Elodie asks me.

"Ohhh, pretty good. I'm done with a couple of contracts now."

"And you're not going to look for new business."

"Not right now."

"I can't believe how much you've cut back." She shakes her head. "You, the workaholic."

I wrinkle my nose. "I know."

She opens her mouth but hesitates. "Okay, I'm going to ask you something. Does cutting back on your work have anything to do with your marriage ending?"

I blink at her.

"I always had the feeling that you blame yourself for Trevor cheating on you. Because you worked so much."

I suck on my bottom lip.

"Not that you were responsible," she adds. "He's an asswipe. But..." Her forehead creases. "Are you cutting back on your work to try to keep that from happening again?"

I look across the room. She's right. I did blame myself. And I thought I was over that. *Is* that why I've reduced my client list?

"Are you mad at me?" Elodie asks, forehead creased.

"No. No." I turn back to her. "I'm seriously thinking about it, because it's a good question."

"Okay."

"No. That's not why I've reduced my workload. I know my workaholic tendencies were an attempt to boost my self-esteem. To make me feel like my goals mattered as much as Trevor's. But I don't feel like that with Ford. And I know that Trevor alone is responsible for his cheating. The truth is, it was really hard, working long hours when the team got into the playoffs, and then house hunting, and moving two places, selling our condos. Decorating this place." I wave a hand. "I was looking at veterinary technologist programs, at community college. It's not a veterinarian degree, but it's a shorter program and I'd be working with animals."

"Really?"

"Yeah." I smile. "Ford encouraged me to look into schools, even if I wanted to become a Doctor of Veterinarian Medicine. He wanted me to have my dream. But I still love my work, and life is really full right now and..." I stop. And swallow past the catch in my esophagus. I meet her eyes. "And I love it. I love them."

Elodie smiles and hugs me. "I'm happy for you, hon."

I squeeze her back. "Thank you."

She draws back. "But I can't believe you sent clients to Haven!"

"She's good at her job." I pull condiments out of the fridge. "I'm over it all. Things haven't worked out so well for her. I know it's not my problem, but I feel bad for her. She's a single mom and that's not easy."

"You're a better person than I am."

"Eh." I shake my head. "No, I'm not."

"Have you heard anything from her?"

"No. It doesn't matter. Can you carry these out?" I indicate the tray of condiments, paper plates, cups, and cutlery.

"Sure."

I pick up the tray of chicken breasts and we go back out.

Ford's teammates are all yakking away, happy and relaxed. Most of them went away to other homes for the summer and are now returning to New Jersey as training camp starts in a couple of weeks. I think they had a good summer and a much-needed rest after grueling playoffs.

Ford was nominated for the Vezina Trophy, but he didn't win. He didn't win the Jennings Trophy either, which is awarded to the goalie with the fewest goals scored against him. I knew he'd be disappointed, and he was a bit, but his attitude about that has changed. That doesn't mean he doesn't work just as hard; he totally does. And he played fantastic in the playoffs. But that's what matters to him—playing the best he can for his teammates and the fans. The awards are nice, but not the most important thing.

He smiles down at me when I set down the chicken. "Hey, beautiful."

"Hi. You ready to cook?"

"With you?" He gives me a dirty smirk. "Always."

"Haha." I grin. "I know."

He moves closer. "It's not that I'm always horny," he says in my ear. "It's just that you're always sexy."

I look up at him through my eyelashes. "Sweet talker."

"Just wait till later. I'll sweet talk you out of your clothes and into bed."

"Get a room," Marek says to us, shaking his head.

I grin.

There's more puppy and child commotion around us and while Ford cooks I deal with that, until Grandma and Grandpa (Archibald) come and take Tilly and my parents take Kiki. I move around and talk to the other WAGs who are there, sip a glass of wine, and occasionally supervise the barbecue.

Just as we're about to eat, the thunderstorm that's been threatening all day arrives with a loud clap of thunder. Rain pelts down as everyone grabs stuff and runs for the house.

"Oh, noooo!" I cry as I try to corral a frisky pup and a toddler who wants to stand in the rain.

Inside, everyone's laughing and shaking water off themselves.

"It couldn't have held off just a little longer?" I complain.

"It's fine," Ford says. "We'll just move in here."

I give him a long look.

"What?"

I grin. "*You're* the one calming *me* down about the change in plans."

"He's a new man," Ben says with a laugh and a clap on Ford's shoulder. "Mr. Chill."

"As if," Mabel scoffs. "He's still as anal as ever."

"Don't say that word." Ben winces.

Mabel bursts out laughing. "Why, honey? What's wrong with it?"

"Uh oh. Someone had a bad experience," Crusher speaks up. "You need lots of lube for that, you know."

It's a good thing our kitchen is big, as everyone crowds around the island. Ford finds an umbrella and goes out to finish cooking. Our dining table isn't big enough for everyone, but we all find places to sit. Ford sits with Tilly, cutting up her hot dog, dishing out some pasta from the salad for her. It's a little chaotic and not exactly what I planned, but it's fine.

Later, when our guests have departed, Tilly's in bed, and Kiki is conked out on the rug in the living room, Ford takes my hand and pulls me through the living room and into the TV room, which has a built-in desk at one end. This is his office. Apparently, he needs an office.

"What are you doing?" I ask.

"I have something to show you."

"Oooh. That sounds fun."

"Okay, who's the perv now?"

I laugh. "I can't top you."

"True. But I'm a perv in a romantic way."

I kiss his cheek.

He picks up an envelope off the desk, opens it, and hands me some papers.

"What is this?" I glance up at him.

"The paperwork for you to adopt Tilly."

I suck in a breath and press my hand to my throat where my heart has lodged.

It's not a surprise. We talked about it. I want to do it. He wants me to do it. We cried.

But it's really happening.

I look back up at him with misty eyes. "Thank you."

He smiles, a smile so full of love and affection and support. "This makes me happy, too."

"I'm glad."

I'm going to be Tilly's mom, officially. I love her so much. Someone asked me the other day how I could love her since she's not my biological child. I thought that was such a stupid question. We love all kinds of people who aren't biologically related to us.

There are many kinds of love. I think no two are the same. Love is different for different people.

It's also complicated. I want only the best for Tilly, but I also know that's not possible. There will be times she will be hurt. There will be times she is sad. There will be times she disappoints me or makes me angry. But I will always love her.

The love I have for Ford is different, but no less complex. I expect it will grow and change as we do. He, too, will likely make me angry. We might hurt each other. As with Tilly, I would take away any of his pain if I could. I like Ford and have fun with him. We were friends first. But there's also the sexual attraction. Affection. Loyalty. And more. Love isn't all hugs and kisses and puppies and kittens. It's hard. It's vulnerable. It's sacrifice. It's hurting when someone else hurts.

Because of all those things, it takes courage to love.

I thought it was better to be alone than to get hurt again. I questioned my judgment. And I was afraid. Afraid to fall in love and then lose it again. Afraid of being betrayed or rejected again. Afraid to trust the wrong person. And afraid there was something wrong with me.

I almost let those fears get in the way of loving Ford and being with him. But I chose love.

* * *

MORE FROM KELLY JAMIESON

Another book from Kelly Jamieson, *Crossing the Line*, is available to order now here:

https://mybook.to/CrossingLineBackAd

ACKNOWLEDGEMENTS

Thank you first to everyone at Boldwood Books for working on this book, making it better, and sharing it with the world. To my readers—I love to share my stories with you. I also love to share my passion for hockey along with the passion of two people falling in love. Thank you so much for buying and reading my books—I am forever grateful!

ABOUT THE AUTHOR

Kelly Jamieson is a USA Today bestselling author of over fifty romance novels.

Sign up to Kelly Jamieson's mailing list for news, competitions and updates on future books.

Visit Kelly's website: www.bit.ly/kellyjweb

Follow Kelly on social media here:

- facebook.com/KellyJamiesonRomanceAuthor
- x.com/KellyJamieson
- instagram.com/kellyjamiesonauthor
- bookbub.com/authors/kelly-jamieson
- tiktok.com/@kellyjamiesonauthor

ALSO BY KELLY JAMIESON

ALSO BY KELLY JAMIESON

Crossing the Line

Keeping the Score

Boldwood
EVER AFTER
x♡x♡

JOIN BOLDWOOD'S
**ROMANCE
COMMUNITY**
FOR SWEET AND
SPICY BOOK RECS
WITH ALL YOUR
FAVOURITE
TROPES!

SIGN UP TO OUR
NEWSLETTER

HTTPS://BIT.LY/BOLDWOODEVERAFTER

Boldwood

Boldwood Books is an award-winning fiction publishing company seeking out the best stories from around the world.

Find out more at www.boldwoodbooks.com

Join our reader community for brilliant books, competitions and offers!

Follow us
@BoldwoodBooks
@TheBoldBookClub

Sign up to our weekly deals newsletter

https://bit.ly/BoldwoodBNewsletter